Acclaim for Steven Millhauser's

DANGEROUS LAUGHTER

"Playfully and powerfully explor[es] the freedom of the imagination to reject the ordinary world of the merely real and explore the incredible world of purely aesthetic creation. . . . Devilishly clever." —*Milwaukee Journal Sentinel*

"[Millhauser's] startling, imaginative acts draw us in and then make us question not just what we're seeing but our response to it. . . . A showcase for precise language."

—*Chicago Tribune*

"There is a ferocious restlessness in [these] stories, a mingling of desire and dread. . . . Mesmerizing."

—*O, The Oprah Magazine*

"Explore[s] the bewitching, undefined space between perception and reality, evoking a disquieting supernatural realm that threatens to disrupt the everyday." —*The Washington Post*

"Masterful. . . . As fantastical as each of [Millhauser's] stories may be, they never seem more than a notch away from reality."

—*Time Out New York*

"This is classic Millhauser, and it won't disappoint newcomers or longtime fans." —*Slate*

"Excellent. . . . A substantial treat." —*The New York Sun*

"Millhauser is a superb craftsman whose quirky prose and off-beat subject matters manipulate the fictional narrative to get the most out of every page." —*Pittsburgh Post-Gazette*

"A blend of Hawthorne and Borges, with a hint of Paul Auster. . . . These stories will tug at you long after you've put them down." —*San Antonio Express-News*

"There are few writers in America better at striking the note of longing, of missed opportunity, of life taking uncanny and unfathomable turns. . . . Millhauser is the maestro of the creepy." —*The Buffalo News*

"[Millhauser] seems to have the late Edward Gorey looking over one shoulder, the early Tim Burton looking over the other, and the Addams Family looking on from the wings. . . . American gothic, with a smirk. . . . A magician with words." —*Easy Reader*

"Millhauser's stories take us in both directions at once—the laughing escape of fantasy and the dangerous proximity of the best in modern literature." —*The Austin Chronicle*

Steven Millhauser

DANGEROUS LAUGHTER

Steven Millhauser is the author of numerous works of fiction and was awarded the Pulitzer Prize for *Martin Dressler*. His story "Eisenheim the Illusionist" was the basis of the film *The Illusionist* starring Edward Norton and Paul Giamatti. His work has been translated into fourteen languages. He teaches at Skidmore College.

ALSO BY STEVEN MILLHAUSER

THE KING IN THE TREE

ENCHANTED NIGHT

THE KNIFE THROWER

MARTIN DRESSLER

LITTLE KINGDOMS

THE BARNUM MUSEUM

FROM THE REALM OF MORPHEUS

IN THE PENNY ARCADE

PORTRAIT OF A ROMANTIC

EDWIN MULLHOUSE

DANGEROUS LAUGHTER

THIRTEEN STORIES

STEVEN MILLHAUSER

Vintage Contemporaries
Vintage Books
A Division of Random House, Inc.
New York

FIRST VINTAGE CONTEMPORARIES EDITION, FEBRUARY 2009

The following stories have been previously published, some in slightly different form: "The Dome" in *The American Scholar*; "A Change in Fashion" and "The Wizard of West Orange" in *Harper's Magazine*; "A Precursor of the Cinema" and "The Tower" in *McSweeney's*; "Cat 'n' Mouse," "The Disappearance of Elaine Coleman," "History of a Disturbance," and "In the Reign of Harad IV" in *The New Yorker*; and "Dangerous Laughter," "The Other Town," and "The Room in the Attic" in *Tin House*.

Some of these stories were also published in the following: "Dangerous Laughter" in *The Best of Tin House* (Tin House Books, Portland, 2006); "A Change in Fashion" in *The O. Henry Prize Stories 2008*, edited by Laura Furman (Anchor Books, a division of Random House, Inc., New York, 2008); "The Dome" in *The Pushcart Prize XXXII*, edited by Bill Henderson (Pushcart Press, Wainscott, New York, 2007); and "Cat 'n' Mouse" in *The Story and Its Writer, Seventh Edition*, edited by Ann Charters (Bedford/St. Martin's, New York, 2007).

The Library of Congress has cataloged the Knopf edition as follows:
Millhauser, Steven.
Dangerous laughter : thirteen stories / by Steven Millhauser.—1st ed.
p. cm.
I. Title
PS3563.I422D36 2008
813'.54—dc22 2007022929

Vintage ISBN: 978-0-307-38747-9

Book design by Iris Weinstein

www.vintagebooks.com

Printed in the United States of America
10 9 8 7 6 5 4 3 2

TO ANNA AND JONATHAN

CONTENTS

OPENING CARTOON

CAT 'N' MOUSE

THE CAT IS CHASING the mouse through the kitchen: between the blue chair legs, over the tabletop with its red-and-white-checkered tablecloth that is already sliding in great waves, past the sugar bowl falling to the left and the cream jug falling to the right, over the blue chair back, down the chair legs, across the waxed and butter-yellow floor. The cat and the mouse lean backward and try to stop on the slippery wax, which shows their flawless reflections. Sparks shoot from their heels, but it's much too late: the big door looms. The mouse crashes through, leaving a mouse-shaped hole. The cat crashes through, replacing the mouse-shaped hole with a larger, cat-shaped hole. In the living room they race over the back of the couch, across the piano keys (delicate mouse tune, crash of cat chords), along the blue rug. The fleeing mouse snatches a glance over his shoulder, and when he looks forward again he sees the floor lamp coming closer and closer. Impossible to stop—at the last moment he splits in half and rejoins himself on the other side. Behind him the rushing cat fails to split in half and crashes into the lamp: his head and body push the brass pole into the shape of a trombone. For a moment the cat hangs sideways there, his stiff legs shaking like the clapper of a bell. Then he pulls free and rushes after the mouse, who turns and darts into a mousehole in the baseboard. The cat crashes into the wall and folds up like an accordion.

Slowly he unfolds, emitting accordion music. He lies on the floor with his chin on his upraised paw, one eyebrow lifted high in disgust, the claws of his other forepaw tapping the floorboards. A small piece of plaster drops on his head. He raises an outraged eye. A framed painting falls heavily on his head, which plunges out of sight between his shoulders. The painting shows a green tree with bright red apples. The cat's head struggles to rise, then pops up with the sound of a yanked cork, lifting the picture. Apples fall from the tree and land with a thump on the grass. The cat shudders, winces. A final apple falls. Slowly it rolls toward the frame, drops over the edge, and lands on the cat's head. In the cat's eyes, cash registers ring up NO SALE.

The mouse, dressed in a bathrobe and slippers, is sitting in his plump armchair, reading a book. He is tall and slim. His feet rest on a hassock, and a pair of spectacles rest on the end of his long, whiskered nose. Yellow light from a table lamp pours onto the book and dimly illuminates the cozy brown room. On the wall hang a tilted sampler bearing the words HOME SWEET HOME, an oval photograph of the mouse's mother with her gray hair in a bun, and a reproduction of Seurat's *Sunday Afternoon* in which all the figures are mice. Near the armchair is a bookcase filled with books, with several titles visible: *Martin Cheddarwit*, Gouda's *Faust*, *The Memoirs of Anthony Edam*, *A History of the Medicheese*, the sonnets of Shakespaw. As the mouse reads his book, he reaches without looking toward a dish on the table. The dish is empty: his fingers tap about inside it. The mouse rises and goes over to the cupboard, which is empty except for a tin box with the word CHEESE on it. He opens the box and turns it upside down. Into his palm drops a single toothpick. He gives it a melancholy look. Shaking his head, he returns to his chair and takes up his book. In a bubble above his head a picture appears: he is seated at a long table covered with a white tablecloth. He is holding a fork upright in one fist and a knife upright in the other. A mouse butler dressed in tails sets before him a piece of cheese the size of a wedding cake.

From the mousehole emerges a red telescope. The lens looks to the left, then to the right. A hand issues from the end of the telescope and beckons the mouse forward. The mouse steps from the mousehole, collapses the telescope, and thrusts it into his bathrobe pocket. In the moonlit room he tiptoes carefully, lifting his legs very high, over to the base of the armchair. He dives under the chair and peeks out through the fringe. He emerges from beneath the armchair, slinks over to the couch, and dives under. He peeks out through the fringe. He emerges from beneath the couch and approaches the slightly open kitchen door. He stands flat against the doorjamb, facing the living room, his eyes darting left and right. One leg tiptoes delicately around the jamb. His stretched body snaps after it like a rubber band. In the kitchen he creeps to a moonlit chair, stands pressed against a chair leg, begins to climb. His nose rises over the tabletop: he sees a cream pitcher, a gleaming knife, a looming pepper mill. On a breadboard sits a wedge of cheese. The mouse, hunching his shoulders, tiptoes up to the cheese. From a pocket of his robe he removes a white handkerchief that he ties around his neck. He bends over the cheese, half closing his eyes, as if he were sniffing a flower. With a crashing sound the cat springs onto the table. As he chases the mouse, the tablecloth bunches in waves, the sugar bowl topples, and waterfalls of sugar spill to the floor. An olive from a fallen cocktail glass rolls across the table, knocking into a cup, a saltshaker, a trivet: the objects light up and cause bells to ring, as in a pinball machine. On the floor a brigade of ants is gathering the sugar: one ant catches the falling grains in a bucket, which he dumps into the bucket of a second ant, who dumps the sugar into the bucket of a third ant, all the way across the room, until the last ant dumps it into a waiting truck. The cat chases the mouse over the blue chair back, down the chair legs, across the waxed floor. Both lean backward and try to stop as the big door comes closer and closer.

The mouse is sitting in his armchair with his chin in his hand, looking off into the distance with a melancholy expression. He is thoughtful by temperament, and he is distressed at the necessity of interrupting his meditations for the daily search for food. The search is wearying and absurd in itself, but is made unbearable by the presence of the brutish cat. The mouse's disdain for the cat is precise and abundant: he loathes the soft, heavy paws with their hidden hooks, the glinting teeth, the hot, fish-stinking breath. At the same time, he confesses to himself a secret admiration for the cat's coarse energy and simplicity. It appears that the cat has no other aim in life than to catch the mouse. Although the faculty of astonishment is not highly developed in the mouse, he is constantly astonished by the cat's unremitting enmity. This makes the cat dangerous, despite his stupidity, for the mouse recognizes that he himself has long periods when the cat fades entirely from his mind. Moreover, despite the fundamental simplicity of the cat's nature, it remains true that the cat is cunning: he plots tirelessly against the mouse, and his ludicrous wiles require in the mouse an alert attention that he would prefer not to give. The mouse is aware of the temptation of indifference; he must continually exert himself to be wary. He feels that he is exhausting his nerves and harming his spirit by attending to the cat; at the same time, he realizes that his attention is at best imperfect, and that the cat is thinking uninterruptedly, with boundless energy, of him. If only the mouse could stay in his hole, he would be happy, but he cannot stay in his hole, because of the need to find cheese. It is not a situation calculated to produce the peace of mind conducive to contemplation.

• • •

The cat is standing in front of the mousehole with a hammer in one hand and a saw in the other. Beside him rests a pile of yellow boards and a big bag of nails. He begins furiously hammering and sawing, moving across the room in a cloud of dust that conceals him. Suddenly the dust clears and the cat beholds his work: a long, twisting pathway that begins at the mousehole and passes under the couch, over the back of the armchair, across the piano, through the kitchen door, and onto the kitchen table. On the tablecloth, at the end of the pathway, is a large mousetrap on which sits a lump of cheese. The cat tiptoes over to the refrigerator, vanishes behind it, and slyly thrusts out his head: his eyes dart left and right. There is the sound of a bicycle bell: *ring ring*. A moment later the mouse appears, pedaling fiercely. He speeds from the end of the pathway onto the table. As he screeches to a stop, the round wheels stretch out of shape and then become round again. The mouse is wearing riding goggles, a riding cap, and gloves. He leans his bicycle against the sugar bowl, steps over to the mousetrap, and looks at it with interest. He steps onto the mousetrap, sits down on the brass bar, and puts on a white bib. From a pocket of his leather jacket he removes a knife and fork. He eats the cheese swiftly. After his meal, he replaces the knife and fork in his pocket and begins to play on the mousetrap. He swings on a high bar, hangs upside down by his legs, walks the parallel bars, performs gymnastic stunts. Then he climbs onto his bicycle and disappears along the pathway, ringing his bell. The cat emerges from behind the refrigerator and springs onto the table beside the mousetrap. He frowns down at the trap. From the top of his head he plucks a single hair: it comes loose with the sound of a snapping violin string. Slowly he lowers the hair toward the mousetrap. The hair touches the spring. The mousetrap remains motionless. He presses the spring with a spoon. The mousetrap remains motionless. He bangs the spring with a sledgehammer. The mousetrap remains motionless. He looks at the trap with rage. Cautiously he reaches out a single toe. The mousetrap springs shut with the sound of a slammed iron door. The cat hops about the table holding his trapped foot as the toe swells to the size of a lightbulb, bright red.

The cat enters on the left, disguised as a mouse. He is wearing a blond wig, a nose mask, and a tight black dress slit to the thigh. He has high and very round breasts, a tiny waist, and round, rolling hips. His lips are bright red, and his black lashes are so tightly curled that when he blinks his eyes the lashes roll out and snap back like window shades. He walks slowly and seductively, resting one hand on a hip and one hand on his blond hair. The mouse is standing in the mousehole, leaning against one side with his hands in his pockets. His eyes protrude from their sockets in the shape of telescopes. In the lens of each telescope is a thumping heart. Slowly, as if mesmerized, the mouse sleepwalks into the room. The cat places a needle on a record, and rumba music begins to play. The cat dances with his hands clasped behind his neck, thrusting out each hip, fluttering his long lashes, turning to face the other way: in the tight black dress, his twitching backside is shaped like the ace of spades. The mouse faces the cat and begins to dance. They stride back and forth across the room, wriggling and kicking in step. As they dance, the cat's wig comes loose, revealing one cat ear. The cat dances over to a bearskin rug and lies down on his side. He closes his long-lashed eyes and purses his red, red lips. The mouse steps up to the cat. He reaches into his pocket, removes a cigar, and places it between the big red lips. The cat's eyes open. They look down at the cigar, look up, and look down again. The cat removes the cigar and stares at it. The cigar explodes. When the smoke clears, the cat's face is black. He gives a strained, very white smile. Many small lines appear in his teeth. The teeth crack into little pieces and fall out.

The cat is lying on his back in his basket in the kitchen. His hands are clasped behind his head, his left knee is raised, and his right ankle rests sideways on the raised knee. He is filled with rage at the thought of the mouse, who he knows despises him. He would like to tear the mouse to pieces, to roast him over a fire, to plunge him into a pan of burning butter. He understands that his rage is not the rage of hunger and he wonders whether the mouse himself is responsible for evoking this savagery, which burns in his chest like indigestion. He despises the mouse's physical delicacy, his weak arms thin as the teeth of combs, his frail, crushable skull, his fondness for books and solitude. At the same time, he is irritably aware that he admires the mouse's elegance, his air of culture and languor, his easy self-assurance. Why is he always reading? In a sense, the mouse intimidates the cat: in his presence, the cat feels clumsy and foolish. He thinks obsessively about the mouse and suspects with rage that the mouse frequently does not think about him at all, there in his brown room. If the mouse were less indifferent, would he burn with such hatred? Might they learn to live peacefully together in the same house? Would he be released from this pain of outrage in his heart?

The mouse is standing at his workbench, curling the eyelashes of a mechanical cat. Her long black hair is shiny as licorice; her lips look like licked candy. She is wearing a tight red dress, black fishnet stockings, and red high heels. The mouse stands the mechanical cat on her feet, unzips the back of her dress, and winds a big key. He zips up the dress and aims her toward the mousehole. In the living room, the mechanical cat struts slowly back and forth; her pointy breasts stick out like party hats. The cat's head rises over the back of the armchair. In his eyes appear hearts pierced by arrows. He slithers over the chair and slides along the floor like honey. When he reaches the strutting cat, he glides to an upright position and stands mooning at her. His heart is thumping so hard that it pushes out the skin of his chest with each beat. The cat reaches into a pocket and removes a straw boater, which he places on his head at a rakish angle. He fastens at his throat a large polka-dot bow tie. He becomes aware of a ticking sound. He removes from his pocket a round yellow watch, places it against his ear, frowns, and returns it to his pocket. He bends close to the face of the cat and sees in each of her eyes a shiny round black bomb with a burning fuse. The cat turns to the audience and then back to the dangerous eyes. The mechanical cat blows up. When the smoke clears, the cat's fur hangs from him in tatters, revealing his pink flesh and a pair of polka-dot boxer shorts.

Outside the mousehole, the cat is winding up a mouse that exactly resembles the real mouse. The mechanical mouse is wearing a bathrobe and slippers, stands with hands in pockets, and has a pair of eyeglasses perched at the end of its nose. The cat lifts open the top of the mouse's head, which is attached in the manner of a hinged lid. He inserts a sizzling red stick of dynamite and closes the lid. He sets the mouse in front of the hole and watches as it vanishes through the arched opening. Inside, the mouse is sitting in his chair, reading a book. He does not raise his eyes to the visitor, who glides over with its hands in its pockets. Still reading, the mouse reaches out and lifts open the head of his double. He removes the sizzling dynamite, thrusts it into a cake, and inserts the cake into the mouse's head. He turns the mechanical mouse around and continues reading as it walks out through the arch. The cat is squatting beside the hole with his eyes shut and his fingers pressed in his ears. He opens his eyes and sees the mouse. His eyebrows rise. He snatches up the mouse, opens its head, and lifts out a thickly frosted cake that says HAPPY BIRTHDAY. In the center of the cake is a sizzling red stick of dynamite. The cat's fur leaps up. He takes a tremendous breath and blows out the fuse with such force that for a moment the cake is slanted. Now the cat grins, licks his teeth, and opens his jaws. He hears a sound. The cake is ticking loudly: *tock tock, tock tock.* Puzzled, the cat holds it up to one ear. He listens closely. A terrible knowledge dawns in his eyes.

The cat rides into the living room in a bright yellow crane. From the boom hangs a shiny black wrecking ball. He drives up to the mousehole and stops. He pushes and pulls a pair of levers, which cause the wrecking ball to be inserted into a gigantic rubber band attached to a gigantic slingshot. The rubber band stretches back and back. Suddenly it releases the shiny black ball, which smashes into the wall. The entire house collapses, leaving only a tall red chimney standing amid the ruins. On top of the chimney is a stork's nest, in which a stork sits with a fishing pole. He is wearing a blue baseball cap. Below, in the rubble, a stirring is visible. The cat rises unsteadily, leaning on a crutch. His head is covered with a white bandage that conceals an eye; one leg is in a cast and one arm in a sling. With the tip of his crutch, he moves away a pile of rubble and exposes a fragment of baseboard. In the baseboard we see the unharmed mousehole. Inside the mousehole, the mouse sits in his chair, reading a book.

The mouse understands that the clownishly inept cat has the freedom to fail over and over again, during the long course of an inglorious lifetime, while he himself is denied the liberty of a single mistake. It is highly unlikely, of course, that he will ever be guilty of an error, since he is much cleverer than the cat and immediately sees through every one of his risible stratagems. Still, might not the very knowledge of his superiority lead to a relaxation of vigilance that will prove fatal, in the end? After all, he is not invulnerable; he is invulnerable only insofar as he is vigilant. The mouse is bored, deeply bored, by the ease with which he outwits the cat; there are times when he longs for a more worthy enemy, someone more like himself. He understands that his boredom is a dangerous weakness against which he must perpetually be on his guard. Sometimes he thinks, If only I could stop watching over myself, if only I could let myself go! The thought alarms him and causes him to look over his shoulder at the mousehole, across which the shadow of the cat has already fallen.

The cat enters from the left, carrying a sack over one shoulder. He sets the sack down beside the mousehole. He unties a rope from the neck of the sack, plunges both hands in, and carefully lifts out a gray cloud. He places the cloud in the air above the mousehole. Rain begins to fall from the cloud, splashing down in great drops. The cat reaches into the sack and removes some old clothes. He swiftly disguises himself as a peddler and rings the mouse's bell. The mouse appears in the arched doorway, leaning against the side with his arms folded across his stomach and his ankles crossed as he stares out at the rain. The cat removes from the sack an array of mouse-size umbrellas, which he opens in turn: red, yellow, green, blue. The mouse shakes his head. The cat removes from the sack a yellow slicker, a pair of hip boots, a fishing rod and tackle box. The mouse shakes his head. The cat removes a red rubber sea horse, a compressed-air tank, a diving bell, a rowboat, a yacht. The mouse shakes his head, steps into his house, and slams the door. He opens the door, hangs a sign on the knob, and slams the door again. The sign reads NOT

HOME. The rain falls harder. The cat steps out from under the cloud, which rises above his head and begins to follow him about the room. The storm grows worse: he is pelted with hailstones the size of golf balls. In the cloud appear many golfers, driving golf balls into the room. Forked lightning flashes; thunder roars. The cat rushes around the room trying to escape the cloud and dives under the couch. His tail sticks out. Lightning strikes the tail, which crackles like an electric wire. The couch rises for an instant, exposing the luminous, electrified cat rigid with shock; inside the cat's body, with its rim of spiked fur, his blue-white skeleton is visible. Now snow begins to fall from the cloud, and whistling winds begin to blow. Snow lies in drifts on the rug, rises swiftly up the sides of the armchair, sweeps up to the mantelpiece, where the clock looks down in terror and covers its eyes with its hands. The cat struggles slowly through the blizzard but is soon encased in snow. Icicles hang from his chin. He stands motionless, shaped like a cat struggling forward with bent head. The door of the mousehole opens and the mouse emerges, wearing earmuffs, scarf, and gloves. The sun is shining. He begins shoveling a path. When he comes to the snow-cat, he climbs to the top of his shovel and sticks a carrot in the center of the snowy face. Then he climbs down, steps back, and begins throwing snowballs. The cat's head falls off.

The cat is pacing angrily in the kitchen, his hands behind his back and his eyebrows drawn down in a V. In a bubble above his head a wish appears: he is operating a circular saw that moves slowly, with high whining sounds, along a yellow board. At the end of the board is the mouse, lying on his back, tied down with ropes. The image vanishes and is replaced by another: the cat, wearing an engineer's hat, is driving a great train along a track. The mouse is stretched across the middle of the track, his wrists fastened to one rail and his ankles to the other. Sweat bursts in big drops from the mouse's face as the image vanishes and is replaced by another: the cat is turning a winch that slowly lowers an anvil toward the mouse, who is tied to a little chair. The mouse looks up in terror. Suddenly the cat lets go of the crank and the anvil rushes down with a whistling sound as the winch spins wildly. At the last moment, the mouse tumbles away. The anvil falls through the bubble onto the cat's head.

The cat understands that the mouse will always outwit him, but this tormenting knowledge serves only to inflame his desire to catch the mouse. He will never give up. His life, in relation to the mouse, is one long failure, a monotonous succession of unspeakable humiliations; his unhappiness is relieved only by moments of delusional hope, during which he believes, despite doubts supported by a lifetime of bitter experience, that at last he will succeed. Although he knows that he will never catch the mouse, who will forever escape into his mousehole a half inch ahead of the reaching claw, he also knows that only if he catches the mouse will his wretched life be justified. He will be transformed. Is it therefore his own life that he seeks, when he lies awake plotting against the mouse? Is it, when all is said and done, himself that he is chasing? The cat frowns and scratches his nose.

The cat stands before the mousehole holding in one hand a piece of white chalk. On the blue wall he draws the outline of a large door. The mousehole is at the bottom of the door. He draws the circle of a doorknob and opens the door. He steps into a black room. At the end of the room stands the mouse with a piece of chalk. The mouse draws a white mousehole on the wall and steps through. The cat kneels down and peers into the mousehole. He stands up and draws another door. He opens the door and steps into another black room. At the end of the room stands the mouse, who draws another mousehole and steps through. The cat draws another door, the mouse draws another mousehole. Faster and faster they draw: door, hole, door, hole, door. At the end of the last room, the mouse draws on the wall a white stick of dynamite. He draws a white match, which he takes in his hand and strikes against the wall. He lights the dynamite and hands it to the cat. The cat looks at the white outline of the dynamite. He offers it to the mouse. The mouse shakes his head. The cat points to himself and raises his eyebrows. The mouse nods. The stick of dynamite explodes.

The cat enters on the left, wearing a yellow hard hat and pushing a red wheelbarrow. The wheelbarrow is piled high with boards. In front of the mousehole, the cat puts down the handles of the barrow, pulls a hammer and saw from the pile of boards, and thrusts a fistful of black nails between his teeth. He begins sawing and hammering rapidly, moving from one end of the room to the other as a cloud of dust conceals his work. Suddenly the dust clears and the cat beholds his creation: he has constructed a tall guillotine, connected to the mousehole by a stairway. The blue-black glistening blade hangs between posts high above the opening for the head. Directly below the opening, on the other side, stands a basket. On the rim of the basket the cat places a wedge of cheese. The cat loops a piece of string onto a lever in the side of the guillotine and fastens the other end of the string to the wedge of cheese. Then he tiptoes away with hunched shoulders and vanishes behind a fire shovel. A moment later, the mouse climbs the stairs onto the platform of the guillotine. He stands with his hands in the pockets of his robe and contemplates the blade, the opening for the head, and the piece of cheese. He removes from one pocket a yellow package with a red bow. He leans over the edge of the platform and slips the loop from the lever. He thrusts his head through the head hole, removes the piece of cheese from the rim of the basket, and sets the package in its place. He ties the string to the package, slides his head back through the hole, and fits the loop of the string back over the lever. From his pocket he removes a large pair of scissors, which he lays on the platform. He next removes a length of rope, which he fastens to the lever so that the rope hangs nearly to the floor. On the floor he stands cross-ankled against the wheel of the barrow, eating his cheese. A moment later, the cat leaps onto the platform. He looks up in surprise at the unfallen blade. He crouches down, peers through the head hole, and sees the yellow package. He frowns. He looks up at the blade. He looks at the yellow package. Gingerly he reaches a paw through the opening and snatches it back. He frowns at the string. A cunning look comes into his eyes. He notices the pair of scissors, picks them up, and cuts the string. He waits, but nothing happens. Eagerly he thrusts his head through the opening and reaches for the package. The mouse, eating his cheese with one hand, lazily tugs at the rope with the other. The blade rushes down with the sound of a roaring train; a forlorn whistle blows. The cat tries to pull his head out of the hole. The blade slices off the top half of his head, which drops into the basket and rolls noisily around like a coin. The cat pulls himself out of the hole and stumbles about until he falls over the edge of the platform into the basket. He seizes the top of his head and puts it on like a hat. It is backward. He straightens it with a half turn. In his hand he sees with surprise the yellow package with the red bow. Frowning, he unties it. Inside is a bright red stick of dynamite with a sizzling fuse. The cat looks at the dynamite and turns his head to the audience. He blinks once. The dynamite explodes. When the smoke clears, the cat's face is black. In each eye a ship cracks in half and slowly sinks in the water.

• • •

The mouse is sitting in his chair with his feet on the hassock and his open book facedown on his lap. A mood of melancholy has invaded him, as if the brown tones of his room had seeped into his brain. He feels stale and out of sorts: he moves within the narrow compass of his mind, utterly devoid of fresh ideas. Is he perhaps too much alone? He thinks of the cat and wonders whether there is some dim and distant possibility of a connection, perhaps a companionship. Is it possible that they might become friends? Perhaps he could teach the cat to appreciate the things of the mind, and learn from the cat to enjoy life's simpler pleasures. Perhaps the cat, too, feels an occasional sting of loneliness. Haven't they much in common, after all? Both are bachelors, indoor sorts, who enjoy the comforts of a cozy domesticity; both are secretive; both take pleasure in plots and schemes. The more the mouse pursues this line of thought, the more it seems to him that the cat is a large, soft mouse. He imagines the cat with mouse ears and gentle mouse paws, wearing a white bib, sitting across from him at the kitchen table, lifting to his mouth a fork at the end of which is a piece of cheese.

The cat enters from the right with a chalkboard eraser in one hand. He goes over to the mousehole, bends down, and erases it. He stands up and erases the wall, revealing the mouse's home. The mouse is sitting in his chair with his feet on the hassock and his open book facedown on his lap. The cat bends over and erases the book. The mouse looks up in irritation. The cat erases the mouse's chair. He erases the hassock. He erases the entire room. He tosses the eraser over his shoulder. Now there is nothing left in the world except the cat and the mouse. The cat snatches him up in a fist. The cat's red tongue slides over glistening teeth sharp as ice picks. Here and there, over a tooth, a bright star expands and contracts. The cat opens his jaws wider, closes his eyes, and hesitates. The death of the mouse is desirable in every way, but will life without him really be pleasurable? Will the mouse's absence satisfy him entirely? Is it conceivable that he may miss the mouse, from time to time? Is it possible that he needs the mouse, in some disturbing way?

As the cat hesitates, the mouse reaches into a pocket of his robe and removes a red handkerchief. With swift circular strokes he wipes out the cat's teeth while the cat's eyes watch in surprise. He wipes out the cat's eyes. He wipes out the cat's whiskers. He wipes out the cat's head. Still held in the cat's fist, he wipes out the entire cat, except for the paw holding him. Then, very carefully, he wipes out the paw. He drops lightly down and slaps his palms together. He looks about. He is alone with his red handkerchief in a blank white world. After a pause, he begins to wipe himself out, moving rapidly from head to toe. Now there is nothing left but the red handkerchief. The handkerchief flutters, grows larger, and suddenly splits in half. The halves become red theater curtains, which begin to close. Across the closing curtains, words write themselves in black script: THE END.

VANISHING ACTS

THE DISAPPEARANCE OF ELAINE COLEMAN

THE NEWS OF the disappearance disturbed and excited us. For weeks afterward, the blurred and grainy photograph of a young woman no one seemed to know, though some of us vaguely remembered her, appeared on yellow posters displayed on the glass doors of the post office, on telephone poles, on windows of the CVS and the renovated supermarket. The small photo showed a serious face turned partly away, above a fur collar; the picture seemed to be an enlargement of a casual snapshot, perhaps originally showing a full-length view—the sort of picture, we imagined, taken carelessly by a bored relative to commemorate an occasion. For a time women were warned not to go out alone at night, while the investigation pursued its futile course. Gradually the posters became rain-wrinkled and streaked with grime, the blurred photos seemed to be fading away, and then one day they were gone, leaving behind a faint uneasiness that itself dissolved slowly in the smoke-scented autumn air.

According to the newspaper reports, the last person to see Elaine Coleman alive was a neighbor, Mrs. Mary Blessington, who greeted her on the final evening as Elaine stepped out of her car and began to walk along the path of red slates leading to the side entrance of the house on Willow Street where she rented two rooms on the second floor. Mary Blessington was raking leaves. She leaned on her rake, waved to Elaine Coleman, and remarked on the weather. She noticed nothing unusual about the quiet young woman walking at dusk toward the side door, carrying in one arm a small paper bag (probably containing the quart of milk found unopened in her refrigerator) and holding her keys in the other hand. When questioned further about Elaine Coleman's appearance as she walked toward the house, Mary Blessington admitted that it was almost dark and that she couldn't make her out "all that well." The landlady, Mrs. Waters, who lived on the first floor and rented upstairs rooms to two boarders, described Elaine Coleman as a quiet person, steady, very polite. She went to bed early, never had visitors, and paid her rent unfailingly on the first of the month. She liked to stay by herself, the landlady added. On the last evening Mrs. Waters heard Elaine's footsteps climbing the stairs as usual to her apartment on the second floor in back. The landlady did not actually see her, on that occasion. The next morning she noticed the car still parked in front, even though it was a Wednesday and Miss Coleman never missed a day of work. In the afternoon, when the mail came, Mrs. Waters decided to carry a letter upstairs to her boarder, who she assumed was sick. The door was locked. She knocked gently, then louder and louder, before opening the door with a duplicate key. She hesitated a long time before calling the police.

For days we spoke of nothing else. We read the newspapers ardently, the local *Messenger* and the papers from neighboring towns; we studied the posters, we memorized the facts, we interpreted the evidence, we imagined the worst.

The photograph, bad and blurry though it was, left its own sharp impression: a woman caught in the act of looking away, a woman evading scrutiny. Her blurred eyes were half closed, the turned-up collar of her jacket concealed the line of her jaw, and a crinkled strand of hair came straggling down over her cheek. She looked, though it was difficult to tell, as if she had hunched her shoulders against the cold. But what struck some of us about the photograph was what it seemed to conceal. It was as if beneath that grainy cheek, that blurred and narrow nose with the skin pulled tight across the bridge, lay some other, younger, more familiar image. Some of us recalled dimly an Elaine, an Elaine Coleman, in our high school, a young Elaine of fourteen or fifteen years ago who had been in our classes, though none of us could remember her clearly or say where she sat or what she did. I myself seemed to recall an Elaine Coleman in English class, sophomore or junior year, a quiet girl, someone I hadn't paid much attention to. In my old yearbook I found her, Elaine Coleman. I did not recognize her face. At the same time it didn't seem the face of a stranger. It appeared to be the missing woman on the poster, though in another key, so that you didn't make the connection immediately. The photograph was slightly overexposed, making her seem a little washed out, a little flat—there was a bright indistinctness about her. She was neither pretty nor unpretty. Her face was half turned away, her expression serious; her hair, done up in the style of the time, showed the shine of a careful combing. She had joined no clubs, played no sports, belonged to nothing.

The only other photograph of her was a group picture of our homeroom class. She stood in the third row from the front, her body turned awkwardly to one side, her eyes lowered, her features difficult to distinguish.

In the early days of her disappearance I kept trying to remember her, the dim girl in my English class who had grown up into a blurred and grainy stranger. I seemed to see her sitting at her maplewood desk beside the radiator, looking down at a book, her arms thin and pale, her brown hair falling partly behind her shoulder and partly before, a quiet girl in a long skirt and white socks, but I could never be certain I wasn't making her up. One night I dreamed her: a girl with black hair who looked at me gravely. I woke up oddly stirred and relieved, but as I opened my eyes I realized that the girl in my dream was Miriam Blumenthal, a witty and laughing girl with blazing black hair, who in dream-disguise had presented herself to me as the missing Elaine.

One detail that troubled us was that Elaine Coleman's keys were discovered on the kitchen table, beside an open newspaper and a saucer. The key ring with its six keys and its silver kitten, the brown leather pocketbook containing her wallet, the fleece-lined coat on the back of a chair, all this suggested a sudden and disturbing departure, but it was the keys that attracted our particular attention, for they included the key to her apartment. We learned that the door could be locked in two ways: from the inside, by turning a knob that slid a bolt, and from the outside, with a key. If the door was locked and the key inside, then Elaine Coleman cannot have left by the door—unless there was another key. It was possible, though no one believed it, that someone with a second key had entered and left through her door, or that Elaine herself, using a second key, had left by the door and locked it from the outside. But a thorough police investigation discovered no record of a duplicate. It seemed far more likely that she had left by one of the four windows. Two were in the kitchen–living room facing the back, and two in the bedroom facing the back and side. In the bathroom there was a small fifth window, no more than twelve inches in height and width, through which it would have been impossible to enter or exit. Directly below the four main windows grew a row of hydrangea and rhododendron bushes. All four windows were closed, though not locked, and the outer storm windows were in place. It seemed necessary to imagine that Elaine Coleman had deliberately escaped through a second-floor window, fifteen feet up in the air, when she might far more easily have left by the door, or that an intruder had entered through a window and carried her off, taking care to pull both panes back into place. But the bushes, grass, and leaves below the four windows showed no trace of disturbance, nor was there any evidence in the rooms to suggest a break-in.

The second boarder, Mrs. Helen Ziolkowski, a seventy-year-old widow who had lived in the front apartment for twenty years, described Elaine Coleman as a nice young woman, quiet, very pale, the sort who kept to herself. It was the first we had heard of her pallor, which lent her a certain allure. On the last evening Mrs. Ziolkowski heard the door close and the bolt turn in the lock. She heard the refrigerator door open and close, light footsteps moving about, a dish rattling, a teapot whistling. It was a quiet house and you could hear a lot. She had heard no unusual sounds, no screams, no voices, nothing at any time that might have suggested a struggle. In fact it had been absolutely quiet in Elaine Coleman's apartment from about seven o'clock on; she had been surprised not to hear the usual sounds of dinner being prepared in the kitchen. She herself had gone to bed at eleven o'clock. She was a light sleeper and was up often at night.

I wasn't the only one who kept trying to remember Elaine Coleman. Others who had gone to high school with me, and who now lived in our town with families of their own, remained puzzled or uncertain about who she was, though no one doubted she had actually been there. One of us thought he recalled her in biology, sophomore year, bent over a frog fastened to the black wax of a dissecting pan. Another recalled her in English class, senior year, not by the radiator but at the back of the room—a girl who didn't say much, a girl with uninteresting hair. But though he remembered her clearly, or said he did, there at the back of the room, he could not remember anything more about her, he couldn't summon up any details.

One night, about three weeks after the disappearance, I woke from a troubling dream that had nothing to do with Elaine Coleman—I was in a room without windows, there was a greenish light, some frightening force was gathering behind the closed door—and sat up in bed. The dream itself no longer upset me, but it seemed to me that I was on the verge of recalling something. In startling detail I remembered a party I had gone to, when I was fifteen or sixteen. I saw the basement playroom very clearly: the piano with sheet music open on the rack, the shine of the piano lamp on the white pages and on the stockings of a girl sitting in a nearby armchair, the striped couch, some guys in the corner playing a child's game with blocks, the cigarette smoke, the bowl of pretzel sticks—and there on a hassock near the window, leaning forward a little, wearing a white blouse and a long dark skirt, her hands in her lap, Elaine Coleman. Her face was sketchy—dark hair some shade of brown, grainy skin—and not entirely to be trusted, since it showed signs of having been infected by the photograph of the missing Elaine, but I had no doubt that I had remembered her.

I tried to bring her into sharper focus, but it was as if I hadn't looked at her directly. The more I tried to recapture that evening, the more sharply I was able to see details of the basement playroom (my hands on the chipped white piano keys, the green and red and yellow blocks forming a higher and higher tower, someone on the swim team moving his arms out from his chest as he demonstrated the butterfly, the dazzling knees of Lorraine Palermo in sheer stockings), but I could not summon Elaine Coleman's face.

According to the landlady, the bedroom showed no signs of disturbance. The pillow had been removed from under the bedclothes and placed against the headboard. On the nightstand a cup half filled with tea rested on a postcard announcing the opening of a new hardware store. The bedspread was slightly rumpled; on it lay a white flannel nightgown printed with tiny pale-blue flowers, and a fat paperback resting open against the spread. The lamp on the nightstand was still on.

We tried to imagine the landlady in the bedroom doorway, her first steps into the quiet room, the afternoon sunlight streaming in past the closed venetian blinds, the pale, hot bulb in the sun-streaked lamp.

The newspapers reported that Elaine Coleman had gone on from high school to attend a small college in Vermont, where she majored in business and wrote one drama review for the school paper. After graduation she lived for a year in the same college town, waitressing at a seafood restaurant; then she returned to our town, where she lived for a few years in a one-room apartment before moving to the two-room apartment on Willow Street. During her college years her parents had moved to California, from where the father, an electrician, moved alone to Oregon. "She didn't have a mean bone in her body," her mother was quoted as saying. Elaine worked for a year on the town paper, waited on tables, worked in the post office and a coffee shop, before getting a job in a business supply store in a neighboring town. People remembered her as a quiet woman, polite, a good worker. She seemed to have no close friends.

I now recalled catching glimpses of a half-familiar face during summers home from college, and later, when I returned to town and settled down. I had long ago forgotten her name. She would be standing at the far end of a supermarket aisle, or on line in a drugstore, or disappearing into a store on Main Street. I noticed her without looking at her, as one might notice a friend's aunt. If our paths crossed, I would nod and pass by, thinking of other things. After all, we had never been friends, she and I—we had never been anything. She was someone I'd gone to high school with, that was all, someone I scarcely knew, though it was also true that I had nothing against her. Was it really the missing

Elaine? Only after her disappearance did those fleeting encounters seem pierced by a poignance I knew to be false, though I couldn't help feeling it anyway, for it was as if I ought to have stopped and talked to her, warned her, saved her, done something.

My second vivid memory of Elaine Coleman came to me three days after my memory of the party. It was sometime in high school, and I was out walking with my friend Roger on one of those sunny autumn afternoons when the sky is so blue and clear that it ought to be summer, but the sugar maples have turned red and yellow, and smoke from leaf fires stings your eyes. We had gone for a long walk into an unfamiliar neighborhood on the other side of town. Here the houses were small, with detached garages; on the lawns you saw an occasional plastic yellow sunflower or fake deer. Roger was talking about a girl he was crazy about, who played tennis and lived in a fancy house on Gideon Hill, and I was advising him to disguise himself as a caretaker and apply for a job trimming her rosebushes. "The yard move," I said. "It gets 'em every time." "She would never respect me," Roger answered seriously. We were passing a garage where a girl in jeans and a dark parka was tossing a basketball into a hoop without a net. The garage door was open and you could see old furniture inside, couches with lamps lying on them and tables holding upside-down chairs. The basketball hit the rim and came bouncing down the drive toward us. I caught it and tossed it back to the girl, who had started after it but had stopped upon seeing us. I recognized Elaine Coleman. "Thanks," she said, holding the basketball in two hands and hesitating a moment before she lowered her eyes and turned away.

What struck me, as I remembered that afternoon, was the moment of hesitation. It might have meant a number of things, such as "Do you and Roger want to shoot a few?" or "I'd like to invite you to shoot a basket but I don't want to ask you if you don't really want to" or maybe something else entirely, but in that moment, which seemed a moment of uncertainty, Roger glanced sharply at me and mouthed a silent "No." What troubled my memory was the sense that Elaine had seen that look, that judgment; she must have been skilled at reading dismissive signs. We walked away into the blue afternoon of high autumn, talking about the girl on Gideon Hill, and in the clear air I could hear the sharp, repeated sound of the basketball striking the driveway as Elaine Coleman walked back toward the garage.

Is it true that whatever has once been seen is in the mind forever? After my second memory I expected an eruption of images, as if they had only been waiting for the chance to reveal themselves. In senior year of high school I must have seen her every day in English class and homeroom, must have passed her in the halls and seen her in the cafeteria, to say nothing of the inevitable chance meetings in the streets and stores of a small town, but aside from the party and the garage I could summon no further image, not one. Nor could I see her face. It was as if she had no face, no features. Even the three photographs appeared to be of three different people, or perhaps they were three versions of a single person no one had ever seen. And so I returned to my two memories, as if they contained a secret that only intense scrutiny could bring to light. But though I saw, always more clearly, the chipped yellowish-white keys of the piano, the glittering stockings, the blue autumn sky, the sun glinting into the shadowy garage with its chairs and tables and boxes, though I saw, or seemed to see, the scuffed black loafer and white ribbed sock of a foot near the piano and the sparkling black shingles on the garage roof, I could not see more of Elaine Coleman than I had already remembered: the hands in the lap, at the party; the moment of hesitation, in the driveway.

During the first few weeks, when the story still seemed important, the newspapers located someone named Richard

Baxter, who worked in a chemical plant in a nearby town. He had last seen Elaine Coleman three years ago. "We went out a few times," he was quoted as saying. "She was a nice girl, quiet. She didn't really have all that much to say." He didn't remember too much about her, he said.

The bafflement of the police, the lack of clues, the locked door, the closed windows, led me to wonder whether we were formulating the problem properly, whether we were failing to take into account some crucial element. In all discussions of the disappearance only two possibilities, in all their variations, were ever considered: abduction and escape. The first possibility, although it could never be entirely discounted, had been decisively called into question by the police investigation, which found in the rooms and the yard no evidence whatever of an intruder. It therefore seemed more reasonable to imagine that Elaine Coleman had left of her own volition. Indeed it was tempting to believe that by an act of will she had broken from her lonely routine and set forth secretly to start a new life. Alone, friendless, restless, unhappy, and nearing her thirtieth birthday, she had at last overcome some inner constriction and surrendered herself to the lure of adventure. This theory was able to make clever use of the abandoned keys, wallet, coat, and car, which became the very proof of the radical nature of her break from everything familiar in her life. Skeptics pointed out that she wasn't likely to get very far without her credit card, her driver's license, and the twenty-seven dollars and thirty-four cents found in her wallet. But what finally rendered the theory suspect was the conventional and hopelessly romantic nature of the imagined escape, which not only required her to triumph over the quiet habits of a lifetime, but was so much what we might have wished for her that it seemed penetrated by desires not her own. Thus I wondered whether there might not be some other way to account for the disappearance, some bolder way that called for a different, more elusive, more dangerous logic.

The police searched the north woods with dogs, dragged the pond behind the lumberyard. For a while there were rumors that she'd been kidnapped in the parking lot where she worked, but two employees had seen her drive off, Mary Blessington had waved to her in the evening, and Mrs. Ziolkowski had heard her closing the refrigerator door, rattling a dish, moving around.

If there was no abduction and no escape, then Elaine Coleman must have climbed the stairs, entered her apartment, locked her door, put the milk in the refrigerator, hung her coat over the back of a chair, and—disappeared. Period. End of discussion. Or to put it another way: the disappearance must have taken place *within the apartment itself.* If one ruled out abduction and escape, then Elaine Coleman ought to have been found somewhere in her rooms—perhaps dead in a closet. But the police investigation had been thorough. She appeared to have vanished from her rooms as completely as she had vanished from my mind, leaving behind only a scattering of clues to suggest she had ever been there.

As the investigation slowly unraveled, as the posters faded and at length disappeared, I tried desperately to remember more of Elaine Coleman, as if I owed her at least the courtesy of recollection. What bothered me wasn't so much the disappearance itself, since I had scarcely known her, or even the possible ugliness of that disappearance, but my own failure of memory. Others recalled her still more dimly. It was as if none of us had ever looked at her, or had looked at her while thinking of something more interesting. I felt that we were guilty of some obscure crime. For it seemed to me that we who had seen her now and then out of the corner of our eyes, we who had seen her without seeing her, who without malice had failed to give her our full attention, were already preparing her for the fate that overtook her, were already, in a sense not yet clear to me, pushing her in the direction of disappearance.

It was during this time of failed recollection that I had what can only be called a pseudo-memory of Elaine Coleman, which haunted me precisely to the extent that I did not know how much of her it contained. The time was two or three years before the disappearance. I remembered that I was at a movie theater with a friend, my friend's wife, and a woman I was seeing then. It was a foreign movie, black and white, with subtitles; I remembered my friend's wife laughing wildly at the childish translation of a curse while the actor on the screen smashed his fist against a door. I recalled a big tub of popcorn that the four of us passed back and forth. I recalled the chill of the air-conditioning, which made me long for the heat of the summer night. Slowly the lights came on, the credits continued to roll, and as the four of us began making our way up the crowded aisle I noticed a woman in dark clothes rising from a seat near the far aisle. I caught only a glimpse of her before looking irritably away. She reminded me of someone I half knew, maybe the girl from my high school whom I sometimes saw and whose name I had forgotten, and I didn't want to catch her eye, didn't want to be forced to exchange meaningless, awkward words with her, whoever she was. In the bright, jammed lobby I braced myself for the worthless meeting. But for some reason she never emerged from the theater, and as I stepped with relief into the heat of the summer night, which already was beginning to seem oppressive, I wondered whether she'd hung back on purpose because she had seen me turning irritably away. Then I felt a moment of remorse for my harshness toward the half-seen woman in the theater, the pseudo-Elaine, for after all I had nothing against her, the girl who had once been in my English class.

Like a detective, like a lover, I returned relentlessly to the few images I had of her: the dim girl at the party, the girl with the basketball who lowered her eyes, the turned-away face in the yearbook picture, the blurred police photo, the vague person, older now, whom I nodded to occasionally in town, the woman in the theater. I felt as if I'd wronged her in some way, as if I had something to atone for. The paltry images seemed to taunt me, as if they held the secret of her disappearance. The hazy girl, the blurred photo . . . Sometimes I felt an inner shaking or trembling, as if I were on the verge of an overwhelming revelation.

One night I dreamed that I was playing basketball with Elaine Coleman. The driveway was also the beach, the ball kept splashing in shallow water, but Elaine Coleman was laughing, her face was radiant though somehow hidden, and when I woke I felt that the great failure in my life was never to have evoked that laughter.

As the weather grew colder, I began to notice that people no longer wanted to talk about Elaine Coleman. She had simply disappeared, that was all, and one day she'd be found, or forgotten, and that would be that. Life would go on. Sometimes I had the impression that people were angry at her, as if by disappearing she had complicated our lives.

One sunny afternoon in January I drove to the house on Willow Street. I knew the street, lined now with bare, twisted maples that threw long shadows across the road and onto the fronts of the houses opposite. A brilliant blue mailbox stood at one corner, beside a telephone pole with a drum-shaped transformer high up under the crossarm. I parked across from the house, but not directly across, and looked at it furtively, as if I were breaking a law. It was a house like many on the block, two-storied and wood-shingled, with side gables and a black roof. The shingles were painted light gray and the shutters black. I saw pale curtains in all the windows, and the path of red slates leading to the door in the side of the house. The door had two small windows near the top, and they too were curtained. I saw a row of bare bushes and a piece of the backyard, where a bird feeder hung from a branch. I tried to imagine her life there, in the quiet house, but I could imagine nothing, nothing at all. It seemed to me that she had never lived there, never gone to my high school—that she was the town's dream, as it lay napping in the cold sun of a January afternoon.

I drove away from that peaceful, mocking street, which seemed to say, "There's nothing wrong here. We're a respectable street. You've had your look, now give it up," but I was farther than ever from letting her go. Helplessly I rummaged through my images, searched for clues, sensed directions that led nowhere. I felt her slipping from me, vanishing, a ghost-girl, a blurred photo, a woman without features, a figure in dark clothes rising from her seat and floating away.

I returned to the newspaper reports, which I kept in a folder on my night table. One detail that struck me was that the landlady had not actually seen Elaine Coleman on the final evening before her disappearance. The neighbor, who had waved to her at dusk, had not been able to make her out all that well.

Two nights later I woke suddenly, startled as if by a dream, though I could recall no dream. A moment later the truth shook me like a blow to the temple.

Elaine Coleman did not disappear suddenly, as the police believed, but gradually, over the course of time. Those years of sitting unnoticed in corners, of not being looked at, must have given her a queasy, unstable sense of herself. Often she must have felt almost invisible. If it's true that we exist by impressing ourselves on other minds, by entering other imaginations, then the quiet, unremarkable girl whom no one noticed must at times have felt herself growing vague, as if she were gradually being erased by the world's inattention. In high school, the process of blurring begun much earlier had probably not yet reached a critical stage; her face, with its characteristically lowered and averted eyes, had grown only a little uncertain. By the time she returned from college, the erasure had become more advanced. The woman glimpsed in town without ever being seen, the unimagined person whom no one could recall clearly, was growing dim, fading away, vanishing, like a room at dusk. She was moving irrevocably toward the realm of dream.

On that last evening, when Mary Blessington waved to her in the dusk without really seeing her, Elaine Coleman was scarcely more than a shadow. She climbed the stairs to her room, locked the door as usual, put the milk in the refrigerator, and hung her coat over the back of a chair. Behind her the secondhand mirror barely reflected her. She heated the kettle and sat at the kitchen table, reading the paper and drinking a cup of tea. Had she been feeling tired lately, or was there a sense of lightness, of anticipation? In the bedroom she set her cup of tea down on a postcard on her nightstand and changed into her heavy white nightgown with its little blue flowers. Later, when she felt rested, she would make dinner. She pulled out the pillow and lay down with a book. Dusk was deepening into early night. In the darkening room she could see a shadowy nightstand, the sleeve of a sweater hanging on a chair, the faint shape of her body on the bed. She turned on the lamp and tried to read. Her eyes, heavy lidded, began to close. I imagined a not-unpleasant tiredness, a feeling of finality, a sensation of dispersion. The next day there was nothing but a nightgown and a paperback on a bed.

It may have been a little different; one evening she may have become aware of what was happening to her, she may, in a profound movement of her being, have embraced her fate and joined forces with the powers of dissolution.

She is not alone. On street corners at dusk, in the corridors of dark movie theaters, behind the windows of cars in parking lots at melancholy shopping centers illuminated by pale orange lamps, you sometimes see them, the Elaine Colemans of this world. They lower their eyes, they turn away, they vanish into shadowy places. Sometimes I seem to see, through their nearly transparent skin, a light or a building behind them. I try to catch their eyes, to penetrate them with my attention, but it's always too late, already they are fading, fixed as they are in the long habit of not being noticed. And perhaps the police, who suspected foul play, were not in the end mistaken. For we are no longer innocent, we who do not see and do not remember, we incurious ones, we conspirators in disappearance. I too murdered Elaine Coleman. Let this account be entered in the record.

THE ROOM IN THE ATTIC

I

WAKERS AND DREAMERS

I FIRST SAW WOLF in March of junior year. This isn't his story, but I suppose I ought to begin with him. I had slung myself into my seat with the careful nonchalance of which I was a master, and had opened my ancient brownish-red copy of *The Mayor of Casterbridge,* which held nothing of interest for me except the little threads of unraveling cloth along the bottom of the front cover, when I became aware of someone in the row on my right, two seats up. It was as if he'd sprung into existence a moment before. I was struck by his light gray suit—no one in our school wore a suit—and by the top of a paperback that I saw tugging down his left jacket pocket. I felt a brief pity for him, the new kid in the wrong clothes, along with a certain contempt for his suit and a curiosity about his book. He seemed to be studying the back of his left hand, though for a moment I saw him look toward the row of tall windows along the side of the room. One of them stood open, on this mild morning in 1959, held up by an upside-down flowerpot, and for some reason I imagined him striding across the room, pushing the window higher, and stepping through.

When everyone was seated, Mrs. Bassick asked the new boy to stand up. It was an act he performed with surprising grace—a tall young man, sure of himself, unsmiling but at ease in his light gray suit, his hair curving back above his ears and falling in strands over his forehead, his long hands hanging lightly at his sides, as if it were nothing at all to stand up in a roomful of strangers with all eyes on you, or as if he simply didn't care: John Wolfson, who had moved to our town from somewhere else in Connecticut, welcome to William Harrison High. He sat down, not quickly or clumsily as I would have done, and leaned back in an attitude of polite attention as class began. Five minutes later I saw his left hand slip into his jacket pocket and remove the paperback. He held it open on his lap during the rest of class.

Later that day I passed him in the hall and saw that he had shed his jacket and tie. I imagined them hanging forlornly on a hook in his locker. The next day he appeared in a new set of clothes, which he wore with casual ease: chinos, scuffed black loafers with crushed-looking sides, and a light blue long-sleeved shirt with the cuffs rolled back twice over his forearms. I envied his ease with clothes; girls smiled at him; within a week we were calling him Wolf and feeling that he was part of things, as if he'd always been among us, this stranger with his amused gray eyes. Rumor had it that his father had been transferred suddenly from another part of Connecticut; rumor also had it that Wolf had flunked out of prep school or been thrown out for unknown reasons that seemed vaguely glamorous. He was slow-smiling, amiable, a little reserved. What struck me about him, aside from his untroubled way of fitting in, was the alien paperback I always saw among his schoolbooks. The book marked him. It was as if to say he'd gotten rid of the suit, but refused to go further. That, and the slight reserve you could feel in him, his air of self-sufficiency, the touch of mockery you sometimes felt in his smile—it all kept him from being simply popular. Sometimes it seemed to me that he had made an effort to look exactly like us, so that he could do what he liked without attracting attention.

We fell into an uneasy friendship. I too was a secret reader, though I kept my books at home, in my room with the wide bookcase and the old living-room armchair with a sagging cushion. But that wasn't the main thing. I thought of myself, in those days, as someone in disguise—beneath the obedient son, beneath the straight-A student, the agreeable well-brought-up boy with his friends and his ping-pong and his semiofficial girl-friend, there was another being, restless, elusive, mocking, disruptive, imperious, and this shadowy underself had nothing to do with that other one who laughed with his friends and went to school dances and spent summer afternoons at the beach. In a murky sense I felt that my secret reading was a way of burrowing down to that underplace, where a truer or better version of myself lay waiting for me. But Wolf would have none of it. "A book," he declared, "is a dream-machine." He said this one day when we were sitting on the steps of the town library, leaning back against the pillars. "Its purpose," he said, "is to take you out of the world." He jerked his thumb toward the doors of the library, where I worked for two hours a day after school, three days a week. "Welcome to the dream-factory." I protested that for me a book was something else, something to get me past whatever was standing in my way, though I didn't know what it was that was in my way or what I wanted to get to on the other side. "What gets in your way," Wolf said, as if he'd thought about it before, "is all this"—he waved vaguely at Main Street. "Stores, houses, classrooms, alarm clocks, dinner at six, a sound mind in a healthy body. The well-ordered life." He shrugged and held up a book. "My ticket out of here." He gave that slow lazy smile of his, which had, I thought, a touch of mockery in it.

He invited me to his house, one warm April day, when all the windows stood open and you could see out past the baseball field to the railroad tracks running behind it. We left together after school, I walking beside my bike as my books jumped in the dented wire basket, Wolf strolling beside me with a nylon jacket flung over one shoulder like a guy in a shirt ad and his books clutched at his hip. I lived in a newish neighborhood of ranch houses not far from the beach, but Wolf lived on the other side of town, out past the thruway, where the houses grew larger, the trees thicker and greener. We entered the shade of the thruway overpass, filled with the roar of eighteen-wheelers rumbling over our heads, then cut across a small park with slatted benches. After a while we found ourselves walking along a winding road, bordered by short brown posts with red reflectors. Here the houses were set far back from the street behind clusters of pine and oak and maple. At a driveway with a high wooden fence along one side and a high hedge on the other, we turned in and climbed a curving slope.

Around the bend, Wolf's house appeared. Massive and shadowy, it seemed to stand too close to me as I bent my neck back to look up at the row of second-floor windows with their black shutters. The house was so dark that I was surprised to notice it was painted white; the sun struck through the high trees onto the clapboards in small bright bursts of white and burned on the black roof shingles.

"Welcome to Wolfland," he said—and raising his right arm, he moved his long hand in a slow, graceful flourish, shaped like a tilde.

He opened the front door with a key and I followed him into

a living room so gloomy that it felt as if heavy curtains had been closed across the windows. In fact the curtains were open and the windows held upward-slanted blinds that gave a broken view of sun-mottled branches. In the sunnier kitchen he tossed his books onto a table on which sat a gardening glove and an orange box of Wheaties, picked up a note that he read aloud—"Back later. Love, M"—and led me back into the living room, where a stairpost stood at the foot of a carpeted stairway. Upstairs we walked along a dusky hall with closed doors. Wolf stopped at the last one, which he opened by turning the knob and pushing with the toe of his loafer. Repeating his flourish, and adding a little bow, as if he were acting the part of a courtier paying homage to his lord, he waited for me to enter.

I stepped into a dark brown sunless room with drawn shades. One of the shades was torn at the side, letting in a line of light. "Watch out," Wolf said, "don't move," as he crossed the room to an old brass floor lamp with a fringed yellowish shade and pulled the chain. The light, dark as butterscotch, shone on an old armchair that sat in a corner and looked wrong in some way. But what struck me was the book-madness of the place—books lay scattered across the unmade bed and the top of a battered-looking desk, books stood in knee-high piles on the floor, books were crammed sideways and right side up in a narrow bookcase that rose higher than my head and leaned dangerously from the wall, books sat in stacks on top of a dingy dresser. The closet door was propped open by a pile of books, and from beneath the bed a book stuck out beside the toe of a maroon slipper.

"Have a seat," Wolf said, indicating the armchair, which I now saw was without legs. I sat down carefully in the low chair, afraid I might knock over the book piles that lay on the floor against each arm. Wolf yanked back the spread with its load of books, which went tumbling against the wall, and lay down on his back with his head against a pillow, one arm behind his neck and his ankles crossed. That afternoon he told me that the difference between human beings and animals was that human beings were able to dream while awake. He said that the purpose of books was to permit us to exercise that faculty. Art, he said, was a controlled madness, which was why the people who selected books for high school English classes were careful to choose only false books that were discussable, boring, and sane, or else, if they chose a real book by mistake, they presented it in a way that ignored everything great and mad about it. He said that high school was for morons and mediocrities. He said that his mother had agreed never to enter his room so long as he changed his sheets once a week. He said that books weren't made of themes, which you could write essays about, but of images that inserted themselves into your brain and replaced what you were seeing with your eyes. There were two kinds of people, he said, wakers and dreamers. Wakers had once had the ability to dream but had lost it, and so they hated dreamers and persecuted them in every way. He said that teachers were wakers. He spoke of writers I'd never heard of, writers such as William Prescott Pearson, A. E. Jacobs, and John Sharp, his favorite, who wrote terrific stories like "The Elevator," about a man who one day enters an elevator in a fifty-six-story office building and never comes out except to use the public bathrooms and the food machines, and "The Infernal Roller Coaster," about a roller coaster that goes up and up and never reaches the top, but whose masterpiece was a five-hundred-page novel that takes place entirely during the blink of an eye. Compared with these works, things like *Silas Marner* and *The Mayor of Disasterbridge* were about as interesting as newspaper supplements advertising vacuum cleaners.

"Care to see the attic?" he said suddenly. In the warm cave of books I had half closed my eyes, but Wolf had risen from the bed and was already standing at the door. I followed him out into the dusk of the hall, past the top of the stairway, to an unpainted door that looked like the door of a linen closet. It opened to reveal a flight of wooden steps. Up we went into that hot attic, where tawny sunlight streamed through a small round window, fell against bare floorboards and splintery rafters, and weakened into a brown darkness. As we passed along, I made out old couches and bureaus and armchairs, as if we'd broken into the furniture department of a big-city store. Then we came to a high old-fashioned record cabinet, which rose up to my chest; Wolf opened the top to reveal a dim turntable, on which lay a ghostly white bear with outstretched arms. He next led me to a wooden wall with a door; it opened onto a short hall, with a door on each side. He stopped at the left-hand one, knocked lightly with a single knuckle, and bent forward as if to listen.

"My sister's room," he then said, and ushered me in.

When he closed the door behind us I found myself in total darkness. I had the sensation that Wolf was standing close to me, but I could not see him there. Then I felt something on my upper arm and jerked away, but it was only Wolf's hand, guiding me. Slowly he moved me forward through the blackness, as I held up an arm as if to protect my face from branches in a forest. "Sit here," he whispered. He placed my hand on what seemed to be the high back of an upholstered chair, with a row of metal buttons running across the top.

I felt my way around the chair and sat down, while I sensed Wolf settling into another seat nearby. I was sitting in a straight-backed stiff chair with hard, upholstered arms, the sort of chair you might find in the ornate parlor of an aging actress in a black-and-white movie. "Isabel," he said quietly, "are you awake?" I strained my eyes in that thick darkness, but I could see nothing at all. It struck me that it was all a hoax, an audacious joke meant to ridicule me in some way. At the same time I listened for the slightest sound and narrowed my eyes until they trembled with the effort to see. Anything could have been in that room.

"She's asleep," Wolf said, and I thought: Perfect, a perfect trick. I imagined him looking at me with a superior smile.

"Wolf?" a voice whispered, but so lightly that I wondered whether I had imagined it.

"Isabel," Wolf's voice said. "Are you up? I brought a visitor."

Something stirred. I heard a sound as of bedclothes, and what seemed like a faint sigh, and somewhere in that darkness I heard the word "Hello."

"Say hello to Isabel," Wolf said.

"Hello," I said, feeling irritable and absurd.

"Tell her your name," Wolf said quietly, as if I were a shy six-year-old child, and I would have said nothing, but who knew what was going on, there in the dark.

"David," I said. "Dave."

"Two names," the voice said; there was more rustling. "Two are better than one." I wondered whether Wolf had learned the trick of throwing his voice.

"Do you like my name, David Dave?"

I hesitated. "Yes," I said. "I do."

"Uh-uh-uh," she said playfully, and I imagined a finger wagging in the dark. "You had to think about it."

"But I do," I said, thinking quickly. "I was listening to the sound of it, in my mind."

"Oh, that was a good answer, David Dave, a very good answer. I don't believe you, not for a second, but I won't make you pay a penalty, this time. So hey, how do you like my room? No no, don't worry, just kidding. What's Wolfie been telling you about me?"

"Not too much, actually."

"Oh good, then you can make me up. Isabel, or The Mystery of the Haunted Chamber. Hoooo, I'm feeling tired. Will you come back and sit with me again, David Dave?"

"Yes," I said. "I will. Definitely."

I heard a long yawn, and a mumbled phrase that sounded like "See ya later, alligator," and then I felt Wolf's hand on my arm and he was leading me out of the dark room and shutting the door carefully behind him. We walked in silence down the wooden steps and the carpeted steps into the gloom of the living room. Evidently it was time to go. Maybe he didn't want me to question him about that little game of his, up there in the dark. If he wished to be enigmatic, that was fine with me.

"She likes you," he said at the front door, standing with his forearm up against the jamb and his other hand clasping his raised shoulder. He lowered his voice to say, "Don't worry about anything." "Okay," I said, "I won't," and walked down the front steps to my bike, with its dented wire basket filled with books. I kicked up the stand, swung my leg over the seat, and gave a wave as I started down the winding drive. At the bend I glanced back at the house, rising in a kind of twilight, then whipped around to watch the shade-darkened drive as I rushed downhill between the high fence and the hedge, and when I burst onto the street I had to tighten my eyes in the sudden harsh light of the afternoon sun.

II

ADVENTURES IN THE DARK

All the way home, along hot streets printed with the curved shadows of telephone wires, I saw the high dark house, the cave of books, the black chamber. It all reminded me of something, and as I rode through the shade of the thruway overpass and broke into the sun it came to me: the darkness of the movie theater, the sun-striped lobby, the emergence into the glare of a summer afternoon. I had always liked that moment of confusion, when your mind is possessed by two worlds at once: the hard sidewalk with its anthills and its silver gum wrapper, the swordfight in the high room with the crimson curtain. But soon the grainy sidewalk, the brilliant yellow fire hydrant, the flash of sun on the fender of a passing car, the jewel-green traffic light, become so vivid and exact that the other pictures grow dim, and you can hardly summon up the vague dark house, the book piles on the floor, the dim voice in the dark. I had the feeling that if I turned my bike around and rode back I'd find nothing at all—only a winding road lined with trees and a few dark posts with red reflectors.

At home I greeted my mother in the sunny kitchen, where she held up her hands to show me her flour-covered fingers and smoothed back a lock of hair with the back of a wrist. In my room I tossed my books on the bed and slumped down next to them with my neck against the wall and my legs dangling over the side. My wooden bookcase, painted a shiny gray, filled me with irritation. Here and there among the books were spaces given over to other things—old board games, a wooden box of chess pieces with a sliding top, two collections of stamps, a varnished bowl I had made in woodshop in the seventh grade. On top was my display of minerals, each with its label, and then came a globe on a brass stand, an electric clock with a visible cord, and a radiometer with vanes spinning in the light. Even the books exasperated me: they stood in neat rows, held tightly in place by green metal bookends with cork-lined bases.

On the beige wall and part of my bureau, long stripes of sunlight, thrown from the open slats of my blinds, lay tipped at an angle.

That night I woke in the dark. But I saw at once that it wasn't dark: light from a streetlamp glimmered on the globe, on the leather edges of the blotter on my desk, on the metal curve of the shade of the floor lamp beside my reading chair. Suddenly I thought: The attic was empty, no one was there—and I fell asleep.

The next day I saw Wolf in English, French, and American History. I passed him twice in the halls, saw him leaving the cafeteria as I entered, and spoke with him briefly after school, checking my watch as we stood on a plot of brownish grass near the bridge that crossed the railroad tracks and led to the center of town. I had to get over to the library and work my two-hour shift. Wolf stood smoking a cigarette with his thumb hooked in his belt and his eyes narrowed against the updrifting bluish smoke. He said nothing about his house, nothing about Isabel, and as I walked down toward Main Street I felt a ripple of anger, as if something had been taken away from me. I could forgive the deception but not the silence. On the second floor of the library, where I stood removing books from a metal cart and studying the white Dewey decimal numbers on the back before placing the books on the shelves, I recalled his book-mad room and wondered whether I had fallen asleep there, in that stumpy armchair, and dreamed my visit to his invisible sister.

It was like that for the rest of the week: a few meetings in class, a few words after school. It was as if he'd invited me on an adventure and changed his mind. I felt like the victim of an unpleasant joke and vowed to stay out of his way. That weekend I set up my ping-pong table in the garage and called up my friends Ray and Dennis. My mother brought out glasses of lemonade heavy with ice cubes and we ate fistfuls of pretzel sticks and ran after the white ball as it rolled down the driveway toward the street, where kids from next door were playing Wiffle ball with a yellow plastic bat and a man with a strap around his waist stood leaning away from the top of a telephone pole. Afterward we sat on the screened back porch and played canasta on the green card table. On Monday I worked again at the library, and on Tuesday, a day off, Wolf invited me to his house.

It was still there at the top of the curving drive, less dark than I had remembered it, the clapboards distinctly white in the broken shade of the pines and Norway maples. As we walked through the living room toward the stairs, a tall handsome woman in khaki Bermuda shorts and a white halter entered from the kitchen, carrying a trowel in one hand and wearing on the other a grass-stained glove. I saw at once that she was Wolf's mother—saw it by something in the cheekbones, in the eyes, in the air of careless authority with which she inhabited her body. She thrust the trowel into the gardening glove, reached out her long bare hand, and shook hands firmly. "I'm John's mother," she said. For a moment I wondered who John was. "Sorry for the mess. You must be David."

"He is, and then again he isn't," Wolf said, and throwing an arm across her shoulders he added, "What mess?" As she turned to him with a look of loving exasperation, she raised the back of her hand to her temple and smoothed away a piece of dark hair—and suddenly I imagined a world of mothers with hands dipped in work, raising their wrists gracefully to smooth back their hair.

In his room with the drawn shades he sat in the legless armchair with his feet up on the bed, while I lay across the bed with my neck against the wall, one foot on the floor and one ankle resting on my knee. He spoke only about Isabel. She was shy, extremely shy—hence the meeting in the dark. Whenever she met someone new—an ordeal she preferred to avoid—she insisted on the condition of absolute darkness. Thick curtains hung over the windows of the attic room. But don't worry—when she got to know me better, when she got used to me, he was sure she'd come out of the dark. Besides, she didn't *only* stay in her room—sometimes she came down for dinner or walked around the house. It was only strangers who made her nervous. He appreciated my willingness to visit her, she needed to see people, god did she need to see people, though not just any old moronic people. As soon as he'd met me, he'd been sure. Truth was, about a year ago she'd had some kind of—well, they called it a breakdown, though in his opinion her nervous system had discovered a brilliant way of allowing her to do whatever she wanted without having to suffer the boredom of good old high school and all the rest of the famous teenage routine. She hadn't attended school for the last year, but the board of education had allowed her to study at home and take the tests in her room. She was much more studious than he was, always memorizing French irregular verbs and the parts of earthworms. She was a year younger than we were. He himself would love to have a nice little breakdown, to use that word, though frankly he'd prefer to call it a fix-up, but he suffered from an embarrassing case of perfect health, he couldn't even manage to catch a cold, something must be wrong with him.

Wolf reached under his chair, brought up a pack of cigarettes, and held it out to me with raised eyebrows. He shrugged, thrust one into his mouth, and lit up. "It all depends on how you define health," he said. He drew the smoke deep into his lungs and, raising his chin so that his face was nearly horizontal, blew a slow stream of smoke toward the ceiling. When he was done he raised a shade, opened the window, and made little brushing motions with his hands toward the screen. He blew at the screen with short quick bursts of breath. Then he shut the window and jerked down the shade.

He turned to face me, leaning back against the window frame with his hands in his pockets and his ankles crossed.

"Do you have a girlfriend?" he asked.

It wasn't a question I was expecting. "Yes and no," I finally said.

"Brilliant answer," Wolf said, with his slow lazy smile. He pushed with his shoulders against the window frame and stood up. "Shall we?" He nodded toward the door.

I followed him up the wooden steps into the sun-streaked dark attic. In the little hall he whispered, "She's expecting you." At the last door he knocked with his hand held sideways, using a single knuckle. He opened the door—in the dim light of the hall I caught sight of the edge of a bureau with a shadowy hairbrush on top—and a moment later I was in utter darkness. He led me to the high-backed chair, and as I sat upright against the stiff back and gripped the chair arms, I felt like the wooden carving of a king.

"Welcome, stranger," the voice said. It seemed to be coming from a few feet away, as if from someone sitting up in bed. "What brings you to these parts?" I had the feeling that Wolf was staring at me in the dark.

"I was looking for the post office," I said.

"This here's the 'lectric company, mister," Isabel said.

The black room, the stiff chair, the word " 'lectric," the sense that I was being tested in some way, all this made me break into a sharp, nervous laugh.

I could feel Wolf rising from his chair. "I'll be in my room. Just ring if you need anything." I heard his footsteps on the rug. The door opened and closed quickly.

"Did he say 'ring'?"

"I've got a bell."

"Oh—your Isa-bell."

"Do you always make jokes?"

"Only in the dark."

"And when it gets light?"

"Dead serious."

"Lucky it's dark. Let's play a game."

"In the dark?"

"You'll see."

I tried to imagine some mad game of Monopoly, in which you had to select your piece by touch, trying to distinguish the ship from the car, then rolled the dice across an invisible board and carefully felt their smooth sides to find the slightly recessed dots. I was wondering how I might contrive to move my piece along an unseen board when I felt something soft against my fingers and snatched my hand away.

"Here," Isabel said. "Tell me what it is. You can only use one hand."

I reached out my hand and felt a soft pressure against the palm. I closed my fingers over something furry or fuzzy and roundish, with a hardness under the fur. On one side the fur gave way to a smoothness of cloth. It felt familiar, this roundish furryish thing about the size of my palm, but though I kept turning it over and stroking it with my thumb, I couldn't figure it out.

"Give up?" she said. "Actually, I should have told you—it's part of something."

"Is it part of a stuffed animal?"

"Well, no. Close. Actually—you'll kill me—it's an earmuff. It came off that metal thing that goes over your head."

She next passed me an object that was hard and thin and cool, which immediately shaped itself against my fingers as a teaspoon.

"That was way too easy," I said.

"Well, I felt guilty. Try this one."

It was small and curved, with a clip of some sort attached to it, and suddenly I knew: a barrette. There followed a hard leathery object that was easy—an eyeglass case—and then a mysterious cloth strip with tassels that turned out to be a bookmark, and then a papery spongy object with a string attached that I triumphantly identified as a tea bag. Once, as she passed me a small glass object, I felt against the underside of my fingers the light pressure of her fingertips. And once, after a pause in which I heard sounds as of shifting cloth, she let fall into my outstretched hand a longish piece of fabric that she immediately snatched away, saying "That wasn't fair," bursting into a laugh at my protest, and refusing to identify it, even as I imagined her slipping back into a shirt or pajama top.

After the touching game she asked me to describe my room. I told her about my bookcase, my armchair with the sagging cushion, and my wall lamp that could be pulled out on a fold-up metal contraption, but she kept asking for more details. "I can't *see* anything," she said, sounding exasperated. I tried to make her see the X-shaped crosspieces of the unfolding wall lamp over my bed, and then I described, with fanatical care, the six-sided quartz crystal, the pale purple fluorite crystal in the shape of a tetrahedron, and the amethyst geode in my mineral collection. When it was her turn, she described a cherrywood box on her desk, with four compartments. One held a small pouch of blue felt tied with leather thongs and containing a silver dollar and an Indian-head penny, the second held a pair of short red-handled scissors, the third a set of tortoiseshell barrettes, and the fourth a small yellowish ivory figurine, a Chinese sage seated with his legs crossed and holding an open book in his lap. One of his hands was broken off at the wrist, he wore a broad-brimmed conical hat, the ivory pages of the book were wavy—and as she described the ivory man in the compartment of the cherrywood box, I seemed to see, taking shape in the darkness, a faint and tremulous Chinese sage, hovering at the height of my head.

We were playing Ghost when I was startled by a knock at the

door. Quickly the door opened and closed; I was aware of a momentary change in the quality of blackness but saw nothing. "It's nearly five-thirty," Wolf said—he knew I was expected home by six. "See you, stranger," Isabel said as Wolf led me toward the door. Downstairs I greeted his mother, who was standing in the living room with her arms reaching up to the top of a drooping curtain. When she turned to look at me, keeping one hand on the curtain and waving the fingers of her other hand, I saw that her mouth was full of safety pins.

I now began to visit Wolf's house after school on Tuesdays and Thursdays, when I was free of the library, and on weekend afternoons. I would climb the stairs to Wolf's room, where we talked for a while, and then he would rise from the chair or bed very slowly, as if he were being tugged back by a tremendous force, and lead me up to the attic. At the door of Isabel's room he knocked with one knuckle, lightly, twice. Without waiting for a reply, he held open the door and closed it quickly behind me before returning to his room. If he cared that I was spending less time with him than with his sister, he never showed it. If anything, he seemed eager for me to visit her—it was as if he thought I might cure her in some way. Exactly what it all meant I didn't know, couldn't care. I knew only that I needed to visit Isabel, to be with her in that room. The darkness excited me—I could feel it seize me and draw me in. Everything in me seemed to quicken there.

The darkness, the hidden face, the secret room, the unseeing of Isabel—it all soon came to feel as much a part of her as her voice. If I tried to picture her, I saw a wavering shadowy image that hardened gradually into a tall girl in Bermuda shorts, holding a trowel. Sometimes, before she faded away, I saw gray, amused eyes—Wolf's eyes. She loved games, all sorts of games, and it occurred to me that one thing we were doing in that room was playing the game of darkness. She was like a child who closes her eyes, stretches out her arms, and pretends to be blind. For all I knew, she might really be blind—she might really be anything. Whatever she was, I had to go there, to the dark at the top of the house.

In one of our kitchen drawers, the one to the right of the silverware drawer, there were two flashlights, a regular one and a very small one, the size of a fountain pen. One day not long after my first visit, I slipped the small flashlight into my pocket and carried it with me into the darkness of Isabel's room. My plan was to take it out during one of our games, fiddle with it, and shine it suddenly and briefly, as if by accident, at Isabel. She would spring into existence—at last!—if only for a second, before vanishing into the hidden world. I would apologize and we would continue as before.

As I sat in the stiff chair, holding the little flashlight and listening to Isabel tell me about a new word game she'd invented, I kept waiting for the right moment. I could hear her shifting in the bed—I imagined her moving her arms about as she talked. Then I imagined her sleeves, perhaps pajama sleeves, slipping back along her gesturing forearms. At that instant my desire to see her, to strip her of darkness, became so ferocious that I raised my fingertips to my throat and felt the thudding of my blood. I imagined her startled eyes, brilliant with fear. It seemed to me that to shine the light at Isabel, to expose her to my greedy gaze, would be like tearing off her clothes. With a feeling of shame, of sorrow, and of something that felt like gratitude, I returned the light to my pocket.

And settling into the chair, as the afternoon's deep night flowed into me, I wondered at my ignorance; for I saw that what held me there was the darkness, the lure of an unseen, mysterious world.

Meanwhile, in the unmysterious world outside Wolfland, I burst out laughing in the cafeteria, raised my hand in American

History, banged my locker shut. I shelved books in the library, drank cherry Cokes at Lucy's Luncheonette, and went miniature golfing on Friday nights with Ray and Dennis, while cars rolled by on the Post Road with their windows open and tough-looking boys with slicked-back hair slapped their hands on car tops to blasts of rock 'n' roll. At every moment I felt invaded by Isabel, but at the same time I had trouble remembering her exactly, in the world beyond her room. The sunlit realm kept threatening to make a ghost of her, or to erase her entirely, and I began to look forward to the coming of night, when she grew more vivid in my mind.

One Saturday morning as I was walking in town, on my way to buy a birthday card for a girl in my French class, I was shocked to see Isabel strolling out of Mancini's drugstore. Her dark hair, cut short, was held back by a glossy barrette, and her short-sleeved white blouse was tucked into her jeans, which were rolled up to midcalf. A navy-blue pocketbook, slung over her left shoulder, kept bumping against her right hip. Although I knew that Isabel never left her house, that I had allowed a scattering of details, which must have been collecting in my mind, to attach themselves to this stranger strolling out of Mancini's drugstore, still my heart beat hard, my breath came quick, and not until later that afternoon, when I climbed the wooden stairs, did I grow calm in the rich blackness of Isabel's chamber.

Sometimes when I sat with her in the dark I wondered whether she was deformed in some way. I imagined a twisted mouth, a smashed nose, a mulberry birthmark spreading like a stain across her face. As a ghost-swarm of ugly Isabels rose in my mind, I felt repelled not so much by the images as by something in myself that was creating them, and as if in protest another kind of Isabel began to appear, blue-eyed Isabels and smiling Isabels, Isabels in red shorts, Isabels in faded jeans with a dark blue patch in back where a pocket had torn off, Isabels in white bathing suits wiping their glistening arms with beach towels, until my brain was so filled with false Isabels that I pressed my hands against the sides of my head, as if to crush them to death.

One night I thought: The blackness is a poison that soaks into my skin and makes me insane. During these seizures I have delusions that I call Isabel. The thought interested me, excited me, as if I had found the solution to a difficult problem in trigonometry, but as the night wore on, the idea grew less and less interesting until it left me feeling bored and indifferent.

One afternoon as we were playing the game of objects, Isabel said, "Now hold out your hand palm up, this is a tricky one." I was instantly alert; something in her voice betrayed a secret excitement. Holding out my hand as she had instructed, I heard some movement on the bed. A moment later I felt a softly hard, heavyish object lowered slowly onto my palm. A confusion came over me, I began to close my fingers over it, suddenly there was a wild laugh near my ear and she snatched the strange object away, crying, "Couldn't you guess? Couldn't you guess?" but I had already recognized, lying for a moment in the palm of my hand, Isabel's warm forearm.

As the evenings became hotter, I found it difficult to sit at my desk doing homework in the light of my twin-bulb fluorescent lamp. I had always found it pleasing and even soothing to complete homework assignments: the carefully numbered answers, the crisp sound of turned pages, the red and yellow and green index tabs, the clean white notebook paper with its orderly rows of blue lines and the pale red line running down the side. Now it all irritated me, as if I were being distracted from the real business of life. Through the screens of my partly open windows I could hear the sounds of my neighborhood at dusk: low voices in a nearby yard, the rising and falling hum of a distant lawnmower, dishes clinking from an open window, the slam of a car door, a girl's high laughter. I began memorizing the sounds and collecting new ones, so that I could report them to Isabel: footsteps in another room, which might be my father going into the kitchen for a box of crackers or my mother coming in from the back porch; the sound of a garage door being lowered; the wheels of a passing bicycle rustling in the sand at the side of the street. The sounds pleased me, because I could bring them to Isabel, but at the same time they disturbed me, for it was as if the world that separated me from Isabel were growing thicker and more impenetrable as I listened.

At night I kept waking up and falling asleep, as Isabels tumbled through my mind. In the mornings I felt sluggish and heavy-headed, and sometimes during the day I would catch my mother looking at me in the way she did when I was coming down with something.

One afternoon toward the middle of June, Isabel seemed a little distracted. It was hot in the attic room and the darkness seemed thick and soft, like wool. I could hear her shifting about on the bed, and then I heard another sound, as of fingers stroking cloth, but silkier. "What are you doing, Isabel?" "Oh, brushing my hair." I imagined the brush I'd half glimpsed on the bureau as it pulled its way through stretched-out hair that kept changing from dark to blond to reddish brown. I heard the clunk of what I thought must be a brush on a table and suddenly she said, "Would you like to see my room?" My hands clutched the arms of the chair—I imagined a burst of light, like a blow to my forehead. Isabel laughed; her laughter sounded cruel; I knew nothing about this girl in the dark, who was suddenly going to reveal herself to me in some violent way; I could feel an Isabel rising in my mind, but her head was the head of some girl in my English class, which faded away and was replaced by another head; something touched my arm. "Get up," her voice said, very close to me.

Holding my wrist in her hand, she led me through the dark

and placed my hand on cool wood surfaces, roundish knobs, soft protuberances, velvety edges. Images of drawers and padded seats and velvet jewel boxes floated in my mind. After a while I felt against my palm the familiar back of my upholstered chair with its row of metal buttons. "Is the tour over, Isabel?" "One more item of interest." She took a step and, still holding my wrist, placed my hand on a rumpled softness that felt like a sheet. "Tour over," she said, and released my wrist. I heard a creak, a rustling, silence.

"So how do you like my room?" she asked, in a voice that came from the other end of the bed.

"It's very— it's very—," I said, searching for the exact word.

"You probably ought to lie down, you know. If you're tired."

I climbed tensely onto the bed, pressing my knees into the mattress, and began crawling across it toward her voice. "Nnnn!" I said, snatching my hand away as something moved out of reach. The bed seemed long, longer than the entire room, though I was moving so slowly that I was almost motionless. "Are you there?" I said to the dark. Isabel said nothing. I patted about: a pillow, another pillow, a sheet, a turned-back spread. "Where are you?" I asked the dark. "Here," she whispered, so close that I could feel her breath against my ear. I reached out and felt empty air. "I can't see you, Isabel." Deep in the room I heard a burst of laughter. "Can you fly, Isabel? Is that your secret?" I listened to the room. "Are you anywhere?" Still kneeling on the bed, but raising my upper body, like a rearing horse, I swept out both hands, my fingertips fluttering about, stroking the dark. From the pillow and sheets came a fresh, slightly soapy scent. I lay down on my stomach, pressing my cheek into a pillow and inhaling the scent of Isabel. In the darkness I closed my eyes. Somewhere I heard a sound, as of a foot knocking against a piece of furniture. Then I felt a pushing-down in the mattress. Something hard pressed against the side of my arm. I felt the hardness with my fingertips and suddenly understood that I was touching a face. It pulled away. "Isabel," I said. "Isabel, Isabel, Isabel." Nothing was there. In the thick darkness I felt myself dissolving, turning into black mist, spreading into the farthest reaches of the room.

III

REVELATION

On a brilliant afternoon in July, under a sky so blue that it seemed to have weight, the beach towels on the sand reminded me of the rectangles of color in a child's paint box. Here and there a slanted beach umbrella partly shaded a blanket. Under the wide umbrellas, thermos jugs and cooler chests and half-open picnic baskets stood among yellow water wings and green sea monsters. On my striped towel, in the fierce sun, I leaned back on both elbows and stared off past my ankle bones at the place where the rippling dry sand changed to flat and wet. Low waves broke slowly in uneven lines. The water moved partway up the beach and slid back, leaving a dark shine that quickly vanished.

People were walking about, sitting up on blankets, running in and out of the water. A tall girl with a blond ponytail and coppery glistening legs came walking along the wet sand. Her bathing suit was so white that it looked freshly painted. Her sticking-out breasts looked hard and sharp, like funnels. A small rubber football flew spinning through the bright blue air. In the sand a gull walked stiffly and half lifted its wings. Down in the shallow water a thick-chested senior in a tight bathing suit crouched on his hands and knees, so that I could see the blond hairs glowing on his lower spine—suddenly a lanky junior with hard-muscled legs came running down the beach into the water, flung his hands onto the back of his kneeling friend, and flipped gracefully into the air, landing in the water with a splash. Tilted bottles of soda gleamed here and there in the sand beside beach towels, a girl in a turquoise two-piece stood by the foot of the lifeguard stand, looking up and shading her eyes, and high in the sky a yellow helicopter seemed stuck in the thick blue heavy summer air.

Laughing, whooping, running their hands through their wet hair, Ray and Dennis came striding toward me, kicking up bursts of sand. They picked up their towels and stood rubbing their chests and arms. Water streamed from their bathing suits.

"So guess who I ran into down by the jetty," Ray said, laying out his towel carefully in the sand. "Joyce. She said Vicky thinks you're mad at her." He threw himself facedown on the towel.

"I'm not mad at her. I just want—I just need—"

"Ah just *want,*" Dennis said, holding up his hands as if they were poised over a guitar. "Ah just *need.*" He strummed the guitar.

Summer had come, season of sweet loafing. I spent long hours lying on the beach, playing ping-pong in my shady garage, and reading on the screened back porch, where thin stripes of sun and shade fell across my book from the bamboo blinds. Even my job at the library seemed a lazy sort of half-dreaming, as I wheeled my cart slowly between high dim shelves pierced by spears of sun. But as I lay on the beach running my fingers through the warm sand, as I bent over to retrieve a ping-pong ball from a cluster of broken-toothed rakes and shiny red badminton poles rusting at the bottom, all the time I was waiting for

Isabel. She slept until one or two in the afternoon. No one was allowed to visit her till the middle of the day. Wolf himself never rose before noon and seemed amused at what he called my peculiar habits. "The early bird catches the worm," he said, "but who wants the worm?" I found myself rising later and later in the morning, but there were always hours of sunshine to get through before I arrived in the dark.

"Up so soon?" my father said, glancing at me over the tops of his eyeglasses as he bent toward his lunch in the sunny kitchen.

Sometimes, to pass the time, I took long drives with Ray and Dennis, when Dennis could borrow his mother's car. My plan had been to get my license as soon as school was out, but I woke each day feeling tired and kept putting it off. We would drive along the thruway until we saw the name of some little town we didn't know. Then we drove all over that town, passing through the business district with its brick bank trimmed in white and its glass-fronted barbershop with the slow-turning reflection of a striped pole before heading out to the country lanes with their lonely mailboxes and their low stone walls, and ended up having lunch at some diner where you could get twenty-two kinds of pancake and the maple syrup came in glass containers shaped like smiling bears. Dennis wore sunglasses and drove with one wrist resting on the wheel. In his lamplit room with the drawn shades, Wolf had told me how he'd taken the written test six months ago without once opening the boring manual. "And?" I asked. He smiled, raised a finger, and drew it across his throat.

And at last I made my way up the wooden stairs and disappeared in the dark. "Isabel," I would say, standing by the chair, "are you awake?" Or: "Isabel, are you there?" Sometimes I felt a touch on my arm and I would reach out, saying, "Isabel? Is that you?" as my hand grasped at air. Then I would hear her laughing quietly from the bed or across the room or just behind me or who knew where. She would say, "Welcome, stranger," or "Lo, the traveler returns," or nothing at all. Then I would make my way over to the bed and pat my way along the side and lie down, hoping for a fleeting touch, hoping she would be there.

I visited her every day. When I wasn't working at the library, I rode my bike to her house at three in the afternoon; in Isabel's room I would forget the other world so completely that sometimes when I came downstairs I was startled to see the lamps in the living room glowing bright yellow. Through the front window I could see the porch light shining on black leaves. Then I would phone my parents with apologies and ride my bike home to a reheated dinner, while my mother looked at me with her worried expression and my father asked if I'd ever happened to hear of a clever little invention called the wristwatch. At night I could hear my mother and father talking about me in low voices, as if there were something wrong with me.

On the three afternoons a week I worked at the library, I would ride over to Wolf's house after dinner and not return until after midnight. Sometimes Wolf's mother, who liked to stay up late watching old movies on a little ten-inch television in the darkened living room, offered to drive me home. I would sit with her on the couch for a while, watching a snippet of black-and-white movie: an unshaven man in a rumpled suit stumbling along a dusty street in a Mexican town, a woman in a phone booth frantically dialing as she looked about in terror. Then I would load my bike into the trunk of the car and sit with Wolf's mother in front. On the way to my house, along dark streets that glowed now and then under the yellow light of a streetlamp, she would talk about Wolf: he'd failed three subjects, could you believe it, he was smart as a whip but had always hated school, she was worried about him, I was a good influence. Then with her long fingers she would light up a cigarette, and in the dark car streaked with passing lights I would see her eyes—Wolf's eyes—narrow against the upstreaming smoke.

At times it seemed to me that I inhabited two worlds: a sunny and boring day-world that had nothing to do with Isabel, and a rich night-world that was all Isabel. I soon saw that this division was false. The summer night itself, compared with Isabel's world, was a place of light: the yellow windows of houses, the glow of streetlamps, the porch lights, the headlights of passing cars, the ruby taillights, the white summer moon in the deep blue sky. No, the real division was between the visible world and that other world, where Isabel waited for me like a dark dream.

One afternoon as I stood by the chair I felt something press against my foot. "Isabel, is that you?" In the blackness I listened, then bent over the bed. I patted the covers and began crawling across, all the way to the pillows, but Isabel wasn't there. I heard a small laugh, which seemed to come from the floor. Carefully stepping from the bed I kneeled on the carpet, lifted the spread, and peered into blackness, as if I were looking for a cat. "Come on, Isabel," I said, "I know you're there," and reached my hand under. I felt something furry against my fingers and snatched my hand away. I heard a dim sound, the furry thing pressed into my arm—and closing my hand over it, I drew out from under the bed an object that wasn't a kitten. From the top of the bed Isabel said, "Did you find what you were looking for, David Dave?" but ignoring her I pressed the thick, furry slipper against my face.

Sometimes I tried to imagine her in the world of light. She lay next to me on the beach, on her own towel, with a thin line of sand in between—and though I could see, in my mind, that thin line of sand, and the ribbed white towel with a blue eyeglass case in one corner and a bottle of suntan lotion in another, though I could see a depression in the towel where she had kneeled, and a glitter of sand scattered across one corner, though I could see, or almost see, a wavering above the towel, a trembling of air, as if the atmosphere were thickening, I could not see Isabel.

But in the dark there was only Isabel. She would touch me

and vanish—a laughing ghost. Sometimes, for an instant, my fingers grazed some part of her. She allowed me to lie down on the bed beside her but not to reach out. I could hear her breathing next to me, and along my side I could feel, like a faint exhalation, her nearby side, so close that my arm-hairs bristled. These were the rules of the game, if it was a game—I didn't care, felt only a kind of feverish calm. I needed to be there, needed the dark, the games, the adventure, the kingdom of her room. I needed—I didn't know what. But it was as if I were more myself in that room than anywhere else. Outside, in the light, where everything stood revealed, I was somehow hidden away. In Isabel's dark domain, I lived inside out.

Meanwhile I was getting up later and later. One day after lunch my mother said to me, "You're looking tired, Davy. This friend of yours . . . Wouldn't it be better if you stayed home today?" And looking anxiously at me she placed on my forehead the cool backs of her fingers.

"Don't," I said, jerking my head away.

One afternoon I found Isabel in the dark. Instead of walking to the right of my chair, as I usually did, I changed my mind at the last moment and walked to the left—and suddenly I stumbled against her, where she'd been crouching or lying, and I fell. I disentangled myself in a great flailing rush, and as I did so I felt for an instant, against my ribs, a slippery silky material that slid over something soft that suddenly vanished.

Because she had asked me about the beach, I began to bring her things: a smooth stone, a mussel shell, the claw of a small crab. I collected impressions for her, too, like the dark shine of the sand as the waves slid back, or the tilted bottles of soda beside the beach towels. The soda itself looked tilted, against the slanted glass, but was actually level with the sand. She always wanted to see more—the exact shape of a wave, the pattern of footprints in a sandbar—and I felt myself becoming a connoisseur of sensations, an artist of the world of light.

But what I longed for was the dark room, the realm, the mystery of Isabel-land. There, the other world dissolved in a solution of black. There, all was pleasure, strangeness, and a kind of sensual promise that drifted in the air like a dark perfume.

"Do you know what this is?" she said. "One hand. Come on. Guess."

In my palm I felt a soft, slinky thing, which filled my hand slowly, as if lowered from a height.

"Is it a scarf?" I said, rubbing it with my thumb as it spilled over the sides of my hand.

"A scarf!" she said, bursting into wild laughter.

One day Dennis said to me, "So what's with you and Vicky?" We were sitting on my front steps, watching people on the way to the beach, with their towels and radios.

"Nothing's with me and Vicky."

"Okay, okay," he said. "Jesus."

Sometimes I had the sense that Isabel was revealing herself to me slowly, like a gradually materializing phantom, according to a plan that eluded me. If I waited patiently, it would all become clear, as if things were moving toward some larger revelation.

"You're so good for me," she said, whispering near my ear. I felt her hand squeeze my hand. In the dark I smelled a faint soapy scent and a more tangy, fleshy odor. When I reached out I felt her pillow beside me, still warm from her head.

On the beach one day as I lay thinking of Isabel, I overheard a girl saying, ". . . August already and he hasn't even sent me one single solitary . . ." Something about those words troubled me. As I pressed my chest and stomach against the hard-soft sand under my towel, trying to capture, for Isabel, the precise sensation of hard and soft, it came to me: what troubled me was the knowledge that time was passing, that it was already August—August, the second half of summer, August, the deceitful month. Still the hot days seem to stretch on and on, just as they did in July, but you know that instead of a new summer month shimmering in the distance, there's no longer any protection from September—and you can almost see, far off in the summery haze, the first breath-clouds forming in the brisk autumn air.

It was about this time that I noticed a little change in Isabel. She was growing restless—or perhaps she was only searching for a new game. Now when I arrived she was almost never in bed, but was somewhere else in the room, standing or moving about. One afternoon when I entered the dark I could hear her in an unfamiliar place. "Where are you?" I said. "Over here. Be done in a sec." I heard a wooden sliding, a creak, a rustling, a slide and thump, as of a closed drawer. There was a ripply, cloth-y sound, a snap, more rustling. "There!" Isabel said. "You can come over now." I advanced slowly, holding out an arm. "Sorry!" I said, and snatched my hand away. "Fresh!" said Isabel. "So! How do you like it?" She seized my wrist and placed my hand on her upper arm and then for a moment on her hip. "It's a new dress," she said. "Stockings, too. Or scarves, according to *some* people." I heard scritch-scratchy sounds, as if she were rubbing her knees together. "So! Can you dance?" A hand grasped my hand and set it on her waist. On the fingers of my other hand I felt the grope of a closing hand. Fingers seized my waist. "*One* two three *one* two three!" she chanted, as she began to waltz in the dark—and I, who had taken dance lessons in the eighth grade, led her round and round as she hummed "The Vienna Waltz," till she smacked into something and cried, "Don't stop!"—and as I turned round and round in that room, knocking into things that fell over, I felt her hair tickling my face, I smelled a faint perfume that made me think of oboes and bassoons, I pressed my fingers against the hard, rippling small of her back as she hummed louder and louder and something went rolling across the room and burst against a wall.

Because the bed was almost always empty, I no longer hesitated by the chair. Instead I went straight past it and lay down on my back with my head on a pillow and waited for her to present herself. After a while she would greet me and sit down on the chair with her feet on the bed. Then she would talk to me about her plans for the future—she wanted to be a doctor, she wanted to help people, she wanted to travel—while I lay in the dark and tried to imagine Isabel stepping from an airplane, in some bright airport, somewhere.

It was during one of these afternoons in early August, when she sat in the chair with her bare feet resting near my lower leg, that she told me about an idea she'd been turning over in her mind. She'd been thinking about it, actually, for a long time, though she hadn't been ready to face it, really. But now, thanks to me, she felt she had the courage to do it. Of course, it wasn't the sort of thing you would just go ahead and do without giving it a whole lot of thought—you had to sort of sneak up on it, in your mind. And that's just what she'd been doing, over these last weeks, and it felt right, so right, it really did. And so, to make a long story short, or a short story long, she was going to break out of the dark—let in the light—before the month was over.

A moment later she said, "You're not saying anything."

I said, "Are you really sure you—"

"Absolutely," Isabel said.

Now whenever I entered she was full of plans. At first she'd thought to change things gradually—a dim candle at one end of the room, then on my next visit a lamp on the bed table, and finally the opened curtains—but the more she thought about it, the more she liked the idea of announcing the new era dramatically. A complete break—that was the way to go. And once the darkness was gone, why, she could do anything—anything. She felt it in her bones. She'd always wanted to learn how to play tennis, for example, and had foolishly put it off. She wanted to see people, do things. She missed her aunt in Maine. She and I could go rowing together—there must be lakes around here. We could go swimming at that beach of mine. And as I lay back against the pillows, listening to her as she sat on the chair with her legs on the bed, I could feel her kicking her heels in excitement.

One afternoon as I climbed the carpeted stairs, on my way to the wooden stairs that led to the attic, it struck me that I hadn't seen Wolf for quite some time. I had visited him occasionally, on the way to Isabel's room, but not for the past few weeks or so, and I felt a sudden desire to see him now. I knocked on his door with a single knuckle—two light raps—and after a pause I heard the word "Enter," uttered in a tone of mock solemnity.

I pushed open the door and saw in the mildly sunny room a big new desk against one wall. Wolf was sitting at it with his back to me, bent over a notebook. The shades had been replaced by white blinds, and through the open slats I saw sun-struck green leaves and bits of blue sky. The tall narrow bookcase was still there, fastened upright against the wall, but the stray piles of books were gone, in place of the sunken chair stood a red leather armchair with a red leather hassock, the room had an air of studious neatness.

Wolf turned to glance over his shoulder. When he saw me he frowned and then slowly began to smile; as his smile became fixed, his frown gradually lessened without disappearing entirely. With a flourish he indicated the red leather armchair.

As I walked over to it, he jerked his thumb at the desk. "The new dispensation." He shrugged. "It's very interesting. They want me to do well in school, but they think I read too much. Books as the enemy. Hence our new friend here. I call him Fred." He patted the desk as if it were a big, friendly dog. "They think it's good for my—what was that word they used? Oh yes: character."

I sat down in the new chair, placing one leg on the hassock, while Wolf half rose and swung around in his wooden chair so that he straddled it, facing me. His crossed forearms rested on the back. On the bed I noticed a new plaid spread.

"And what have you been up to, David Dave?" he asked, looking at me with his air of amusement.

"Oh, you know. The library. Ping-pong. Nothing much. You?"

He shrugged a single shoulder. "The salt mines." He nodded toward the desk. "Summer school. Punishment for dereliction of duty. Have I mentioned that I flunked three subjects? A family secret."

I lowered my eyes.

"And look at this neat little number." He swung an arm back to the desk and held up a booklet. "Driver's manual. From the Department of Motor Vehicles, with love." He tossed it back. "My father was very clear. Failure will no longer be tolerated." He shrugged again. "They think I'm a bad influence on myself." Wolf smiled. "They want me to be more like—well, like you."

"Me!"

"Sure, why not? Straight A's, the good life, all that jazz. A solid citizen."

"They're wrong," I said quietly, and then: "Don't be like me!" It came out like a cry.

"If you say so," he said, after a pause.

We sat for a while in silence. I looked at the big pale desk, with its shiny black fluorescent light and its green blotter in a dark leatherish frame, at the new plaid bedspread, at the clean bright blinds. "Well then," I said, "I guess—" and rose to go. Wolf said nothing. At the door I turned to look back at him, and he gave me that slow lazy smile, with its little touch of mockery.

In the darkness of Isabel's chamber her plans were taking

shape. The great event would take place on the last day of August, three days before the start of school. I lay on the bed remembering the first time I had entered the room; it seemed a long time ago. "Isabel," I said, "do you remember—" "Are you listening?" she said sharply, and for a moment I did not know what she was talking about.

One night I woke and saw Isabel very clearly. She was wearing white shorts and a bright red short-sleeved blouse. She was leaning back on both hands, with her legs stretched out and her face tilted back, her hair bound in a ponytail and her mouth radiantly smiling. Her face was vague, except for the smile, with its perfectly shaped small white teeth and its thin line of glistening pink between the bright teeth and the upper lip. I fell asleep, and when I woke again I saw the same image, sharp and bright, and understood instantly where it had come from: I saw the dentist's waiting room, the sunny glass table with the magazines, the glossy page advertising a special brand of toothpaste that whitened as it cleaned.

In the last days of August I had the sense of a distant brightness advancing, like an ancient army in a movie epic, the sun flashing on the polished helmets and on the tips of the upraised swords.

On the day before the final day, I said to Isabel, "Come over here." My voice startled me with its harshness, its tone of aggrieved authority. There was silence in the dark. Then I felt, in the mattress, the pressure of a form, as she climbed onto the bed and settled down beside me. "It'll be all right," she whispered. "You'll see." I could feel her like a heat along my side. My cheek itched, as if tickled by Isabel's hair or perhaps by a high ripple in the rumpled spread. My eyes were wide open. Images rose up and drifted away: a Chinese sage reading a book, bursts of sunlight on shady clapboards, a gray jacket hanging on a hook.

On the morning of the last day of August I woke unusually

early. Even my parents were still asleep. I drank a glass of orange juice in the bright kitchen, tried to read on the back porch, and at last decided to go to the beach. As I stepped onto the sand I was surprised to see a scattering of people, standing about or lying on towels, and I wondered whether they were there because they had stayed all night. The tide was in. Over the water the sky was so blue that it reminded me of an expensive shirt I had seen in a department store. I laid out my towel, with my bottle of suntan lotion in one corner and my book in another, and then I set off on a walk along the wet sand by the low waves. Farther out the water solidified into patches of deep purplish blue and streaks of silver. In the shiny dark sand I saw my footprints, which stood out pale for a moment before the dark wetness soaked back. I tried to imagine a second pair of footprints walking beside mine, first pale and then dark, vanishing in the frilly-edged sheets of water thrown forward by the breaking waves. People were arriving at the beach, carrying towels and radios. Far up on the sand, a girl sat up, poured lotion into her hand, and began caressing her arm slowly, stretching it out and turning it back and forth. When I reached the jetty I walked out onto the rocks, sat for a while on the warm stone with my legs in the water, then swam out until I was tired. Back on my towel I lay down and felt the sun burning off the waterdrops. A girl from my French class waved to me and I waved back. Families with beach umbrellas were coming over the crest of sand by the parking lot. The beach was filling up.

I arrived at Isabel's house toward three in the afternoon. At the door Wolf's mother appeared in green shorts and a yellow halter, with a pocketbook over her shoulder and car keys hanging from her hand. "Go on in," she said, "I'm in a rush," and hurried down the steps. In the driveway she turned and called, "John's out. She's expecting you." I passed through the cool dim living room, climbed the carpeted steps to the second floor, and looked at the familiar hall with its closed doors before climbing into the attic. At the top of the stairs I passed through the sun-striped darkness into the second hall and quietly entered Isabel's chamber.

"Oh there you are," she said, with a mixture of impatience and excitement.

"I went to the beach," I said, looking around at the dark. Parts of it were more familiar than others—the part that held the chair, the part that held the bed—and I wondered if I could memorize the different parts by concentrating my attention.

"I'm very excited!" cried Isabel, and I heard her do a little dance-step on the carpet.

Slowly I walked over to the bed and lay down.

"What are you doing, what are you doing?" Isabel said, stamping her foot.

"Doing? Just lying here, Isabel, thinking how peaceful it is. You know, I went for a swim this morning and I'm—"

"You're such a tease!" she cried. "You can't just lie there," she said, much closer, and I felt a tug at my sleeve. "You have to get up."

"Isabel, listen. Do you really—"

"Oh what are you talking about? Come on! Come on!" She tugged again and I followed her into the dark. I could feel her excitement like a wind. She drew me across the room and abruptly stopped. I could hear her patting the curtains, groping for the drawstrings. The curtains sounded thick and softly solid, like the side of an immense animal. I imagined the brilliant light outside, raised like a sword. "There!" Isabel said. I heard her tugging, jerking stubbornly, moving her hand about, like a maddened bird trapped in the folds. Something gave way, the top of the curtains began to pull apart, sunlight burst through like a shout, for an instant I saw the slowly separating dark-blue folds, a swirl of glowing golden dust, an edge of raised sleeve, before I flung a hand over my eyes. Thrusting out the other hand, I made my way blindly across the room toward the door as she shouted, "Hey, where're you—" Behind me I heard the curtains scraping back, through my fingers I could feel the room filling with light as if a fire had broken out. I pulled open the door and did not look back. As I fled through the attic and down the first flight of stairs, I saw, beyond the edge of my vision, in that instant before I covered my eyes with my hand, a raised reddish sleeve with a slight sheen to it, slipping down along a ghostly shimmer of sunlit forearm, vague as an agitation of air. At the bottom of the second stairway I waved to Wolf's mother, who turned out to be a jacket on the back of a shadowy chair, hurried through the living room, and escaped through the front door. Only when my bicycle was speeding down the curving drive between the high fence and the hedge did I turn to look back at the house, forgetting that, from this angle, I could see only the pines, the maples, the sunny and shady driveway turning out of sight.

School began three days later. Wolf was in none of my classes and I couldn't find him in the halls. I had never called his house before—somehow our friendship had nothing to do with telephones—but that afternoon I dialed his number. The phone rang fourteen times before I hung up. I imagined the house in ruins, ravaged by sunlight. I looked for Wolf in school the next day, but he wasn't there. No one knew anything about him. That afternoon after school I called in sick at the library and rode over to Wolf's house on my bike. At the top of the curving drive it was still standing there, in shade broken by brilliant points of light. Wolf's mother, wearing jeans and a sweatshirt and holding a pair of pliers in one hand, answered the door. In the darkish living room she sat on the couch and I sat in an armchair, holding a glass of iced tea that I forgot to drink, as she told me that Wolf was attending a special boarding school in Massachusetts.

Hadn't he mentioned it? A liberal curriculum—a very liberal curriculum. As for Isabel, she'd gone to live for a while with her aunt in Maine, where she usually spent her summers and where she was now attending the public high school. Her year off had done her a world of good. Wolf's mother thanked me for being so nice to Isabel, during her convalescence. At the front door she looked at me fondly. "Thank you for everything, David," she said, and reached out her hand. She gave my hand a vigorous shake and stood watching me from the doorway as I rode off on my bike.

That fall I threw myself into my classes, but all I could think of was the room in the attic. It was as if I were missing some part of myself that I had to have but couldn't find anywhere. In mid-October I got my driver's license and began driving around on the weekends in my father's car. I took up with my semiofficial girlfriend and went to dances and football games. One Saturday afternoon I drove into Wolf's neighborhood, but though I slowed down at his driveway, with its scattering of yellow leaves, I passed it without going in. Often I wondered what would have happened if I had turned to look at her, the day the curtains parted. And I saw it clearly: the sun-filled air, the dust swirling in shafts of light, the bright empty room. No, far better to have turned away, to have understood that, for me, Isabel existed only in the dark. Like a ghost at dawn—like the princess of a magic realm—she had to vanish at the first touch of light. So I drove around in my father's car, waiting for something that never came. By spring of senior year I was caught up in so many things that I had trouble remembering what had happened, exactly, in that dark room, in that vague house, on that winding road on the other side of town. Only now and then an image would rise up out of nowhere and make me thoughtful for a while—an ivory sage bent over his book, a furry earmuff, and that slow, lazy smile, with its little touch of mockery.

DANGEROUS LAUGHTER

FEW OF US now recall that perilous summer. What began as a game, a harmless pastime, quickly took a turn toward the serious and obsessive, which none of us tried to resist. After all, we were young. We were fourteen and fifteen, scornful of childhood, remote from the world of stern and ludicrous adults. We were bored, we were restless, we longed to be seized by any whim or passion and follow it to the farthest reaches of our natures. We wanted to live—to die—to burst into flame—to be transformed into angels or explosions. Only the mundane offended us, as if we secretly feared it was our destiny. By late afternoon our muscles ached, our eyelids grew heavy with obscure desires. And so we dreamed and did nothing, for what was there to do, played ping-pong and went to the beach, loafed in backyards, slept late into the morning—and always we craved adventures so extreme we could never imagine them.

In the long dusks of summer we walked the suburban streets through scents of maple and cut grass, waiting for something to happen.

The game began innocently and spread like a dark rumor. In cool playrooms with parallelograms of sunlight pouring through cellar windows, at ping-pong tables in hot, open garages, around yellow and blue beach towels lying on bright sand above the tide line, you would hear the quiet words, the sharp bursts of laughter. The idea had the simplicity of all inspired things. A word, any word, uttered in a certain solemn tone, could be compelled to reveal its inner stupidity. "Cheese," someone would say, with an air of somber concentration, and again, slowly: "Cheese." Someone would laugh; it was inevitable; the laughter would spread; gusts of hilarity would sweep through the group; and just as things were about to die down, someone would cry out "Elbow!" or "Dirigible!" and bursts of laughter would be set off again. What drew us wasn't so much the hidden absurdity of words, which we'd always suspected, as the sharp heaves and gasps of laughter itself. Deep in our inner dark, we had discovered a startling power. We became fanatics of laughter, devotees of eruption, as if these upheavals were something we hadn't known before, something that would take us where we needed to go.

Such simple performances couldn't satisfy us for long. The laugh parties represented a leap worthy of our hunger. The object was to laugh longer and harder than anyone else, to maintain in yourself an uninterrupted state of explosive release. Rules sprang up to eliminate unacceptable laughter—the feeble, the false, the unfairly exaggerated. Soon every party had its judges, who grew skillful in detecting the slightest deviation from the genuine. As long laughter became the rage, a custom arose in which each of us in turn had to step into a circle of watchers, and there, partly through the stimulus of a crowd already rippling with amusement, and partly through some inner trick that differed from person to person, begin to laugh. Meanwhile the watchers and judges, who themselves were continually thrown into outbursts that drove the laugher to greater and greater heights, studied the roars and convulsions carefully and timed the performance with a stopwatch.

In this atmosphere of urgency, abandon, and rigorous striving, accidents were bound to happen. One girl, laughing hysterically on a couch in a basement playroom, threw back her head and injured her neck when it struck the wooden couch-arm. A boy gasping with mad laughter crashed into a piano bench, fell to the floor, and broke his left arm. These incidents, which might have served as warnings, only heightened our sense of rightness, as if our wounds were signs that we took our laughter seriously.

Not long after the laugh parties began to spread through our afternoons, there arose a new pastime, which enticed us with promises of a more radical kind. The laugh clubs—or laugh parlors, as they were sometimes called—represented a bolder effort to draw forth and prolong our laughter. At first they were organized by slightly older girls, who invited "members" to their houses after dark. In accordance with rules and practices that varied from club to club, the girls were said to produce sustained fits of violent laughter far more thrilling than anything we had yet discovered. No one was certain how the clubs had come into being—one day they simply seemed to be there, as if they'd been present all along, waiting for us to find them.

It was rumored that the first club was the invention of sixteen-year-old Bernice Alderson, whose parents were never home. She lived in a large house in the wooded north end of town; one day she'd read in a history of Egypt that Queen Cleopatra liked to order a slave girl to bind her arms and tickle her bare feet with a feather. In her third-floor bedroom, Bernice and her friend Mary Chapman invited club members to remove their shoes and lie down one by one on the bed. While Mary, with her muscular arms, held the chest and knees firmly in place, Bernice began to tickle the outstretched body—on the stomach, the ribs, the neck, the thighs, the tops and sides of the feet. There was an art to it all: the art of invading and withdrawing, of coaxing from the depths a steady outpouring of helpless laughter. For the visitor held down on the bed, it was a matter of releasing oneself into the hands of the girls and enduring it for as long as possible. All you had to do was say "Stop." In theory the laughter never had to stop, though most of us could barely hold out for three minutes.

Although the laugh parlors existed in fact, for we all attended them and even began to form clubs of our own, they also continued to lead a separate and in a sense higher existence in the realm of rumor, which had the effect of lifting them into the inaccessible and mythical. It was said that in one of these clubs, members were required to remove their clothes, after which they were chained to a bed and tickled savagely to the point of delirium. It was said that one girl, sobbing with laughter, gasping, began to move her hips in strange and suggestive ways, until it became clear that the act of tickling had brought her to orgasm. The erotic was never absent from these rumors—a fact that hardly surprised us, since those of us who were purists of laughter and disdained any crude crossing over into the sexual recognized the kinship between the two worlds. For even then we understood that our laughter, as it erupted from us in unseemly spasms, was part of the kingdom of forbidden things.

As laugh parties gave way to laugh parlors, and rumors thickened, we sometimes had the sense that our secret games had begun to spread to other regions of the town. One day a nine-year-old boy was discovered by his mother holding down and violently tickling his seven-year-old sister, who was shrieking and screaming—the collar of her dress was soaked with tears. The girl's pale body was streaked with lines of deep pink, as if she'd been struck repeatedly with a rope. We heard that Bernice Alderson's mother, at home for a change, had entered the kitchen with a heavy bag of groceries in her arms, slipped on a rubber dog-toy, and fallen to the floor. As she sat there beside a box of smashed and oozing eggs and watched the big, heavy, thumping oranges go rolling across the linoleum, the corners of her mouth began to twitch, her lungs, already burning with anger, began to tingle, and all at once she burst into laughter that lashed her body, threw her head back against the metal doors of the cabinet under the sink, rose to the third-floor bedroom of her daughter, who looked up frowning from a book, and in the end left her exhausted, shaken, bruised, panting, and exhilarated. At night, in my hot room, I lay restless and dissatisfied, longing for the release of feverish laughter that alone could soothe me—and through the screen I seemed to hear, along with the crickets, the rattling window-fan next door, and the hum of far-off trucks on the thruway, the sound of laughter bursting faintly in the night, all over our town, like the buzz of a fluorescent lamp in a distant bedroom.

One night after my parents were asleep I left the house and walked across town to Bernice Alderson's neighborhood. The drawn shade of her third-floor window was aglow with dim yellow light. On the bed in her room Mary Chapman gripped me firmly while Bernice bent over me with a serious but not unkind look. Slowly she brought me to a pitch of wild laughter that seemed to scald my throat as sweat trickled down my neck and the bed creaked to the rhythm of my deep, painful, releasing cries. I held out for a long time, nearly seven minutes, until I begged her to stop. Instantly it was over. Even as I made my way home, under the maples and lindens of a warm July night, I regretted my cowardice and longed for deeper and more terrible laughter. Then I wondered how I could push my way through the hours that separated me from my next descent into the darkness of my body, where laughter lay like lava, waiting for a fissure to form that would release it like liquid fire.

Of course we compared notes. We'd known from the beginning that some were more skilled in laughter than others, that some were able to sustain long and robust fits of the bone-shaking kind, which seemed to bring them to the verge of hysteria or unconsciousness without stepping over the line. Many of us boasted of our powers, only to be outdone by others; rumors blossomed; and in this murky atmosphere of extravagant claims, dubious feats, and unverifiable stories, the figure of Clara Schuler began to stand out with a certain distinctness.

Clara Schuler was fifteen years old. She was a quiet girl, who sat very still in class with her book open before her, eyes lowered and both feet resting on the floor. She never drummed her fingers on the desk. She never pushed her hair back over her ear or crossed and uncrossed her legs—as if, for her, a single motion were a form of disruption. When she passed a handout to the person seated behind her, she turned her upper body abruptly, dropped the paper on the desk with lowered eyes, and turned abruptly back. She never raised her hand in class. When called on, she flushed slightly, answered in a voice so quiet that the teacher had to ask her to "speak up," and said as little as possible, though it was clear she'd done the work. She seemed to experience the act of being looked at as a form of violation; she gave you the impression that her idea of happiness would be to dissolve gradually, leaving behind a small puddle. She was difficult to picture clearly—a little pale, her hair dark in some elusive shade between brown and black, her eyes hidden under lowered lids that sometimes opened suddenly to reveal large, startled irises. She wore trim knee-length skirts and solid-colored cotton blouses that looked neatly ironed. Sometimes she wore in her collar a small silver pin shaped like a cat.

One small thing struck me about Clara Schuler: in the course of the day she would become a little unraveled. Strands of hair would fall across her face, the back of her blouse would bunch up and start to pull away from her leather belt, one of her white socks would begin to droop. The next day she'd be back in her seat, her hair neatly combed, her blouse tucked in, her socks pulled up tight with the ribs perfectly straight, her hands folded lightly on her maplewood desk.

Clara had one friend, a girl named Helen Jacoby, who sat with her in the cafeteria and met her at the lockers after class. Helen was a long-boned girl who played basketball and laughed at anything. When she threw her head back to drink bottles of soda, you could see the ridges of her trachea pressing through her neck. She seemed an unlikely companion for Clara Schuler, but we were used to seeing them together and we felt, without thinking much about it, that each enhanced the other—Helen made Clara seem less strange and solitary, in a sense protected her and prevented her from being perceived as ridiculous, while Clara made good old Helen seem more interesting, lent her a touch of mystery. We weren't surprised, that summer, to see Helen at the laugh parties, where she laughed with her head thrown back in a way that reminded me of the way she drank soda; and it was Helen who one afternoon brought Clara Schuler with her and introduced her to the new game.

I began to watch Clara at these parties. We all watched her. She would step into the circle and stand there with lowered eyes, her head leaning forward slightly, her shoulders slumped, her arms tense at her sides—looking, I couldn't help thinking, as if she were being punished in some humiliating way. You could see the veins rising up on the backs of her hands. She stood so motionless that she seemed to be holding her breath; perhaps she was; and you could feel something building in her, as in a child about to cry; her neck stiff; the tendons visible; two vertical lines between her eyebrows; then a kind of mild trembling in her neck and arms, a veiled shudder, an inner rippling, and through her body, still rigid but in the grip of a force, you could sense a presence, rising, expanding, until, with a painful gasp, with a jerk of her shoulders, she gave way to a cry or scream of laughter—

laughter that continued to well up in her, to shake her as if she were possessed by a demon, until her cheeks were wet, her hair wild in her face, her chest heaving, her fingers clutching at her arms and head—and still the laughter came, hurling her about, making her gulp and gasp as if in terror, her mouth stretched back over her teeth, her eyes squeezed shut, her hands pressed against her ribs as if to keep herself from cracking apart.

And then it would stop. Abruptly, mysteriously, it was over. She stood there, pale—exhausted—panting. Her eyes, wide open, saw nothing. Slowly she came back to herself. Then quickly, a little unsteadily, she would walk away from us to collapse on a couch.

These feats of laughter were immediately recognized as bold and striking, far superior to the performances we had become accustomed to; and Clara Schuler was invited to all the laugh parties, applauded, and talked about admiringly, for she had a gift of reckless laughter we had not seen before.

Now whenever loose groups of us gathered to pursue our game, Clara Schuler was there. We grew used to her, waited impatiently for her when she was late, this quiet girl who'd never done anything but sit obediently in our classes with both feet on the floor before revealing dark depths of laughter that left us wondering and a little uneasy. For there was something about Clara Schuler's laughter. It wasn't simply that it was more intense than ours. Rather, she seemed to be transformed into an object, seized by a force that raged through her before letting her go. Yes, in Clara Schuler the discrepancy between the body that was shaken and the force that shook it appeared so sharply that at the very moment she became most physical she seemed to lose the sense of her body altogether. For the rest of us, there was always a touch of the sensual in these performances: breasts shook, hips jerked, flesh moved in unexpected ways. But Clara Schuler seemed to pass beyond the easy suggestiveness of moving bodies and to enter new and more ambiguous realms, where the body was the summoner of some dark, eruptive power that was able to flourish only through the accident of a material thing, which it flung about as if cruelly before abandoning it to the rites of exhaustion.

One day she appeared among us alone. Helen Jacoby was at the beach, or out shopping with her mother. We understood that Clara Schuler no longer needed her friend in the old way—that she had come into her own. And we understood one other thing: she would allow nothing to stop her from joining our game, from yielding to the seductions of laughter, for she lived, more and more, only in order to let herself go.

It was inevitable that rumors should spring up about Clara Schuler. It was said that she'd begun to go to the laugh parlors, those half-real, half-legendary places where laughter was wrung out of willing victims by special arts. It was said that one night she had paid a visit to Bernice Alderson's house, where in the lamplit bedroom on the third floor she'd been constrained and skillfully tickled for nearly an hour, at which point she fainted dead away and had to be revived by a scented oil rubbed into her temples. It was said that at another house she'd been so shaken by extreme laughter that her body rose from the bed and hovered in the air for thirty seconds before dropping back down. We knew that this last was a lie, a frivolous and irritating tale fit for children, but it troubled us all the same, it seized our imaginations—for we felt that under the right circumstances, with the help of a physiologically freakish but not inconceivable pattern of spasms, it was the kind of thing Clara Schuler might somehow be able to do.

As our demands became more exacting, and our expectations more refined, Clara Schuler's performances attained heights of release that inflamed us and left no doubt of her power. We tried to copy her gestures, to jerk our shoulders with her precise rhythms, always without success. Sometimes we imagined we could hear, in Clara Schuler's laughter, our own milder laughter, changed into something we could only long for. It was as if our dreams had entered her.

I noticed that her strenuous new life was beginning to affect her appearance. Now when she came to us her hair fell across her cheeks in long strands, which she would impatiently flick away with the backs of her fingers. She looked thinner, though it was hard to tell; she looked tired; she looked as if she might be coming down with something. Her eyes, no longer hidden under lowered lids, gazed at us restlessly and a little vaguely. Sometimes she gave the impression that she was searching for something she could no longer remember. She looked expectant; a little sad; a little bored.

One night, unable to sleep, I escaped from the house and took a walk. Near the end of my street I passed under a streetlamp that flickered and made a crackling sound, so that my shadow trembled. It seemed to me that I was that streetlamp, flickering and crackling with restlessness. After a while I came to an older neighborhood of high maples and gabled houses with rundown front porches. Bicycles leaned wearily against wicker furniture and beach towels hung crookedly over porch rails. I stopped before a dark house near the end of the street. Through an open window on the second floor, over the dirt driveway, I heard the sound of a rattling fan.

It was Clara Schuler's house. I wondered if it was her window. I walked a little closer, looking up at the screen, and it seemed to me that through the rattle and hum of the fan I heard some other sound. It was—I thought it was—the sound of quiet laughter. Was she lying there in the dark, laughing secretly, releasing herself from restlessness? Could she be laughing in her sleep? Maybe it was only some trick of the fan. I stood listening to that small, uncertain sound, which mingled with the blades of the fan until it seemed the fan itself was laughing, perhaps at me. What did I long for, under that window? I longed to be swept up into Clara Schuler's laughter, I longed to join her there, in her dark room, I longed for release from whatever it was I was. But whatever I was lay hard and immovable in me, like bone; I would never be free of my own weight. After a while I turned around and walked home.

It wasn't long after this visit that I saw Clara Schuler at one of the laugh parlors we'd formed, in imitation of those we had heard about or perhaps had invented in order to lure ourselves into deeper experiments. Helen Jacoby sat on the bed and held Clara's wrists while a friend of Helen's held Clara's ankles. A blond-haired girl I'd never seen before bent over her with hooked fingers. Five of us watched the performance. It began with a sudden shiver, as the short blunt fingers darted along her ribs and thighs. Clara Schuler's head began to turn from side to side; her feet in her white socks stiffened. As laughter rushed through her in sharp shuddering bursts, one of her shoulders lifted as if to fold itself across her neck. Within ten minutes her eyes had grown glassy and calm. She lay almost still, even as she continued to laugh. What struck us was that eerie stillness, as if she'd passed beyond struggle to some other place, where laughter poured forth in pure, vigorous streams.

Someone asked nervously if we should stop. The blond-haired girl glanced at her watch and bent over Clara Schuler more intently. After half an hour, Clara began breathing in great wracking gulps, accompanied by groans torn up from her throat. Helen asked her if she'd had enough; Clara shook her head harshly. Her face was so wet that she glowed in the lamplight. Stains of wetness darkened the bedspread.

When the session had lasted just over an hour, the blond-haired girl gave up in exhaustion. She stood shaking her wrists, rubbing the fingers of first one hand and then the other. On the bed Clara Schuler continued stirring and laughing, as if she still felt the fingers moving over her. Gradually her laughter grew fainter; and as she lay there pale and drained, with her head turned to one side, her eyes dull, her lips slack, strands of long hair sticking to her wet cheek, she looked, for a moment, as if she'd grown suddenly old.

It was at this period, when Clara Schuler became queen of the laugh parlors, that I first began to worry about her. One day, emerging from an unusually violent and prolonged series of gasps, she lay motionless, her eyes open and staring, while the fingers played over her skin. It took some moments for us to realize she had lost consciousness, though she soon revived. Another time, walking across a room, she thrust out an arm and seized the back of a chair as her body leaned slowly to one side, before she straightened and continued her walk as if nothing had happened. I understood that these feverish games, these lavish abandonments, were no longer innocent. Sometimes I saw in her eyes the restless unhappiness of someone for whom nothing, not even such ravishments, would ever be enough.

One afternoon when I walked to Main Street to return a book to the library, I saw Clara Schuler stepping out of Cerino's grocery store. I felt an intense desire to speak to her; to warn her against us; to praise her extravagantly; to beg her to teach me the difficult art of laughter. Shyness constrained me, though I wasn't shy—but it was as if I had no right to intrude on her, to break the spell of her remoteness. I kept out of sight and followed her home. When she climbed the wooden steps of her porch, one of which creaked like the floor of an attic, I stepped boldly into view, daring her to turn and see me. She opened the front door and disappeared into the house. For a while I stood there, trying to remember what it was I had wanted to say to Clara Schuler, the modest girl with a fierce, immodest gift. A clattering startled me. Along the shady sidewalk, trembling with spots of sunlight, a girl with yellow pigtails was pulling a lollipop-red wagon, which held a jouncing rhinoceros. I turned and headed home.

That night I dreamed about Clara Schuler. She was standing in a sunny backyard, looking into the distance. I came over to her and spoke a few words, but she did not look at me. I began to walk around her, speaking urgently and trying to catch her gaze, but her face was always turned partly away, and when I seized her arm it felt soft and crumbly, like pie dough.

About this time I began to sense among us a slight shift of attention, an inner wandering. A change was in the air. The laugh parlors seemed to lack their old aura of daring—they'd grown a little familiar, a little humdrum. While one of us lay writhing in laughter, the rest of us glanced toward the windows. One day someone pulled a deck of cards from a pocket, and as we waited our turn on the bed we sat down on the floor to a few hands of gin rummy.

We tried to conjure new possibilities, but our minds were mired in the old forms. Even the weather conspired to hold us back. The heat of midsummer pressed against us like fur. Leaves, thick as tongues, hung heavily from the maples. Dust lay on polished furniture like pollen.

One night it rained. The rain continued all the next day and night; wind knocked down tree branches and telephone wires. In the purple-black sky, prickly lines of lightning burst forth with troubling brightness. Through the dark rectangles of our windows, the lightning flashes looked like textbook diagrams of the circulation of the blood.

The turn came with the new sun. Mist like steam rose from soaked grass. We took up our old games, but it was as if something had been carried off by the storm. At a birthday party in a basement playroom with an out-of-tune piano, a girl named Janet Bianco, listening to a sentimental song, began to behave strangely. Her shoulders trembled, her lips quivered. Mirthless tears rolled along her cheeks. Gradually we understood that she was crying. It caught our attention—it was a new note. Across the room, another girl suddenly burst into tears.

A passion for weeping seized us. It proved fairly easy for one girl to set off another, who set off a third. Boys, tense and embarrassed, gave way slowly. We held weep-fests that left us shaken and thrilled. Here and there a few laugh parties and laugh clubs continued to meet, but we knew it was the end of an era.

Clara Schuler attended that birthday party. As the rage for weeping swept over us, she appeared at a few gatherings, where she stood off to one side with a little frown. We saw her there, looking in our direction, before she began to shimmer and dissolve through our abundant tears. The pleasures of weeping proved more satisfying than the old pleasures of laughter, possibly because, when all was said and done, we weren't happy, we who were restless and always in search of diversion. And whereas laughter had always been difficult to sustain, weeping, once begun, welled up in us with gratifying ease. Several girls, among them Helen Jacoby, discovered in themselves rich and unsuspected depths of unhappiness, which released in the rest of us lengthy, heartfelt bouts of sorrow.

It wasn't long after the new craze had swept away the old that we received an invitation from Clara Schuler. None of us except Helen Jacoby had ever set foot in her house before. We arrived in the middle of a sunny afternoon; in the living room it was already dusk. A tall woman in a long drab dress pointed vaguely toward a carpeted stairway. Clara, she said, was waiting for us in the guest room in the attic. At the top of the stairs we came to a hallway covered with faded wallpaper, showing repeated waterwheels beside repeated streams shaded by willows. A door with a loose knob led up to the attic. Slowly we passed under shadowy rafters that slanted down over wooden barrels and a big bear in a chair and a folded card-table leaning against a tricycle.

Through a half-open door we entered the guest room. Clara Schuler stood with her hands hanging down in front of her, one hand lightly grasping the wrist of the other.

It looked like the room of someone's grandmother, which had been invaded by a child. On a frilly bedspread under old lace curtains sat a big rag doll wearing a pink dress with an apron. Her yellow yarn hair looked as heavy as candy. On top of a mahogany chest of drawers, a black-and-white photograph of a bearded man sat next to a music box decorated with elephants and balloons. It was warm and dusty in that room; we didn't know whether we were allowed to sit on the bed, which seemed to belong to the doll, so we sat on the floor. Clara herself looked tired and tense. We hadn't seen her for a while. We hardly thought about her. It occurred to me that we'd begun to forget her.

Seven or eight of us were there that day, sitting on a frayed maroon rug and looking awkwardly around. After a while Clara tried to close the door—the wood, swollen in the humid heat, refused to fit into the frame—and then walked to the center of the room. I had the impression that she was going to say something to us, but she stood looking vaguely before her. I could sense what she was going to do even before she began to laugh. It was a good laugh, one that reminded me of the old laugh parties, and a few of us joined her uneasily, for old times' sake. But we were done with that game, we could scarcely recall those days of early summer. And, in truth, even our weeping had begun to tire us, already we longed for new enticements. Maybe Clara had sensed a change and was trying to draw us back; maybe she simply wanted to perform one more time. If she was trying to assert her old power over us, she failed entirely. But neither our halfhearted laughter nor our hidden resistance seemed to trouble her, as she abandoned herself to her desire.

There was a concentration in Clara Schuler's laughter, a completeness, an immensity that we hadn't seen before. It was as if she wanted to outdo herself, to give the performance of her life. Her face, flushed on the cheek ridges, was so pale that laughter seemed to be draining away her blood. She stumbled to one side and nearly fell over—someone swung up a supporting hand. She seemed to be laughing harder and harder, with a ferocity that flung her body about, snapped her head back, wrenched her out of shape. The room, filled with wails of laughter, began to feel unbearable. No one knew what to do. At one point she threw herself onto the bed, gasping in what appeared to be an agony of laughter. Slowly, gracefully, the big doll slumped forward, until her head touched her stuck-out legs and the yellow yarn hair lay flung out over her feet.

After thirty-five minutes someone rose and quietly left. I could hear the footsteps fading through the attic.

Others began to leave; they did not say good-bye. Those of us who remained found an old Monopoly game and sat in a corner to play. Clara's eyes had taken on their glassy look, as cries of laughter continued to erupt from her. After the first hour I understood that no one was going to forgive her for this.

When the Monopoly game ended, everyone left except Helen Jacoby and me. Clara was laughing fiercely, her face twisted as if in pain. Her skin was so wet that she looked hard and shiny, like metal. The laughter, raw and harsh, poured up out of her as if some mechanism had broken. One of her forearms was bruised. The afternoon was drawing on toward five when Helen Jacoby, turning up her hands and giving a bitter little shrug, stood up and walked out of the room.

I stayed. And as I watched Clara Schuler, I had the desire to reach out and seize her wrist, to shake her out of her laughter and draw her back before it was too late. No one is allowed to laugh like that, I wanted to say. Stop it right now. She had passed so far beyond herself that there was almost nothing left—

nothing but that creature emptying herself of laughter. It was ugly—indecent—it made you want to look away. At the same time she bound me there, for it was as if she were inviting me to follow her to the farthest and most questionable regions of laughter, where laughter no longer bore any relation to earthly things and, sufficient to itself, soared above the world to flourish in the void. There, you were no longer yourself—you were no longer anything.

More than once I started to reach for her arm. My hand hung in front of me like some fragile piece of sculpture I was holding up for inspection. I saw that I was no more capable of stopping Clara Schuler in her flight than I was of joining her. I could only be a witness.

It was nearly half past five when I finally stood up. "Clara!" I said sharply, but I might as well have been talking to the doll. I wondered whether I'd ever spoken her name before. She was still laughing when I disappeared into the attic. Downstairs I told her mother that something was wrong, her daughter had been laughing for hours. She thanked me, turned slowly to gaze at the carpeted stairs, and said she hoped I would come again.

The local paper reported that Mrs. Schuler discovered her daughter around seven o'clock. She had already stopped breathing. The official cause of death was a ruptured blood vessel in the brain, but we knew the truth: Clara Schuler had died of laughter. "She was always a good girl," her mother was quoted as saying, as if death were a form of disobedience. We cooperated fully with the police, who found no trace of foul play.

For a while Clara Schuler's death was taken up eagerly by the weeping parties, which had begun to languish and which now gained a feverish new energy before collapsing decisively. It was late August; school was looming; as if desperately we hurled ourselves into a sudden passion for old board games, staging fierce contests of Monopoly and Risk, altering the rules in order to make the games last for days. But already our ardor was tainted by the end of summer, already we could see, in eyes glittering with the fever of obsession, a secret distraction.

On a warm afternoon in October I took a walk into Clara Schuler's neighborhood. Her house had been sold. On the long front steps sat a little girl in a green-and-orange-checked jacket, leaning forward and tightening a roller skate with a big silver key. I stood looking up at the bedroom window, half expecting to hear a ghostly laughter. In the quiet afternoon I heard only the whine of a backyard chain saw and the slap of a jump rope against a sidewalk. I felt awkward standing there, like someone trying to peek through a window. The summer seemed far away, as distant as childhood. Had we really played those games? I thought of Clara Schuler, the girl who had died of a ruptured blood vessel, but it was difficult to summon her face. What I could see clearly was that rag doll, slowly falling forward. Something stirred in my chest, and to my astonishment, with a kind of sorrow, I felt myself burst into a sharp laugh.

I looked around uneasily and began walking away. I wanted to be back in my own neighborhood, where people didn't die of laughter. There we threw ourselves into things for a while, lost interest, and went on to something else. Clara Schuler played games differently. Had we disappointed her? As I turned the corner of her street, I glanced back at the window over her dirt driveway. I had never learned whether it was her room. For all I knew, she slept on the other side of the house, or in the guest room in the attic. Again I saw that pink-and-yellow doll, falling forward in a slow, graceful, grotesque bow. No, my laughter was all right. It was a salute to Clara Schuler, an acknowledgment of her great gift. In her own way, she was complete. I wondered whether she had been laughing at us a little, up there in her attic.

As I entered the streets of my neighborhood, I felt a familiar restlessness. Everything stood out clearly. In an open, sunny garage, a man was reaching up to an aluminum ladder hanging horizontally on hooks, while in the front yard a tenth-grade girl wearing tight jeans rolled up to midcalf and a billowy red-and-black lumberjack shirt was standing with a rake beside a pile of yellow leaves shot through with green, shading her eyes and staring up at a man hammering on a roof. The mother of a friend of mine waved at me from behind the shady, sun-striped screen of a porch. Against a backboard above a brilliant white garage door, a basketball went round and round the orange rim of a basket. It was Sunday afternoon, time of the great boredom. Deep in my chest I felt a yawn begin; it went shuddering through my jaw. On the crosspiece of a sunny telephone pole, a grackle shrieked once and was still. The basketball hung in the white net. Suddenly it came unstuck and dropped with a smack to the driveway, the grackle rose into the air, somewhere I heard a burst of laughter. I nodded in the direction of Clara Schuler's neighborhood and continued down the street. Tomorrow something was bound to happen.

HISTORY OF A DISTURBANCE

YOU ARE ANGRY, Elena. You are furious. You are desperately unhappy. Do you know you're becoming bitter?—bitter as those little berries you bit into, remember? in the woods that time. You are frightened. You are resentful. My vow must have seemed to you extremely cruel, or insane. You are suspicious. You are tired. I've never seen you so tired. And of course: you are patient. You're very patient, Elena. I can feel that patience of yours come rolling out at me from every ripple of your unforgiving hair, from your fierce wrists and tense blouse. It's a harsh patience, an aggressive patience. It wants something, as all patience does. What it wants is an explanation, which you feel will free you in some way—if only from the grip of your ferocious waiting. But an explanation is just what's not possible, not now and not ever. What I can give you is only this. Call it an explanation if you like. For me it's a stammer—a shout in the dark.

Do things have beginnings, do you think? Or is a beginning only the first revelation of something that's always been there, waiting to be found? I'm thinking of that little outing we took last summer, the one up to Sandy Point. I'd been working hard, maybe too hard, I had just finished that market-penetration study for Sherwood Merrick Associates, it was the right time to get away. You packed a picnic. You were humming in the kitchen. You were wearing those jeans I like, the ones with the left back pocket torn off, and the top of your bathing suit. I watched as you sliced a sandwich exactly in half. The sun struck your hands. Across your glowing fingers I could see the faint liquidy green cast by the little glass swan on the windowsill. It occurred to me that we rarely took these trips anymore, that we ought to do it more often.

Then we were off, you in that swooping straw hat with its touch of forties glamour, I in that floppy thing that makes me look like a demented explorer. An hour later and there was the country store, with the one red gas pump in front, there was the turn. We passed the summer cottages in the pines. The little parking lot at the end of the road was only half full. Over the stone wall we looked down at the stretch of sand by the lake. We went down the rickety steps, I with the thermos and picnic basket, you with the blanket and towels. Other couples lay in the sun. Some kids were splashing in the water, which rippled from a passing speedboat that made the white barrels rise and fall. The tall lifeguard stand threw a short shadow. Across the lake was a pier, where some boys were fishing. You spread the blanket, took off your hat, shook out your hair. You sat down and began stroking your arm with sunblock. I was sitting next to you, taking it all in, the brown-green water, the wet ropes between the white barrels, the gleam of the lotion on your arm. Everything was bright and clear, and I wondered when the last time was that I'd really looked at anything. Suddenly you stopped what you were doing. You glanced around at the beach, raised your face to the sky, and said, "What a wonderful day!" I turned and looked out at the water.

But I wasn't looking at the water. I was thinking of what you had just said. It was a cry of contentment, a simple expression of delight, the sort of thing anyone might say, on such a day. But I had felt a little sharp burst of irritation. My irritation shocked me. But there it was. I'd been taking in the day, just like you, happy in all my senses. Then you said, "What a wonderful day!" and the day was less wonderful. The day—it's really indecent to speak of these things! But it's as if the day were composed of many separate and diverse presences—that bottle of soda tilted in the sand, that piece of blue-violet sky between the two dark pines, your green hand by the window—which suddenly were blurred together by your words. I felt that something vast and rich had been diminished somehow. I barely knew what you were talking about. I knew of course what you were talking about. But the words annoyed me. I wished you hadn't spoken them. Something uncapturable in the day had been harmed by speech. All at once my irritation passed. The day, which had been banished, came streaming back. Spots of yellow-white sun trembled in brown tree-shadows on the lake-edge. A little girl shouted in the water. I touched your hand.

Was that the beginning? Was it the first sign of a disturbance that had been growing secretly? Two weeks later the Polinzanos had that barbecue. I'd been working hard, harder than usual, putting together a report for Warren and Greene, the one on consumer perception of container shapes for sports beverages. I had all the survey results but I was having trouble writing it up, something was off, I was happy to let it go for an evening. Ralph was in high spirits, flipping over the chicken breasts, pushing down tenderly on the steaks. He waved the spatula about in grand style as he talked real estate. That new three-story monster-house on the block, could you believe two mil, those show-off window arches, and did you get a load of that corny balcony, all of it throwing the neighborhood out of whack, a crazy eyesore, but hey, it was driving property values up, he could live with that. Later, in the near-dark, we sat on the screened porch watching the fireflies. From inside the house came voices, laughter. Someone walked slowly across the dark lawn. You were lying in the chaise. I was sitting in that creaky wicker armchair right next to you. Someone stood up from the glider and went into the kitchen. We were alone on the porch. Voices in the house, the shrill cries of crickets, two glasses of wine on the wicker table, moths bumping against the screens. I was in good spirits, relaxed, barely conscious of that report at the edge of my mind. You turned slowly to me. I remember the lazy roll of your head, your cheek against the vinyl strips, your hair flattened on one side, your eyelids sleepy. You said, "Do you love me?" Your voice was flirtatious, easy—you weren't asking me to put a doubt to rest. I smiled, opened my mouth to answer, and for some reason recalled the afternoon at Sandy Point. And again I felt that burst of irritation, as if words were interposing themselves between me and the summer night. I said nothing. The silence began to swell. I could feel it pressing against both of us, like some big rubbery thing. I saw your eyes, still sleepy, begin to grow alert with confusion. And as if I were waking from a trance, I pushed away the silence, I beat it down with a yes yes yes, of course of course. You put your hand on my arm. All was well.

All was not well. In bed I lay awake, thinking of my irritation, thinking of the silence, which had been, I now thought, not like some big swelling rubbery thing, but like a piece of sharp metal caught in my throat. What was wrong with me? Did I love you? Of course I loved you. But to ask me just then, as I was taking in the night . . . Besides, what did the words mean? Oh, I understood them well enough, those drowsy tender words. They meant, Look, it's a summer night, look, the lawn is dark but there's still a little light left in the sky, they meant you wanted to hear my voice, to hear yourself ask a question that would bring you my voice—it was hardly a question at all, rather a sort of touch, rising out of the night, out of the sounds in the house, the flash of the fireflies. But you said, "Do you love me?," which seemed to require me to understand those words and no others, to think what they might exactly mean. Because they might have meant, Do you still love me as much as you once did even though I know you do, or Isn't it wonderful to sit here and whisper together like teenagers on the dark porch, while people are in the bright living room, talking and laughing, or Do you feel this rush of tender feeling which is rising in me, as I sit here, on this porch, at night, in summer, at the Polinzanos' barbecue, or Do you love everything I am and do, or only some things, and if so, which ones; and it seemed to me that that single word, "love," was trying to compress within itself a multitude of meanings, was trying to take many precise and separate feelings and crush them into a single mushy mass, which I was being asked to hold in my hands like a big sticky ball.

Do you see what was happening? Do you see what I'm trying to say?

Despite these warnings, I hadn't yet understood. I didn't, at this stage, see the connection between the afternoon at Sandy Point, the night at the Polinzanos' barbecue, and the report that was giving me so much trouble. I knew something was wrong, a little wrong, but I thought I'd been working too hard, I needed to relax a little, or maybe—I tried to imagine it—maybe the trouble was with us, with our marriage, a marriage problem. I don't know when I began to suspect it was more dangerous than that.

Not long after the Polinzanos' barbecue I found myself at the supermarket, picking up a few things for the weekend. You know how I love supermarkets. It excites me to walk down those big American avenues piled high with the world's goods, as if the spoils of six continents are being offered to me in the aftermath of a triumphant war. At the same time I enjoy taking note of brand-name readability, shelf positioning, the attention-drawing power of competing package designs. I was in a buoyant mood. My work had gone well that day, pretty well. I wheeled my cart into the checkout line, set out my bags and boxes on the rubber belt, swiped my card. The girl worked her scanner and touchscreen, and I watched with pleasure as the product names appeared sharply on the new LCD monitor facing me above her shoulder. Only two years ago I'd designed a questionnaire on consumer attitudes toward point-of-sale systems in supermarket chains. I signed my slip and handed it to the girl. She smiled at me and said, "Have a good day."

Instantly my mood changed. This time it wasn't irritation that seized me, but a kind of nervousness. What was she trying to say to me? I realized that this thought was absurd. At the same time I stared at the girl, trying to grasp her meaning. Have a good day! What were the words trying to say? At the word "have" her front teeth had pressed into her lip: a big overbite. She looked at me. Have a good day! Good day! Have! "What do you—," I said, and abruptly stopped. Things became very still. I saw two tiny silver rings at the top of her ear, one ring slightly larger than the other. I saw the black plastic edge of the credit-card terminal, a finger with purple nail polish, a long strip of paper with a red stripe running along each border. These elements seemed independent of one another. Somewhere a cash tray slid open, coins clanked. Then the finger joined the girl, the tray banged shut, I was standing by my shopping cart, studying the mesh pattern of the collapsible wire basket, trying to recall what was already slipping away. "You too," I said, as I always do, and fled with my cart.

At dinner that evening I felt uneasy, as if I were concealing a secret. Once or twice I thought you were looking at me strangely. I studied the saltshaker, which looked pretty much the way it had always looked, but with, I thought, some slight change I couldn't account for. In the middle of the night I woke suddenly and thought: Something is happening to me, things will never be the same. Then I felt, across the lower part of my stomach, a first faint ripple of fear.

In the course of the next few days I began listening with close attention to whatever was said to me. I listened to each part of what was said, and I listened to the individual words that composed each part. Words! Had I ever listened to them before? Words like crackles of cellophane, words like sluggish fat flies buzzing on sunny windowsills. The simplest remark began to seem suspect, a riddle—not devoid of meaning, but with a vague haze of meaning that grew hazier as I tried to clutch it. "Not on your life." "You bet!" "I guess so." I would be moving smoothly through my day when suddenly I'd come up against one of them, a word-snag, an obstacle in my path. A group of words would detach themselves from speech and stand at mock attention, sticking out their chests, as if to say: Here we are! Who are you? It was as if some space had opened up, a little rift, between words and whatever they were supposed to be doing. I stumbled in that space, I fell.

At the office I was still having difficulties with my report. The words I had always used had a new sheen of strangeness to them. I found it necessary to interrogate them, to investigate their intentions.

Sometimes they were slippery, like fistfuls of tiny silvery fish. Sometimes they took on a mineral hardness, as if they'd become things in themselves, but strange things, like growths of coral.

I don't mean to exaggerate. I knew what words meant, more or less. A cup was a cup, a window a window. That much was clear. Was that much clear? There began to be moments of hesitation, fractions of a second when the thing I was looking at refused to accept any language. Or rather, between the thing and the word a question had appeared, a slight pause, a rupture.

I recall one evening, it must have been a few weeks later, when I stepped from the darkened dining room into the brightly lit kitchen. I saw a whitish thing on the white kitchen table. In that instant the whitishness on the white table was mysterious, ungraspable. It seemed to spill onto the table like a fluid. I felt a rush of fear. A moment later everything changed. I recognized a cup, a simple white cup. The word pressed it into shape, severed it—as if with the blow of an ax—from everything that surrounded it. There it was: a cup. I wondered what it was I'd seen before the word tightened about it.

I said to myself: You've been working too hard. Your brain is tired. You are not able to concentrate your attention. The words you are using appear to be the same words you have always used, but they've changed in some way, a way you cannot grasp. When this report is done, you are going to take a vacation. That will be good.

I imagined myself in a clean hotel, high up, on the side of a mountain. I imagined myself alone.

I think it was at this period that my own talk began to upset me. The words I uttered seemed like false smiles I was displaying at a party I'd gone to against my will. Sometimes I would overhear myself in the act of speech, like a man who suddenly sees himself in a mirror. Then I grew afraid.

I began to speak less. At the office, where I'd established a long habit of friendliness, I stayed stubbornly at my desk, staring at my screen and limiting myself to the briefest of exchanges, which themselves were not difficult to replace with gestures—a nod, a wave, a smile, a shrug. It's surprising how little you need to say, really. Besides, everyone knew I was killing myself over that report. At home I greeted you silently. I said almost nothing at dinner and immediately shut myself up in my study. You hated my silence. For you it was a knife blade aimed at your neck. You were the victim and I was the murderer. That was the silent understanding we came to, quite early. And of course I didn't murder you just once, I murdered you every day. I understood this. I struggled to be—well, noisier, for your sake. The words I heard emerging from my mouth sounded like imitations of human speech. "Yes, it's hot, but not too hot," I said. "I think that what she probably meant was that she." The fatal fissure was there. On one side, the gush of language. On the other—what? I looked about. The world rushed away on all sides. If only one could be silent! In my study I avoided my irritating desk with its neat binders containing bar charts and statistical tables and sat motionless in the leather chair, looking out the window at the leaves of hydrangea bushes. I felt tremendously tired, but also alert. Not to speak, not to form words, not to think, not to smear the world with sentences—it was like the release of a band of metal tightening around my skull.

I was still able to do some work, during the day, a little work, though I was also staring a lot at the screen. I had command of a precise and specialized vocabulary that I could summon more or less at will. But the doubt had arisen, corroding my belief. Groups of words began to disintegrate under my intense gaze. I was like a man losing his faith, with no priest to turn to.

Always I had the sense that words concealed something, that if only I could abolish them I would discover what was actually there.

One evening I looked for a long time at my hand. Had I ever seen it before? I suppressed the word "hand," rid myself of everything but the act of concentration. It was no longer a hand, not a piece of flesh with nails, wrinkles, bits of reddish-blond hair. There was only a thing, not even that—only the place where my attention fell. Gradually I felt a loosening, a dissolution of the familiar. And I saw: a thickish mass, yellowish and red and blue, a pulsing thing with spaces, a shaded clump. It began to flatten out, to melt into surrounding space, to attach itself to otherness. Then I was staring at my hand again, the fingers slightly parted, the skin of the knuckles like small walnuts, the nails with vertical lines of faint shine. I could feel the words crawling over my hand like ants on a bone. But for a moment I had seen something else.

I am a normal man, wouldn't you say, intelligent and well educated, yes, with an aptitude for a certain kind of high-level work, but fundamentally normal, in temperament and disposition. I understood that what was happening to me was not within the range of the normal, and I felt, in addition to curiosity, an anger that this had come upon me, in the prime of life, like the onset of a fatal disease.

It was during one of those long evenings in my study, while you prowled somewhere in the house, that I recalled an incident from my childhood. For some reason I was in my parents' bedroom, a forbidden place. I heard footsteps approaching. In desperation I stepped over to the closet, with its two sliding doors, then rolled one door open, plunged inside, pushed it shut. The long closet was divided into two parts, my mother's side and my father's side. I knew at once which side I'd entered by the dresses pressing against my cheeks, the tall pairs of high-heeled shoes falling against my ankles as I moved deeper within. Clumsily I crouched down among the fallen shoes, my head and shoulders buried in the bottoms of dresses. And though I liked the sweetish, urine-sharp smell of the leather shoes, the rub of the dresses against my face, the hems heavy on my shoulders, the faint perfume drifting from folds of fabric like dust from a slapped bed, at the same time I felt oppressed by it all, bound tightly in place by the thick leathery smell and the stony fall of cloth, crushed in a black grip. The dresses, the shoes, the pinkish smell of perfume, the scratchy darkness, all pushed against me like the side of a big cat, thrust themselves into my mouth and nose like fur. I could not breathe. I opened my mouth. I felt the dark like fingers closing around my throat. In terror I stumbled up with a harsh scrape of hangers, pulled wildly at the edge of the door, burst outside. Light streamed through the open blinds. Tears of joy burned on my cheeks.

As I sat in my study, recalling my escape from the dresses, it seemed to me that the light streaming through my parents' blinds, in the empty room, was like the silence around me where I sat, and that the heavy dresses, the bittersweet smell of the shoes, the hand on my throat, were the world I had left behind.

I began to sense that there was another place, a place without words, and that if only I could concentrate my attention sufficiently, I might come to that place.

Once, when I was a student and had decided to major in business, I had an argument with a friend. He attacked business as a corrupt discipline, the sole purpose of which was to instill in people a desire to buy. His words upset me, not because I believed that his argument was sound, but because I felt that he was questioning my character. I replied that what attracted me to business was the precision of its vocabulary—a self-enclosed world of carefully defined words that permitted clarity of thought.

At the office I could see people looking at me and also looking away from me. The looks reminded me of the look I had caught in the eyes of the girl with the little rings in her ear, as I tried to understand her words, and the look in your eyes that night at the Polinzanos' barbecue, when I opened my mouth and said nothing.

It was about this time that I began to notice, within me, an intention taking shape. I wondered how long it had been there, waiting for me to notice it. Though my mind was made up, my body hesitated. I was struck by how like me that was: to know, and not to act. Had I always been that way? It would be necessary to arrange a sick leave. There would be questions, difficulties. But aside from all that, finally to go through with it, never to turn back—such acts were not at all in my style.

And if I hesitated, it was also because of you. There you were, in the house. Already we existed in a courteous dark silence trembling with your crushed-down rage. How could I explain to you that words no longer meant what they once had meant, that they no longer meant anything at all? How could I say to you that words interfered with the world? Often I thought of trying to let you know what I knew I would do. But whenever I looked at you, your face was turned partly away.

I tried to remember what it was like to be a very young child, before the time of words. And yet, weren't words always there, filling the air around me? I remember faces bending close, uttering sounds, coaxing me to leave the world of silence, to become one of them. Sometimes, when I moved my face a little, I could almost feel my skin brushing against words, like clusters of tiny, tickling insects.

One night after you'd gone to bed I rose slowly in my study. I observed myself with surprise, though I knew perfectly well what was happening. Without moving my lips I took a vow.

The next morning at breakfast I passed you a slip of paper. You glanced at it with disdain, then crumpled it in your fist. I remember the sound of the paper, which reminded me of fire. Your knuckles stuck up like stones.

When a monk takes a vow of silence, he does so in order to shut out the world and devote himself exclusively to things of the spirit. My vow of silence sought to renew the world, to make it appear before me in all its fullness. I knew that every element in the world—a cup, a tree, a day—was inexhaustible. Only the words that expressed it were vague or limited. Words harmed the world. They took something away from it and put themselves in its place.

When one knows something like that, Elena, one also knows that it isn't possible to go on living in the old way.

I began to wonder whether anything I had ever said was what

I had wanted to say. I began to wonder whether anything I had ever written was what I had wanted to write, or whether what I had wanted to write was underneath, trying to push its way through.

After dinner that day, the day of the crumpled paper, I didn't go to my study but sat in the living room. I was hoping to soothe you somehow, to apologize to you with my presence. You stayed in the bedroom. Once you walked from the bedroom to the guest room, where I heard you making up the bed.

One night as I sat in my leather chair, I had the sensation that you were standing at the door. I could feel a hot place at the back of my neck. I imagined you there in the doorway, looking at me with cold fascination, with a sort of tender and despairing iciness. I saw your tired eyes, your strained mouth. Were you trying to understand me? After all, you were my wife, Elena, and we had once been able to understand each other. I turned suddenly, but no one was there.

Do you think it's been easy for me? Do you? Do you think I don't know how grotesque it must seem? A grown man, forty-three years old, in excellent health, happily married, successful enough in his line of work, who suddenly refuses to speak, who flees the sound of others speaking, shuns the sight of the written word, avoids his wife, leaves his job, in order to shut himself up in his room or take long solitary walks—the idea is clownish, disgusting. The man is mad, sick, damaged, in desperate need of a doctor, a lover, a vacation, anything. Stick him in a ward. Inject him with something. But then, think of the other side. Think of it! Think of the terrible life of words, the unstoppable roar of sound that comes rushing out of people's mouths and seems to have no object except the evasion of silence. The talking species! We're nothing but an aberration, an error of Nature. What must the stones think of us? Sometimes I imagine that if we were very still we could hear, rising from the forests and oceans, the quiet laughter of animals, as they listen to us talk. And then, lovely touch, the invention of an afterlife, a noisy eternity filled with the racket of rejoicing angels. My own heaven would be an immense emptiness—a silence bright and hard as the blade of a sword.

Listen, Elena. Listen to me. I have something to say to you, which can't be said.

As I train myself to cast off words, as I learn to erase word-thoughts, I begin to feel a new world rising up around me. The old world of houses, rooms, trees, and streets shimmers, wavers, and tears away, revealing another universe as startling as fire. We are shut off from the fullness of things. Words hide the world. They blur together elements that exist apart, or they break elements into pieces, bind up the world, contract it into hard little pellets of perception. But the unbound world, the world behind the world—how fluid it is, how lovely and dangerous. At rare moments of clarity, I succeed in breaking through. Then I see. I see a place where nothing is known, because nothing is shaped in advance by words. There, nothing is hidden from me. There, every object presents itself entirely, with all its being. It's as if, looking at a house, you were able to see all four sides and both roof slopes. But then, there's no "house," no "object," no form that stops at a boundary, only a stream of manifold, precise, and nameless sensations, shifting into one another, pullulating, a fullness, a flow. Stripped of words, untamed, the universe pours in on me from every direction. I become what I see. I am earth, I am air. I am all. My eyes are suns. My hair streams among galaxies.

I am often tired. I am sometimes discouraged. I am always sure.

And still you're waiting, Elena—even now. Even now you're waiting for the explanation, the apology, the words that will justify you and set you free. But underneath that waiting is another waiting: you are waiting for me to return to the old way. Isn't it true? Listen, Elena. It's much too late for that. In my silent world, my world of exhausting wonders, there's no place for the old words with which I deceived myself, in my artificial garden. I had thought that words were instruments of precision. Now I know that they devour the world, leaving nothing in its place.

And you? Maybe a moment will come when you'll hesitate, hearing a word. In that instant lies your salvation. Heed the hesitation. Search out the space, the rift. Under this world there is another, waiting to be born. You can remain where you are, in the old world, tasting the bitter berries of disenchantment, or you can overcome yourself, rip yourself free of the word-lie, and enter the world that longs to take you in. To me, on this side, your anger is a failure of perception, your sense of betrayal a sign of the unawakened heart. Shed all these dead modes of feeling and come with me—into the glory of the fire.

Enough. You can't know what these words have cost me, I who no longer have words to speak with. It's like returning to the house of one's childhood: there is the white picket fence, there is the old piano, the Schumann on the music rack, the rose petals beside the vase, and there, look!—above the banister, the turn at the top of the stairs. But all has changed, all's heavy with banishment, for we are no longer who we were. Down with it. You too, Elena: let it go. Let your patience go, your bitterness, your sorrow—they're nothing but words. Leave them behind, in a box in the attic, the one with all the broken dolls. Then come down the stairs and out into the unborn world. Into the sun. The sun.

IMPOSSIBLE ARCHITECTURES

THE DOME

THE FIRST DOMES, the precursors, appeared here and there in affluent neighborhoods, on out-of-the-way roads, where they attracted a certain attention before growing familiar and nearly invisible. The few outsiders who actually witnessed them tended to dismiss them as follies of the rich, comparable to underground heating pipes for winter gardens or basement bowling alleys with automatic pinsetters. Even the early newspaper reports did not quite know what tone to take, shifting uneasily from technical description to ironic commentary, with moments of guarded praise. And that was hardly surprising, since the domes, while having features that were judged to be admirable, displayed themselves in a way that could readily strike an unsympathetic observer as pretentious or irritating.

Each of the early models, made of transparent Viviglas, was designed to fit directly over a house and its property. Now, emerging from the front or back door in summer, the owner of a dome could step comfortably into a world of air-conditioned lawns and gardens, thanks to a highly efficient system of filters and evaporator coils built into the Viviglas. There were other advantages. Recessed fluorescent lighting with dimmer switches permitted the property to be illuminated at night, so that you could read a book or newspaper in the cool outdoors on the hottest, muggiest evenings. Owners were encouraged to practice their golf swings, play badminton after dark, and enjoy a bit of night gardening, in the always perfect weather under the dome. In fact it was a boast of the manufacturer, much quoted at the time, that "Inside our dome, rain never falls." As if that wasn't enough, the manufacturer promised future models that would heat the enclosures in winter, though a number of difficulties still needed to be ironed out. It was above all as technological achievements that the early domes impressed most observers, who nevertheless remained skeptical. Questions were raised about the extent to which such excesses were likely to be shared by the average American household, since the domes at that time cost nearly as much as the estates they encapsulated. Nor could a number of journalists resist reflecting on the metaphorical implications of those glistening, crystalline structures, which enclosed the rich in little princedoms that insulated them even further from the everyday world.

There were, moreover, serious flaws in the early domes, which became apparent soon enough. Grackles, jays, and sparrows settled in great numbers on the dome-tops, where they blocked the sky and left broad smears of yellowish-white excrement. To make matters worse, many birds, deceived by the transparent Viviglas, flew directly into the thick walls and fell dead or injured to the ground below. Now the manufacturer had to send out daily cleaning crews, who washed the outsides of the domes, gathered up the dead and injured birds, and installed small boxes that made a grinding noise intended to discourage wasps, bees, birds, and Japanese beetles from settling anywhere on the shiny surfaces. Other problems began to reveal themselves. Rainwater as it evaporated left dusty streaks, which had to be removed; airborne particles gradually formed a layer of grime. Trouble developed even on the insides of the domes, where mist from sprinkler systems collected on the inner surfaces, increasing the humidity and obscuring the view. The manufacturer devoted itself assiduously to every complaint, while pointing out in its own defense that many of the little annoyances were due strictly to summer and might be expected to vanish with the season. The owners waited; and as the weather turned cold, frost formed colossal and oppressive patterns on the transparent surfaces, which were further darkened by the falling of the first snow.

One might have been forgiven, at this point, for predicting the death of the domes. In many instances the owners did in fact have them removed, a costly business requiring a small army of workmen and fleets of flatbed trucks. Others remained steadfast through the winter, during which a number of benefits became evident. No snow fell on the walks and driveways, bushes and hedges were protected from harmful layers of ice; the air inside the domes, though still unheated, grew pleasantly warm on cold but sunny afternoons. Such discoveries were offset by a burst of new drawbacks. Accumulations of thick-crusted snow froze to the tops of the domes, while spears of ice clung to the sides, and sweeps of high-drifted snow pressed up against the Viviglas doors. By the end of the first winter, it was clear to most customers that the domes were more trouble than they were worth.

The change came in early spring. Three separate events took place within one crucial ten-day period: the manufacturer discovered a cheaper and stronger substance, Splendimax, that reduced the cost of the domes by half; a pollution alert lasting an entire week drew new attention to the domes as pure environments; and a rash of kidnappings in small towns in Connecticut, Massachusetts, and Vermont led to a sudden interest in the domes as protective shells. Now the domes began to appear in less exclusive neighborhoods, where crowds gathered to watch enormous strips of Splendimax being lowered into place by towering cranes. Newspapers and weekly magazines paid close attention to the new middle-class phenomenon, which some journalists attributed to the influence of the mall, with its habit of combining disparate elements under a single roof. Others saw in the trend still another instance of a disturbing tendency in the American suburb: the longing for withdrawal, for self-enclosure, for expensive isolation.

As the domes began to spread slowly, rival manufacturers produced less costly varieties, composed of improved materials and marketed under an array of names (Vitrilon, XceliPlex, Amphiperm, Colossotherm), often with new and attractive features. One dome was equipped with a heating system for winter, another had retractable panels for controlling frost and mist, and one well-advertised version, promoted by educators, came with an artificial night sky that displayed constellations, planets, and other heavenly bodies, scientifically adjusted to latitude and longitude, which moved slowly across the inner surface and were far more vivid and convincing than those in the actual sky.

Yet this activity too might have run its course, leaving behind a scattering of domed properties in towns that had gone on to new diversions, had it not been for an event that took many observers by surprise. Just when it seemed that the market for domed houses had reached its limit, a developer decided to enclose several blocks of newly constructed homes on fourteen acres of land, beneath a single dome. The vast span of Splendimax rose not only over individual properties but over a small park with swings, a communal swimming pool, a stretch of oak and beech woods, and nine freshly paved streets. Two weeks later, in a nearby town, a gated community voted to endome itself; and as the fashion for doming continued to spread, citizens at town meetings and city halls began to debate the question of enclosing commercial districts and public lands, while keeping them accessible to area residents.

It was during this phase of enlarged domings that the first town voted to enclose itself, in a massive dome that was reputed to be one of the great engineering feats of the new millennium. The immensity of the structure, the sheer drama and bravado of it all, caused a sharp increase of interest, for the new magnitude represented a decision that could no longer be dismissed as a passing trend. Critics attacked the hostile apartness of the town, which in its hemisphere of VeridiGlo was said to resemble a walled medieval city, as if the advance in technology served only to conceal a secret atavism. Admirers, as might be expected, hailed the brilliance of the engineering, the grandeur of technological accomplishment, which placed the new dome in the noble line of the skyscraper, the suspension bridge, the hydroelectric dam, and the ancient pyramid. Others praised the domed town for its clean air—a system of escape vents permitted the expulsion of factory pollutants and gasoline fumes—while several took a more aesthetic approach, finding in the space enclosed by the dome a spirit of gaiety, of pleasurable artifice, reminiscent of the old European plaza with its fountain and shade trees or the American mall with its food court and Santa's workshop, for under the roof of the dome the inhabitants of the town were said to feel a bond of community, a sense of uninterrupted gathering in a special place set aside for their common pleasure.

To the surprise of almost everyone, the new dome did not immediately spawn another. It was as if people felt that the doming process was moving ahead a little too rapidly and required a pause, during which the consequences of the new technology might be studied more carefully. It was recognized, to begin with, that the sheer cost of a dome this size far exceeded the annual budget of all but the wealthiest towns. At the same time, a broad range of practical problems had yet to be solved, such as the efficient flow of traffic into and out of the dome, the pattern and duration of nocturnal illumination, and the seasonal migration of birds living within the structure. People began to wonder whether they would be safer under a dome, or whether a permanent enclosure might prove harmful, in the long run. But even as the issue hung in the balance, decisions were being made in remote rooms, behind closed doors, that would soon change everything.

We live in the aftermath of those decisions. To say that the Dome is the single largest achievement in the history of architecture is inadequate and misleading. It is a leap beyond, into some new domain without a name. The story of its building is well known: the drama of starting on both coasts, the erection of the great pillars, the early collapse of the northwestern foundation, the construction of the offshore airports, the closing of the final gap. Many of us can scarcely remember a time when we did not live beneath a soaring roof of transparent Celestilux.

And yet the achievement is not without its detractors, even today. Critics argue that the Dome represents the complete triumph of the consumer society, of which it is the extravagant and unapologetic symbol. For the Dome, they say, has transformed the entire country into a gigantic mall, whose sole purpose is to encourage feverish consumption. The sensation of being under a common roof, of spending many hours under artificial lights, is said to stimulate in the average citizen a relentless desire to buy. And it remains true that the completion of the Dome has been accompanied by a sharp increase in consumer spending, as if everything beneath the Celestilux roof—houses, lakes, clouds—were being displayed to advantage and offered ceaselessly for sale. Some have even claimed that our Dome is the final flowering of the nineteenth-century department store, of which the American mall was only a transitional, horizontal form. According to this view, the great empty spaces of the Dome will gradually be put to commercial use; there are predictions of transparent floors in the sky, level upon level, connected by hollow Celestilux tubes containing motorized passenger platforms.

But those who dislike the Dome do not simply accuse it of serving the interests of late capitalism. They attack the name itself, arguing that the enclosure follows the irregular shape of the continental United States and is therefore no true dome. Defenders, while not denying that the lower base is irregular, are quick to remind their opponents that at the height of four hundred feet the soaring walls of Celestilux slope inward and gradually provide the base for a classic dome that rises over most of the nation. Indeed, the forging of a true dome above a vast, irregular perimeter is one of the engineering triumphs of the entire project. But defenders are not confined to such quibbles. They point proudly to a host of benefits: the national regulation of climate, the protection of our coasts against hurricanes, the creation of twenty-four-hour illumination and the consequent elimination of time zones, the Celestilux shield against ultraviolet radiation.

Without choosing sides in the debate, we may note a number of subtler changes. Because everything lies beneath a single dome, because everything is, in a very real sense, indoors, our feelings about Nature are no longer the same. The Dome, in a single stroke, has abolished Nature. The hills, the streams, the woods, the fields, all have become elements in a new decor, an artfully designed landscape—designed by the mere fact of existing under the Dome. This experience of landscape as *style* has been called the New Interiority. In former days, a distinction was made between inside and outside: people emerged from their homes or apartments and arrived "outside." Today, one leaves one's dwelling place and steps into another, larger room. The change is dramatic. The world, perceived as an interior, shimmers with artifice. A tree growing in a park is indistinguishable from a lifelike tree in the corner of a restaurant. A lake in the country is a more artful version of a tiled pool in a mall.

This perceptual change has led in turn to another, which has been called the New Miniaturism. Things in the world now appear smaller, more toylike. An object that once towered above us—a tall pine, a steep hill, a snowcapped mountain—is itself dwarfed by the Dome, which by the ever-present fact of its vastness miniaturizes what it encloses. The Mississippi is nothing but a trickle of water in a child's terrarium. The Rockies are only a row of stones in a third-grade diorama. Events themselves, under such conditions, have receded in importance, have become aestheticized. Experience is beginning to feel like a collection of ingeniously constructed arcade games. Is it because, living beneath the Dome, people are reminded of playful worlds in enclosed and festive spaces, such as movie theaters, bowling alleys, laser-tag arenas, video arcades, the old fun houses and circuses? Indeed, one might argue that under the regime of the Dome, the country has become not a mall but an immense hall of entertainment, in which every citizen is a player. Certain unpleasant facts of life—rundown neighborhoods, traffic accidents, robberies, drive-by shootings—are in this view taken less seriously, since they are felt to be part of the artificial displays under the Dome. Death itself is losing its terror, has come to seem little more than a brilliantly contrived effect.

There are rumors of grander plans. At a conference in Oslo, architects and engineers have proposed a transparent globe, supported by massive DuraCryst pillars, which would surround the entire earth. That such a vision shall be fulfilled in our lifetime is unlikely; that it should have been dreamed at all is perhaps inevitable. For under the visible fact of the Dome, it is difficult not to imagine still vaster encompassings. Already, at certain moments, in certain moods, the famous Dome has come to seem a little diminished, a little disappointing. No doubt we shall never rest content until the great All is enclosed in a globe of transparent Astrilume. Then solar systems, galaxies, supernovas, infinite space itself, will become elements of a final masterwork—a never-ending festival, a celestial amusement park, in which every exploding star and spinning electron is part of the empyrean choreography. Meanwhile we walk beneath the Celestilux sky, dreaming of new heavens, of impossible architectures. For a change is in the air. You can feel it coming.

IN THE REIGN OF HARAD IV

IN THE REIGN of Harad IV there lived at court a maker of miniatures, who was celebrated for the uncanny perfection of his work. Not only were the objects of his strenuous art pleasing to look at, but the pleasure and astonishment increased as the observer, bending closer, saw that a passionate care had been lavished on the smallest and least visible details. It was said that no matter how closely you examined one of the Master's little pieces, you always discovered some further wonder.

Among the many tasks of the maker of miniatures was supplying court ladies with carved ivory plants and triple-headed sea monsters for their cabinets of delight, drawing the fur and feathers of fabulous creatures in *The Book of Three Hundred Secrets*, and, above all, replacing the furnishings of the old toy palace, which the King had inherited from his father and which was filled with moldering draperies and cracked wood. The famous toy palace, with its more than six hundred rooms, its dungeons and secret passageways, its gardens and courtyards and orchards, rose to the height of a man's chest and occupied its own chamber, across from the King's library. In return for his duties the maker of miniatures was given a private apartment in the palace not far from the court carpenter, as well as an ermine robe that entitled him to take part in official ceremonies. He was assisted by two youthful apprentices. They roughed out the larger miniatures, such as cupboards and canopy beds, fired the little earthenware bowls in a special kiln, applied the first coat of lacquer to objects made of wood, and saved precious time for the Master by fetching from the palace workshops pieces of ivory, copper, lapis, boxwood, and beechwood. But the apprentices were not permitted to attempt the more difficult labors of the miniaturist's art, such as carving the dragon heads at the feet of table legs, or forging the minuscule copper keys that turned the locks of drawers and chests.

One day, after the completion of an arduous and exhilarating task—he had made for one of the miniature orchards a basket of brilliantly lifelike red-and-green apples, each no larger than the pit of a cherry, and as a finishing touch he had placed on the stem of one apple a perfectly reproduced copper fly—the maker of miniatures felt in himself a stirring of restlessness. It wasn't the first time he had experienced such stirrings at the end of a long task, but lately the odd, internal itching had become more insistent. As he tried to penetrate the feeling, to reveal it more clearly to himself, he thought of the basket of apples. The basket had been unusually satisfying to make because it had presented him with a hierarchy of sizes: the basket itself, composed of separate slats of boxwood bound with copper wire, then the apples, and at last the fly. The tiny fly, with its precisely rendered wings, had caused him the most difficulty and the most joy, and it occurred to him that there was no particular reason to stop at the fly. Suddenly he was seized by an inner trembling. Why had he never thought of this before? How was it possible? Didn't logic itself demand that the downward series be pursued? At this thought he felt a deep, guilty excitement, as if he had come to a forbidden door at the end of a private corridor and heard, as he slowly turned the key, a sound of distant music.

He set out to make an apple basket the size of one of his apples. The new wooden apples, each with a stem and two leaves, were so small that he was able to carve them only with the aid of an enlarging glass, which he set into a supporting frame. But even as he struggled pleasurably over each apple, he realized he was dreaming of the fly, the impossible fly that, as it turned out, was visible only as a speck on the minuscule stem, though it was perfect in every detail when viewed through the glass.

The King, who had praised the original fly, looked at the new basket of apples with astonished delight. When the Master invited him to observe the apples through the glass, the King drew in his breath, appeared to be about to speak, and suddenly clapped his hands sharply, whereupon the Chamberlain strode in. The King instructed him to view the miniature fly through the lens. The Chamberlain, a cold and imperious man, gave a harsh gasp. By the next morning the story of the invisible fly was known throughout the palace.

With new zest, as if he were returning to an earlier and more exuberant period of his life, the middle-aged but still vigorous Master devoted himself to a series of miniatures that in every way surpassed his finest efforts of the past. From the pit of a cherry he carved a ring of thirty-six elephants, each holding in its trunk the tail of the elephant before it. Every elephant possessed a pair of nearly invisible tusks carved out of ivory. One day the Master presented to the King a saucer on which stood an inverted ebony thimble. When the King picked up the thimble, he discovered beneath it a meticulous reproduction of the northwest wing of his toy palace, with twenty-six rooms fully furnished, including a writing table with ostrich-claw legs and a gold birdcage containing a nightingale.

Scarcely had the maker of miniatures completed the thimble palace when he felt a new burst of restlessness. Once embarked on his downward voyage, would he ever be able to stop? Besides, wasn't it plain that the tiny palace, though but partially visible to the unaided eye, revealed itself too readily, without that resistance which was an essential part of aesthetic delight? And he proposed to himself a plunge beneath the surface of the visible, the creation of a detailed world wholly inaccessible to the naked eye.

He began with simple things—a copper bowl, a beechwood box—for the material he worked with was, before magnification, itself invisible and required of him a new degree of delicate manipulation. He quickly recognized the need for more powerful lenses, more subtle tools. From the court carpenter he ordered a pair of complex gripping devices that held his hands still and steadied his fingers. This was no work for an old man, he thought—no, or for a young man either—but only for someone in the full vigor of his middle years.

His first masterpiece in the realm of the invisible was a stag with branching antlers. Through a powerful glass he watched the invisible sharpen into the visible: the head twisted to one side, the mouth slightly open, the lips drawn back to reveal the teeth. He carved it and painted it down to the last detail, tooth and hoof and pale inner ear; and it was said by some that, if you looked very closely through the enlarging glass, you could distinguish the amber irises from the bright black pupils.

No sooner had he finished the stag than he embarked on a far more challenging task: an invisible garden, modeled at first on one of the thirty-nine palace gardens but quickly developing its own more elaborate design. During the early stages a sudden draft destroyed a week's worth of work. With the aid of the court carpenter, for whom he drew up a plan, the maker of miniatures constructed a teakwood box with a sloping top, in which was set a square magnifying lens. Two panels in the sides of the box slid smoothly up and down, so that a pair of hands might be inserted, and the square lens, attached to a system of rods and screws, could be raised and lowered. The intricate and delicate garden, protected from disturbing currents of air, grew slowly until it contained dozens of twelve-sided flower beds, fourteen varieties of fruit tree with individual leaves, a system of crossing paths paved with tesserae of ebony and ivory, onyx fountains carved with legendary creatures, snails under stones.

Although the King expressed wonder and amazement at the garden seen through the glass, and praised the Master's conquest of a new world, he asked many questions about the lens and the teakwood box, as if he suspected them of working a spell. At last the King permitted himself to wonder whether his maker of miniatures might not soon return to the visible miracle of his exquisite palace furniture. In the King's voice the Master heard a tone of unmistakable reproach. As he explained the apparatus and adjusted the lens, it seemed to him that by venturing beyond the visible world he had embarked on a voyage more perilous than he had known.

But already he had thrown himself into the crowning masterpiece of this period: the King's famous toy palace, entirely invisible to the naked eye. The more than six hundred rooms would be completely furnished and scrupulously rendered in every detail, including dovetail joints in the cabinets, working locks on the drawers, and fifteen dozen complete sets of knives, forks, and spoons in chased silver, each with the royal insignia—a crown and crossed swords—worked onto the handle.

During the construction of his palace-beneath-the-glass, the maker of miniatures paid several visits to the original toy palace, and was startled each time by the vast building that towered almost to the height of his shoulders. The chairs in the council chamber were the size of his fists. Ever since his own work had taken its slight and necessary turn, its odd unaccountable swerve away from classic smallness toward another, more dubious realm, his two apprentices had assumed the task of supplying furniture for the King's toy palace. And the Master saw that it was good: they were well suited to large and striking effects, he had perhaps been unduly harsh in limiting them to elementary tasks, in the days when such things concerned him.

One day, while looking at a desk in the King's toy palace, the maker of miniatures fell into a reverie. Fastened to the drawer of the desk was a pair of brass lion's-head handles, which had once seemed to him the height of elegance and had cost him three days of work. The smallest object in the toy palace was a silver needle no thicker than a hair. It occurred to him, not without pride, that the entire palace he was now constructing beneath his glass, with its more than six hundred rooms and its gardens and orchards, could be enclosed by the eye of that needle.

But even as he sank deeply into his little world he felt at the back of his mind a slight itching, as if he knew that his palace, even that, could not satisfy him for long. For such a feat, however arduous, was really no more than the further conquest of a familiar realm, the twilight realm of the world revealed by his glass, and he yearned for a world so small that he could not yet imagine it. As he worked on his palace the craving grew in him, and he seemed to sense dimly, just out of reach beyond his inner sight, a farther kingdom.

He began to see it more clearly, with growing excitement, though he confessed to himself that it was less a seeing than a desire gradually hardening into a certainty. Although he now worked with material so minute that it was invisible to the unaided eye, it remained true that the invisible was made visible by his lens. If to others he seemed a magician who brought the seen out of the unseen, in fact he worked wholly in the visible world. It was an ambiguous and elusive world, which vanished into the invisible as soon as the glass was removed, and yet it was a far cry from the purely invisible realm he sensed just beyond.

And he longed to construct objects so small that they would escape the power of the mediating glass, remain submerged in the dark kingdom of the invisible.

He began as always with a simple object: an oblong ivory box with a sliding top. Although the box was so marvelously small that it remained invisible even through the glass, he continued to make use of his teakwood viewer with the sloping top and movable lens, for the familiar apparatus served to concentrate his attention and steady his fingers. The ivory box, which never once emerged from its hidden world to reveal itself to the eye of the Master, was completed in seven days. With his inner eye he contemplated it coolly and felt a calm elation. Despite the absence of visible evidence, he was certain of its formal perfection, of the elegant precision of its parts—never had he taken so much care.

Immediately he threw himself into a more ambitious task: a beechwood peacock with outspread tail. The enchanting peacock, radiant with unseen colors, took him nearly three weeks, and when he was done he felt ready for the task he had secretly been preparing for: an imaginary kingdom.

And so he set to work on his invisible kingdom, with its walled cities and winding rivers, its forests of beech and fir, its copper mines and temple towers, its spoons and insects. By the end of a year he had completed a single city. The city contained cobbled streets and market squares, baskets of grapes on the fruit sellers' stands, merchants' houses with pillared balconies overlooking courtyards, individual bottles in the glassblowers' shops. He felt tired and exhilarated, and as he imagined all that remained undone, stretching out before him like an immense adventure, he found himself wishing that he could reveal his work to someone, as he had once been able to do. The solitude of his task was never oppressive, but from time to time, in the pauses of his day, he felt a touch of loneliness. The King no longer summoned him, and his apprentices had moved into an adjoining chamber and taken on apprentices of their own.

One afternoon, when he was deep-sunk in his invisible kingdom, there was a rap at the door of his chamber. Half raising his head from the teakwood box, the maker of miniatures called for the visitor to enter. The door opened to admit two of the four new apprentices. They began by apologizing for disturbing the Master at work, but explained that they had long admired his unsurpassed art and could not resist the desire to pay their respects and to beg for news of his latest work, of which they had heard confused and contradictory reports. Their own work was still crude and trifling, they had scarcely the skill with which to fashion the leg of a table, and they hoped that a visit to the Master would instruct and inspire them. The Master knew at once that the apprentices, who were both quite young, were very sure of themselves and were belittling themselves only out of courtly politeness, but the loneliness of his last months was soothed by their words of homage. Giving way to temptation, he moved aside to permit them to view his kingdom through the glass. True, they would be able to see nothing, for he had dropped fully beneath the floor of the visible, but perhaps they could somehow sense, as he could in the darkest depths of his mind, the splendor and precision of his invisible art.

The first apprentice bent over the glass in the sloping top of the teakwood box. After a few moments he stepped aside and allowed the second apprentice to bend over the glass. When both had done looking, the younger of the two said that the Master's work was indeed incomparable. Never in his short life had he seen anything so remarkable in both conception and execution. At once the second apprentice gave voice to his admiration, saying that even in his dreams he had not dared to imagine such loveliness. And indeed it was the highest of all honors simply to be in the presence of so great an accomplishment. Then the two apprentices thanked the Master for dignifying them with his attention and respectfully took their leave. The maker of miniatures, knowing that they had seen nothing, that their words were hollow, and that they would never visit him again, returned with some impatience to his work; and as he sank below the crust of the visible world, into his dazzling kingdom, he understood that he had traveled a long way from the early days, that he still had far to go, and that, from now on, his life would be difficult and without forgiveness.

THE OTHER TOWN

THE OTHER TOWN, the one that exactly resembles our town, lies just beyond the north woods. To get there, we have only to walk through a stretch of shade, over a spongy layer of pine needles and brown-black leaves, and come out in any of the backyards that border the woods—the DeAngelo yard, say, with its flowered beach towels hanging over the back-porch rail and its coil of green hose next to the dented garbage cans, or the Altschuler yard with its tall sugar maple, its yellow Wiffle ball bat lying half in sun and half in shade, and its aluminum chaise longue with strips of orange and white vinyl on which a blue eyeglass case is resting, or the Langley yard with its grass-stained soccer ball, its red-handled jump rope, its tin pie-dish for home plate, and its bags of peat moss and fertilizer leaning up against the side of the detached garage. Those of us who prefer not to go on foot can drive up North Pine or Holbrook, both of which end at Linwood, the street that runs along the front of the houses whose backyards border the woods. From there we can go in any direction, all over the town. If we're in the mood, we can stop wherever we like, walk up to any house, open the front door. We can step inside and explore every room. Later, if we wish, we can drive through the other town's north woods, up the other North Pine or Holbrook. Then we'll come out at the edge of a town that is different from ours, a town with its own style—as if, all along, our trip through the other town had been nothing but a trip through our town, which of course in some sense it always is.

Although we're drawn to the other town because of its startling resemblance to ours—the morning papers lying at the same angles on the same porches, the doors and drawers opened to the identical distances, the same dishes in the dish racks and the same clothes in the laundry baskets—it's also true that we're struck by certain differences. We can hardly fail to notice the separate groups of people, often our own neighbors, crossing lawns, entering and leaving houses, stopping now and then to look about, like tourists visiting a famous spot. Then there are the town guards, in their dark green shirts with yellow armbands, who are visible everywhere—in every house and store, in the two parks, in the high school, in the picnic grounds by the stream before the woods. Here and there we also catch glimpses of the replicators, the ones who see to it that all changes in our town are repeated in the other town, and who do their best to keep out of our way. In addition, there's a sense we all have, an elusive but still quite definite sense, which might be called an intuition of absence: the absence of people living in homes, working in stores, conducting the daily life of a town. For of course no one lives in the other town, which exists solely to be visited by us.

Apart from these large differences, which none of us can help noticing, there are many small discrepancies, usually detectable in one's own duplicated house, as when the crowded kitchen drawer contains the very can opener missing from the drawer in one's own kitchen, or when the tomato plant, tied to a stick with string at the side of the house, bears a tomato of different size, on a different stem. Those of us who are older, and have visited the other town many times, take a special pleasure in detecting such mismatchings, though a few purists among us argue that any difference is a flaw and should never be tolerated.

The origin of the other town remains obscure. Its first appearance in the historical record occurs in 1685, some forty years after the founding of our town, when the building of a new house "and of the same house in the North Towne" is reported, though the mention is so brief and riddling that it has been subject to conflicting interpretations. One town historian has argued that "the same house" refers not to an identical house but to a house in similar style. Another points out that "the North Towne" is itself an expression of uncertain meaning, since it was sometimes used to indicate the northern part of our own town. Not till the middle of the eighteenth century does it become clear that a second town exists to our north, imitating our town and maintained by our residents; in addition to public records, private diaries report visits to the other town, which one citizen calls a "wonder work." Still, many details of reproduction and maintenance remain unclear, and it isn't until the nineteenth century that a full record begins to emerge, including the founding of an early version of town guards and the establishment, in 1882, of the craft of replicators. Such evidence as we have suggests only that the other town arose not long after ours and was in some sense a copy. Even this broad proposition has its dissenters, for some argue that the other town was at first distinct from ours and only gradually took on the quality of imitation.

However that may be, the record for well over one hundred years indicates an increasing concern for meticulous replication. Indeed, there's good reason to think that in earlier years the level of imitation was far less precise than it has since become. Before the establishment of replicators, the business of duplication was carried out by separate groups of craftsmen hired at need by the town council. Since the workers had other business, delay was frequent and the entire system subject to a high degree of disorganization. The importance of the replicators lay above all in their being full-time employees engaged in a single undertaking. But whereas the original replicators were expected to attend mostly to houses and their furnishings, our present-day replicators are responsible for all elements of decor, from the paving of streets and the renovation of public buildings to the daily adjustment of levels of salt in the saltshakers and the arrangement of forks in the silverware drawers. Groups of "watchers," working in our town, report on their laptops all daily changes, which the replicators in turn bring about in the other town. During prime visiting hours, from 8 a.m. to 10 p.m., the replicators bring adjustments up to date every two hours, so that, for example, a package delivered to a front porch in our town will also appear on the front porch of the identical house in the other town; because of the difference in time, it's possible for someone who receives a package in our town to drive to the other town and await the same package, which always arrives, though later; such discrepancies seem inevitable, although the replicators have reduced the time lag significantly during the last decade and foresee an era of temporal simultaneity.

Recently the art of replication has reached new levels of mastery. Replicators can reproduce the precise grain of a weathered shingle, the pattern of mud spray on the side of a car, the faint discoloration on the rim of an old coffee cup, the design of cracks on a glued-together porcelain rooster on the kitchen windowsill. A more difficult challenge lies in the realm of Nature. The arrangement of twigs and branches on a specific sycamore, the exact position of blossoms on a flowering rhododendron, the structure of petals in a particular white rose, all present challenges of design, patterns of apparent randomness within a complex order, which have taxed the skills of master craftsmen. Only two generations ago, replicators did little more than select real plants, restricting their attention to size, shape, and number: a medium-sized wild cherry for the side yard, three azaleas and a well-trimmed snowball bush under the front windows. But complaints about discrepancies led to a decade of radical artifice. Suddenly every Norway maple with its precise system of leaves and branches, every spirea bush and marigold, was replicated in the master workshops and planted in the yards of the other town. This in turn led to a new outburst of complaints, since the artificial plants and trees, though convincing at first, gradually gave off an air of falsity. We're now in the midst of a more satisfactory experiment, in which the real and the replicated are carefully intermingled: among the branches of the actual shagbark hickory, a few artificial branches; among the real leaves, the cunning leaves of a master replicator.

Although most of us simply enjoy visiting the other town without thinking very much about it, there are those who can't help wondering why it is there at all. Some say the other town serves as a welcome distraction from the cares of our own town—for them it's a kind of superior amusement park, where we can forget our worries and take delight in a world of sensations. If a window is broken in our town, we rush to have it fixed, we can't rest until the damage is repaired. But in the other town we note with pleasure the skill with which the pattern of broken glass has been imitated, we point admiringly at the shards of glass lying on the living room rug.

Such arguments, others claim, are suitable only for children. The real value of the town, in their opinion, lies in the way it permits us to see our own town more clearly or completely. Preoccupied as we are with domestic and financial cares, we pass through our lives noticing so little of what's really around us that we might be said to inhabit an invisible town; in the other town, the visible town, our attention is seized, we feel compelled to look at things closely, to linger over details that would otherwise fail to exist at all. In this way the other town leads us to a fuller or truer grasp of things. Far from being a childish diversion intended to distract us from more serious concerns, it's a necessary stage away from the simplicities of childhood and into the richness of adult understanding.

For my part, I think there is some truth to both these theories, but I believe the other town serves another purpose as well. Although it strives to resemble our town precisely, in fact it offers us freedoms unthinkable at home. There, we can penetrate other houses at will, cross forbidden boundaries, climb unfamiliar stairways, enter secret rooms. All that is closed to us, in our town, is open there, all that's hidden is seen. This shattering of constriction, this sensation of expansion, of exhilarating release, is in my view the real purpose of the other town, which for all its stillness invites us into a world of dangerous and criminal pleasures.

Our urge to explain the other town, to justify its existence, is not without practical import. The other town is maintained by our workers and paid for by our taxes. Voices are regularly raised in opposition to the whole foolish enterprise, despite the sense shared by most of us that life without the other town would be unsatisfactory, in some way difficult to explain. Repeatedly we hear that the other town is simply unnecessary. We already have a town, the argument goes—a second one, exactly resembling it, is entirely superfluous, not to say absurd, all the more so because no one lives there and no use is made of it, apart from visits that draw people away from more profitable pursuits. This objection shades quickly into a purely material one: the other town represents a shocking waste of land and money. The material argument generally includes proposals to make the existing houses available for sale, to build new homes and low-rise apartments, to develop a senior-citizen center—in short, to make use of the other town in ways that would benefit everyone.

Such ideas are vigorously supported by a small but aggressive group who attack the other town on moral grounds, arguing that the so-called pleasures it offers are disgusting and corrupt. What after all can be said in favor of the pleasure of spying on the lives of one's neighbors, of violating private property, of undermining the laws of our town? These moralists object in particular to the invasion of homes, above all their own homes, especially late at night, when visitors are allowed to explore any unlit room with flashlights supplied by guards. The visitors—we ourselves—are accused of having an unhealthy interest in secret and sexual matters, in hidden things of every description, and in truth we've become quite good at finding and interpreting signs: the black half-slip and the twisted jeans on the throw rug by the rumpled bed, the burst of red wine on the kitchen wall.

But the moralists don't stop here. They go on to accuse the other town of encouraging indecent behavior in our children. A recent incident has inflamed their anger. A band of six children, ranging in age from nine to twelve, was caught roaming through a house on Warren Street, in our town, when the owners were away. A valuable table had been damaged by knife cuts, a bedroom wall defaced with an image of male genitalia scrawled in ink. Those who defend the other town against charges of corrupting our children argue that incidents of this kind are quite rare, that parents themselves are to blame for failing to enforce the distinction between our town and the other town, that in any case childhood disobedience won't vanish if the other town is abolished. In my view, all such defenses are a mistake, since their very existence lends legitimacy to the objections they seek to remove. Far better to listen with melancholy patience, nodding slowly now and then, with a slight narrowing of the eyes, as if smoke is drifting against your face.

In addition to those who attack the other town in every possible way, there are those who support the idea of a second town but object to what they consider a grotesque obsession with replication. It's precisely the differences, they insist, that make the other town worth visiting. Some go so far as to say that the differences are too subtle and ought to be increased and exaggerated. They propose fantastical dwellings, streets of alabaster and gold, underground dream-parks, unearthly towers. Others claim that the existing discrepancies are already so vivid and abundant that larger departures would seem childish and crude.

In spite of these noisy quarrels and harsh attacks, which have plagued us during our entire history, one thing remains certain: the other town is there. Tirelessly it exercises its powers of attraction even on those who protest against it, and perhaps especially on them. Scarcely a week passes when we don't make our way, by foot or by car, through the north woods and into the other town, a town so exactly like our own that for a moment a confusion comes over us, before we remember where we are. Then we wander across backyards, noting details that might have escaped our attention, walk along streets that are just like our streets, except for certain differences, check to see whether the new stop sign has gone up, enter a neighbor's house to explore a rumor of adultery—the necktie over the clock radio, the blue bra draped over the cordovan loafer—or observe the work of a replicator rearranging chairs, opening a door, placing a cup in the sink.

Sometimes the tug of our daily lives prevents us from visiting the other town as often as we might like. Then a restlessness comes over us, an unease, a kind of physiological unhappiness. We stop whatever we're doing—mowing the lawn, lifting the groceries from the trunk of the car—and listen. For it's as if the other town, which is far quieter than ours, is producing a hum, a melody, that we strain to hear. Then we know the time is coming when, in sudden obedience to an inner command, we'll look around quickly, check our watches, and leave for a visit.

So powerful, in fact, is the pull of the other town that some citizens arrange their lives so as to spend as much time there as possible. These fanatics enter every attic and cellar, examine every tree and bush, taking scrupulous note of discrepancies and successful simulations. Once they return home they always turn their talk to the other town, or else sit restlessly alone, as if waiting for something, so that it might be said of them that their real existence is over there, beyond the north woods, while our town, rising up before their eyes, must seem to them a vision or dream.

It even happens now and then that someone will try to take up residence in the other town—an act forbidden by law. Teenagers, in particular, attempt to hide there after closing time at midnight, though only last year a husband and wife, both in their forties, were discovered by a guard at three in the morning in the bedroom of a house on Sagamore Road. Repeated violations are punished by penalties of enforced absence, which are considered so harsh that they are usually commuted to community service. One group of teenage girls, who call themselves The River, hid in the other woods repeatedly and were finally forbidden to enter the other town for a year. They seemed chastened, performed odd jobs around town, and met quietly at one another's houses, where they sat on front porches on hot summer evenings listening to the radio, tapping cigarette ash into the air, and pressing against their collarbones cool bottles of soda glittering with droplets of condensation. One night seven of them were arrested in the dark living room of the Lorenzo house in the other town. As it turned out, they had patiently dug a tunnel, night after night, from the north woods into the forbidden world, where they held secret meetings for weeks before being discovered by a guard.

We who are not fanatics, we common citizens who take life as it comes—we're content to know that the other town is always there, awaiting our visit. Indeed we prefer things this way and feel no desire to cross over permanently. For what would be the point of that? Our lives are here, in our town. It's here that we work, marry, raise our children, and die. The other town is by nature the town that's other—if we moved there, it would at that moment cease to be what it is. For we understand in our bones, without worrying it into thought, that the attraction of the other town lies precisely in its being over there. And we understand something else, though less clearly. The other town, when we enter it, suddenly casts over our town a thereness, an otherness, which we find pleasing, if a little confusing. It's almost as if we can't feel our town, cannot know about it, until we're there, in the other town, imagining our town on the other side of the woods. So perhaps it's true, after all, that when we visit the other town we aren't escaping from our town, as some say, but entering it at last.

But these are difficult questions, which we're content to leave to those who are gifted in thinking about such things. For our part, it's enough to know that each town is there, offering itself to us in its own way. For our town, too, invites our attention, though sometimes we're aware of it only when we enter the other town. In this sense it might be said that our town requires the other, much as the other town depends on ours. Or perhaps the two towns together form a separate town, a third town, and it's in this third town that we truly live.

But again I feel like someone who has managed to wander off into the shade of high trees, up there in the woods. Far better to stick to the path, in my opinion. For there, on one of the trails between the two towns, you can decide to come out in either direction: into a sudden backyard, where every blade of grass and drooping dandelion shows itself like a flame, where a bright blue watering can stands before the half-painted lattices at the base of an old back porch, through which protrude pricker branches and a cluster of sun-struck leaves—or, in the other direction, into the picnic area on our side of the woods, with its brown stream, its swings on long chains, and its unpainted wooden tables, on one of which a pinecone as long as a cigar lies beside a brilliant red paper cup. Though both directions have something to be said for them, there's also a third way, which is the one I like best. That's when you can stop for a moment, midway along the path, and turn your head in both directions: toward the other town, which shimmers through the thick branches of oak and pine, and toward our town, almost obscured by the woods but still showing through. Exactly where I am, when I stand there and look both ways, who can say? It's just for a little while, before I move on.

THE TOWER

DURING THE COURSE of many generations the Tower grew higher and higher until one day it pierced the floor of heaven. Amidst the wild rejoicing, the overturned flagons and the clashing cymbals, a few thoughtful voices made themselves heard, for the event had long been anticipated and was known to be attended by certain difficulties.

No one could deny, for example, that the remarkable height of the Tower, which was undoubtedly its most striking and brilliant achievement, was itself a cause for concern, since those who lived on the plain below couldn't possibly climb to the top within the short space of a lifetime. Inhabitants of the city or the surrounding countryside could at best begin the upward journey, without the slightest hope of nearing the end. Otherwise they could do nothing but remain where they were and wait impatiently for news to reach them from above. Even those who had taken up residence in the Tower could in no way be assured of success—many were now too old for climbing, others lived too far from the top, while still others, though vigorous and within reach, had lost their early fervor and chose not to continue the arduous ascent. It was soon clear that only a small number of devout pilgrims were likely to arrive at the ultimate destination, in addition of course to the company of workers who had completed the final stages of the Tower and were in fact the first to enter the domain of heaven. But the workers were slaves, trained by masons to lay brick upon fire-baked brick on a coating of bitumen, and otherwise uneducated, superstitious, and unreliable. It came as no surprise that their reports were unsatisfactory, especially since their words were passed down from person to person, sometimes shouted at a distance or repeated by a half-drunk servant, and thus hardly more trustworthy than an outright lie. Those living on the plain heard of a brightness, a radiance, a luminous whiteness, but it wasn't clear what the first visitors actually saw, if indeed they saw anything, although one report, greeted with a mixture of eagerness and distrust, spoke of streets paved with emeralds and gold.

Because the Tower had been the one great fact in everyone's life during the immense period of its construction, the problem of ascent had been discussed almost from the beginning. When, after several generations, the Tower had reached a certain height, mathematical calculations proved that no one could climb even that far in the course of an entire lifetime. A number of families therefore came to a decision. They chose a son and his bride and instructed them to climb as far as possible into the inconceivably high yet still far from complete Tower, there to settle in one of the new chambers that had begun to be fashioned for townspeople with a taste for height. In their new quarters they were to bear children, who in turn would one day continue to ascend. In this way a family could climb the Tower in carefully regulated stages, generation after generation.

But this method of ascent led to a second problem, which hadn't been anticipated. As dwellers in the plain climbed the Tower, their relation to the world below became less and less definite; after a certain point, a climber understood that he could no longer return to the plain during his lifetime. Such people, and there were many, found themselves neither on earth nor in heaven, but in some in-between realm, in which it was easy to feel deprived of the pleasures of both places. One solution to this problem was for people to remain in a comparatively low portion of the always rising Tower, too high to descend to the plain, but close enough to those below for tales of the plain to reach them within a reasonable stretch of time; meanwhile, from a much greater distance, reports of heaven could find their way down. The drawback of this solution was that the farther from the top a climber found himself, the less reliable the reports from above were likely to be. For this reason, many in-betweeners climbed as high as they could, in order to be closer to the upper reports, with the corresponding disadvantage of receiving from below reports that grew less trustworthy as the height increased.

Just as the problem of reaching the top of the Tower had led to a number of unforeseen difficulties and confusions, so a host of purely technical problems had arisen during the long labor of construction. The original plan had called for a spiral ramp running around the outside of the Tower, along which lines of workers could transport fire-baked bricks and buckets of bitumen. But at the height of a thousand feet—a height three times greater than any tower had ever attained—it became clear that the original calculations had failed to anticipate the actual strains on so vast a structure. It was therefore necessary to widen the base to nearly four times its original dimensions—a labor that caused the destruction of large sections of the city. And so a second Tower, as it were, grew up around the first, to the height of a thousand feet. At that point a single Tower continued to rise, but now containing an inner ramp that was the continuation of the original outer pathway. The Tower now had two circular paths, an inner and an outer, both of which were used by workers who, as the Tower rose higher, began to work inward from the outer ramp, and outward from the inner ramp, and who began to leave, along the inner ramp, small hollows used as storage and resting spaces.

As the Tower rose still higher, workers encountered another problem. How could they transport new bricks to the always rising top of the Tower? For already, even at this very early stage of construction, it took many days for the bricks to be moved from the kilns in the brickmakers' workshops to the upper rim of the Tower, by means of solid-wheeled carts pulled by two men round and round the gently sloping ramps. The problem was solved by assigning special workers, called carriers, to levels separated by thousand-foot intervals. From each level the carriers moved bricks to the next carrier above, who brought them to the next carrier, and so on. The carriers, who of necessity became permanent dwellers in the Tower, enlarged the storage and resting spaces into primitive dwelling places, which later were elaborated into one of the Tower's most striking features.

For once the carriers had begun to live in the Tower, bringing with them their wives and children, the notion of permanent residence began to take hold. Toward the end of the second generation, when the Tower was already so high that it disappeared into the brilliant blue sky, like a long pole thrust into deep water until the end trembles, shimmers, and vanishes entirely, the King of Shinar, renowned for his piety, ordered workers to prepare a court high in the clouds, where he intended to spend his remaining days in fasting and prayer. When the court was ready, the forty-year-old King left his palace, and in the company of his Queen, his sons, his diviners, his concubines, his courtiers, his menservants, and his musicians began the long climb up the inner ramp of the Tower; by the time he arrived in his new quarters he was an old man, his Queen long dead, his sons solemn with middle age, but he took up residence in the broad halls and richly appointed chambers that stretched away on both sides of the inner ramp.

News of the high court spread quickly. It soon became fashionable for merchant families and even skilled laborers to arrange for living quarters within the Tower, far above the roofs of the temples and the royal palace, higher than the smoke of sacrificial fires, higher, it was said, than the dreams of young women fetching water from wells on rich blue summer afternoons. In this manner the city on the plain was gradually drawn inside the great Tower. The Disappearance, as it was later called, came about in part because of the example of the pious King, but in part, too, because it was terribly oppressive for people to live at the foot of an enormous heaven-seeking Tower, which threw its shadow farther than a man could travel in a month and which, even at a distance, loomed like a raised arm about to strike a blow. Slowly the dwellings of the city were abandoned, the streets deserted, the gardens run to seed; the poor now gathered in ramshackle huts attached to the vast base of the Tower; after a time there was nothing left in the ruined city but wild sheep and lean oxen roaming the weed-grown streets, frogs in the wells, snakes and scorpions in the abandoned temples and dwelling places.

But no sooner had the Tower swallowed the city than a new desire arose, which no one could have foreseen. Even those who had thought long and hard about the Tower, in the days when the city flourished—the temple priests, the royal household, the administrative officials, the chief scribes—even they had failed to imagine one small but eventful change: a gradual loss of mystery and power, in the glorious structure that rose higher than the flight of eagles but that had come to seem, as the years passed, just a little familiar. The Tower had, after all, been in existence for as long as anyone could remember. Although it was growing higher, day by day, it was always the same size to those within it and even to those few who had remained in the surrounding countryside, for the work at the top took place in invisible regions far beyond the range of earthbound sight. At the same time, even among people who believed firmly that the Tower would one day reach heaven, the early expectation of a rapid and almost miraculous success had long been abandoned. It was therefore natural enough to feel that the rise toward heaven was, in a sense, part of the unchanging essence of the Tower, that the act of completion belonged to a different tower, a dream tower, a tower out of childhood stories, and was in any case an event so far in the future that it no longer had direct force in the lives of any but a handful of fanatical believers. There thus arose, in the hearts of the Tower dwellers, a nostalgia for the plain, for the shouts of the marketplace, the sunlight falling past the awnings onto heaps of apricots and figs, the sun and shade of the courtyards, the whitewashed temples, the outlying gardens shaded by date palms. And it came to pass that after a time many of the Tower dwellers began to descend and take up their old lives in the shadow of the Tower, rebuilding their ruined homes, planting their gardens outside the city walls, and gathering daily around the stalls in the market.

When, therefore, the Tower was completed, it contained a considerable population who lived on nearly every level, in chambers varying from primitive caves to rich halls painted with red, black, and lapis-blue hunting scenes, above a thriving city that had already forgotten its earlier abandonment and decay. The news of the successful completion led to a number of immediate changes. The city dwellers, who for their entire lives had scarcely given a thought to the perpetually unfinished Tower in their midst, suddenly stared up at a new, mysterious Tower, an unknown Tower, a Tower that had sprung out of the old one in a single, exhilarating leap. Tower-fever swept the populace. Helplessly caught up in the new upward-flowing excitement, people began the impossible climb, without any hope of reaching the top. Meanwhile those already living in the Tower were shaken by the news—some rushed to begin the final ascent, others, far below, drove themselves to climb higher, while still others, though remaining in their chambers for reasons of health or spiritual feebleness, kept raising their eyes nervously, as if their ceilings would burst, as they awaited word from returning travelers.

And the travelers returned. It was all a little puzzling to those who didn't travel, and even to the travelers themselves. No one, to be sure, had spoken of remaining permanently in heaven, in the days of the rising Tower. But the vision of a new life in the upper world had always shone out as a promise, especially to families who had climbed higher in successive generations and were waiting for the news that heaven had at last been reached. Now the way was suddenly open, yet there proved to be little inclination for settlement. People rushed in, stayed for a few days, or a few years, and then returned, with the exception of a handful who disappeared and were said to have lost their way in those white, unmapped spaces. Of the many reasons for return, two made a deep impression on those who were waiting anxiously for news from above. First, when all was said and done, when experiences of every kind were taken into account and carefully considered, the upper realm was somehow not what anyone had been led to imagine. The many reports of a brightness, of a blinding radiance, while attractive in their way, tended to suggest an absence of objects, a lack of the visible and tangible, which however wondrous was also somewhat tiring. Even those who claimed to see angels and gates of sapphire and streets of gold, or those who, seeing nothing but brightness, were filled with unspeakable bliss, soon came to feel that heaven, in some indefinable but unmistakable way, was unsuitable for permanent residence by the living.

The second reason took many by surprise. Those who flung themselves headlong into heaven discovered that they still carried with them, however dimly, images of the life their forefathers had left behind, down there on the legendary plain. So in the hearts of even the most fervent pilgrims there existed a counterpressure, a tug downward, toward the half-remembered land, the place of origin.

Thus it came about, after the completion of the Tower, that there was movement in two directions, on the inner ramp that coiled about the heart of the structure: an upward movement of those who longed to reach the top, or to settle on a level that would permit their children or their children's children to reach the top, and a downward movement of those who, after reaching the top, longed to descend toward the plain below, or who, after climbing partway, felt a sudden yearning for the familiar world.

But these two movements, which together constituted a vertical way of life, were offset by a third movement. Many inhabitants of the Tower who had taken up permanent residence in order to prepare for the ascent of the next generation were too old, or too tired, or too distracted by the life around them, to desire a change in either direction. And so, in addition to the upward and downward migrations, which took place along the inner ramp, there was a horizontal life that flourished in the many chambers that stretched away on both sides of the inner ramp on every level, to the center of the Tower in one direction and to the outer edge in the other. The horizontalists raised children, visited back and forth, and engaged in a communal life much like that of the city far below. Metalworkers, goldsmiths, leather workers, weavers, and reed workers set up workshops and did a thriving business. Communities of tenants established small gardens and sheep pens, to supplement deliveries of grain and fruit from the distant plain. Only sometimes, in the bustle of daily life, would a Tower dweller recall the fabled structure stretching high above, impossibly high, all the way to heaven, and grow quiet for a time.

Although the two ways of life, the vertical and horizontal, proceeded independently within the Tower, they intersected at the arched doorways of chambers directly bordering the inner ramp, where travelers passed up and down. After a while the borderers began to offer inexpensive meals to hungry travelers, who were tempted by the great tureens of soup and the loaves of unleavened bread baking in clay ovens to rest awhile on their upward or downward journeys. For an additional fee, posted on wooden signs, travelers could sleep beneath goat's-hair blankets in chambers furnished with reed mats, wool rugs, or mattresses filled with straw. Sometimes a traveler, weary of the long journey, and yielding to the seductive peace of the chambers, chose to stay and become a member of the horizontal world; now and then a chamber dweller, stirred by the continual movement of travelers making their way to the top or descending toward the plain, joined the upward or downward flow. But in general the two ways of life opposed each other in equal measure, within the great Tower, as if the two lines of force were part of the system of architectural stresses crucial to the cohesion of the building.

Because of the extreme height of the Tower, which always disappeared from view and therefore was, for the most part, invisible, it was inevitable that rumors should arise concerning its permanence and strength. Cracks appeared in chamber walls, chunks of brightly colored glazed brick on the exterior wall broke off and fell onto the outer ramp, where they occasionally tumbled along and startled travelers, and in the high winds of the upper regions the Tower often swayed, causing ripples of panic among the inhabitants, while those who lived on the plain below, looking up, seemed to see, just beyond the limits of their sight, an entire world about to fall. Then teams of workers would swarm up along the outer ramp to repair the cracks, replace the damaged bricks, and strengthen broad sections of the Tower by propping the inner walls with powerful cedar beams that came from the mountains of Lebanon. On the plain below, an early system of soaring buttresses—a stupendous architectural feat in itself—was reinforced by a massive array of additional supports, which extended high over the streets, over the temples and the royal palace, the river and the marketplace, reaching beyond the fortified walls of the city, out into the distant countryside.

Meanwhile reports of heaven continued to sift down through the Tower, and reports of the plain drifted up, at times mingling and growing confused. People began to dream of climbing to the top of the Tower and entering a world of green fields and flocks of sheep, or descending to a land of blinding radiance. In this swirl of downward nostalgia and upward longing, a curious sect arose, deriding the delusions of climbers and proclaiming that heaven lay below—a wondrous place of twisting streets, market-place stalls heaped with fruit, and two-story houses with wooden galleries running along inner courtyards. But this was only an extreme instance of the many common confusions of that time. Reports of heaven by actual visitors often seemed unconvincing or deceptive, while people who had never left the Tower began to add colorful touches and even to invent journeys of their own. For the tale-tellers, many of whom came to believe their own stories, heaven was always a sensual delight, a city whose great gates were covered with emeralds and sapphires, beryl and chrysoprase, topaz and jasper, while inside rose towers of silver and gold. The imaginary heaven proved far more compelling than the reported one, which was difficult to visualize and in any case had become half dream by the time it reached the lower regions of the Tower; and if the mixture of elaborations, inventions, distortions, and truths stirred in some a desire to see for themselves, in others it produced a tiredness, a spiritual heaviness, which led them to forgo the exertions of the vertical life and to rest content with the milder, more tangible pleasures of a horizontal existence.

It was about this time that the first rumors arose concerning deeper flaws in the Tower. The cracks, the pieces of fallen brick, even the swaying itself, were said to be common and superficial signs, true of every building, whereas the great Tower, which rose so fearfully high that it attained a different order of being, was subject to stresses and strains unknown to the architecture of the everyday world. There was talk of a hidden flaw, a continuous line or fracture running along the entire length of the Tower, somewhere on the inside; and although no one was able to point to the line itself, it was said that, if you listened closely, you could hear, deep inside the Tower, a faint sound like the creaking of many ships in the harbor beyond the marketplace.

What had the dwellers in the plain expected of heaven? Some had hoped to penetrate a mystery, others to outwit death—as if, by appearing bodily in heaven, they would no longer be required to die—still others to take part in a grand adventure, some to be reunited with those who had been buried in the earth, others to feel happiness after a life of hardship and sorrow. If heaven did not directly disappoint every expectation, it was also somehow not what most people had looked forward to, during the generations of hope. What could they make of that white radiance? One difficulty, debated at length by the temple priests, was that the heaven witnessed by travelers was not necessarily the true heaven, which some insisted was inapprehensible by the senses and could be known solely by the spirit unencumbered by the body. According to this argument, even those pilgrims who saw shining towers and heard choruses of unearthly music were deceived by organs of sense that could not but distort the experience of a nonterrestrial and immaterial place.

In the midst of such discussions, it was perhaps not surprising that the Tower itself should be called into question. Troubling whispers began to be heard. Was it possible that the great Tower didn't actually exist? After all, no one had ever seen the entire structure, which kept vanishing from sight no matter where you stood. Except for a handful of visible bricks, the whole thing was little more than a collection of rumors, longings, dreams, and travelers' tales. It was less than a memory. The Tower was a prodigious absence, a soaring void, a pit dug upward into the air. It was as if each part of the visible Tower had begun to dissolve under the vast pressure of the invisible parts, operating in every direction.

A time soon came when all those who had been alive during the completion of thc Tower passed into the enigma of death, leaving behind a new generation, who had never known a world without the perfected Tower. The other Tower—the striving Tower, the always rising and changing and ungraspable Tower—retreated into the realm of hearsay, of legend. Now the new Tower was the stuff of daily life: an immobile Tower, rigid with completion. Though not without splendor, it lacked the sharp mystery of unachieved things. Even the ascent to heaven no longer seemed remarkable, though travelers still returned with tales of a dazzling radiance. As for the descent to earth, it had become little more than a humdrum journey, a change of residence such as many inhabitants of the Tower undertook from time to time.

And a listlessness came over the Tower dwellers, a languor of spirit, punctuated by bursts of excitement that quickly died away. People began to say that things had been better in the old days, before the Tower had brought heaven within reach. For in those days, they said, the dwellers in the plain lived in a continual state of joyful anticipation, of radiant hope, as they stared up at the Tower that grew higher and higher in the bright blue welcoming sky.

But now a shadow seemed to have fallen across that sky—or perhaps it was a shadow across the heart, darkening the sight. People began to turn elsewhere for the pleasures of the unknown and the unseen. It was a time of omens, of dire prophesies, of feverish schemes that led to nothing. Passions swept through souls and ravaged them like diseases. A mother strangled her child when a man with wings whispered in her ear. A young man, declaring he had learned the secret of flight, leaped to his death from the outer ramp. One day a group of plains dwellers suddenly decided to escape from the Tower, which they said crushed them by its heavy presence. With tents and walking staffs they traveled across the countryside and out into the desert. Months from home, wandering exhausted in a strange land where cattle had horns twisted in spirals, where stones had the gift of speech, they looked up and saw the far Tower, rising forever into the sky like a howl of laughter.

Others, rejecting flight as useless, argued that a new work was necessary, an all-consuming task as great as the Tower itself. In this way arose the idea of a second Tower—a reverse Tower, pointing downward, toward the infernal regions. People were struck with astonishment. How could they have failed to think of it before? The land of no return, the abode of death: the mere idea of it filled them with strange, delicious shudders. Everyone suddenly longed to wander in the domain of darkness, beneath the earth, where dim figures brushed past with haunted eyes. A wealthy woman in a high chamber held an Underworld party, to which guests came dressed as dark phantoms and pale corpses. Dim oil lamps cast a gloomy half-light. One young woman, of high beauty and mournful eyes, wore only her own flesh, as a symbol of all that passes away. Meanwhile an architect and three assistants drew up the plans of a new Tower; a committee gave its approval; teams of laborers began digging inside the base of the old Tower. They had gone down nearly two hundred feet before interest began to waver, excitement turned elsewhere, the project was abandoned forever.

In this atmosphere of weariness and restlessness, of sudden yearnings that collapsed into torpor, the Tower itself was often neglected. Here and there old cracks reappeared in the bricks of a chamber wall, the inner ramp was riddled with hollows, glazed bricks on the exterior wall lost their luster and were severely damaged by wind and rain. Piles of rubble rose on the outer ramp. The workers, whose task it was to maintain the Tower, seemed to move slowly and heavily, as if the atmosphere around them had thickened; sometimes they sat down and leaned their heads back against the wall, closing their eyes. A rumor arose: the workers had all died, only their sad ghosts drifted along the spiral paths. In the innermost chambers, the Tower dwellers often felt drowsy and would nod abruptly into sleep, like children falling into a well. Later they would wake suddenly, looking about with startled eyes. Down below, in the city, a young girl dreamed that she was pouring water from a jar. As she poured, the water turned to blood. Inside the Tower, the sound of creaking ships grew louder.

One afternoon a boy playing in a street beside a whitewashed wall looked up at the Tower and did not move. Suddenly he began to run. In another part of the city, a woman drawing water from a well raised her eyes. The handle spun round and round as the bucket plunged. High up in the Tower a pilgrim on the inner ramp reached out a hand to steady himself against a wall. On a table in a high chamber, a bowl of figs began to slide. Down below, on one of the buttresses, a row of sparrows rose into the air with beating wings, like the sound of a shaken rug. A wine cup rolled along the floor, smacked into a wall. A wagon, beside a sack of grain, fell through the air. Far away, a shepherd looked up from his flock. He bent his head back, shading his eyes.

HERETICAL HISTORIES

HERE AT THE HISTORICAL SOCIETY

WE HERE AT the Historical Society are tireless in pursuit of the past. Although we work from eight-thirty to five-thirty, Tuesday through Saturday, and Sundays from twelve to five, many of us may be found here in the evenings as well, often as late as midnight, to say nothing of Monday, our official day of rest, for there are always new artifacts to label and classify, facts to assess, reports to be written, projects to be advanced. Despite our long hours, about which no one complains, our labor represents only the outward sign of an inward devotion that never ceases. At home, among our families, we think about some piece of business that hasn't yet been completed, on after-dinner strolls along the maple-lined streets of our town we recall a memorandum that needs to be consulted before tomorrow's meeting, in the midst of our most intimate embraces we picture, for a moment, the new report that awaits our attention, and even in sleep our minds are invaded by images of bursting walls and falling towers that we recognize, upon waking, as nightmare visions of piles of unpacked crates in the shadowy storage rooms beneath our exhibits. All things considered, I think it's fair to say that we never stop working, here at the Historical Society.

It is therefore misleading and, if I may say so, wildly irresponsible for anyone to suggest that certain recent changes have somehow called into question our love for the past. The past is our passion and our life. It is our reason for existing. We're proud, here at the Historical Society, to occupy the same building as the founders of our association. Located on historic Old Main Street, directly across from the town hall on the green, our white-shingled dwelling, shaded by two-hundred-year-old sycamores, was erected as a private residence in 1867 and purchased by the town six years later for the use of the new Historical Society. With its steep central gable and its ivy-covered chimney running the length of one wall, our home retains the essential shape of the original residence, while benefiting from two major alterations: the addition in 1899 of two rooms in the back, and the construction in 1945–46 of the handsome south wing, which now houses our research library and our extensive archives. Despite serious problems of space—we can scarcely accommodate our steadily growing collections—we resist all temptation to move to a larger and more up-to-date building, for from our front windows we can look out across Old Main Street at the eighteenth-century town hall and the war memorial commemorating the Revolutionary War dead. Both stand on the seventeenth-century green itself, where a granite boulder with a bronze plaque marks the year of our incorporation, 1648. In one of our second-floor exhibit rooms we have a musket dating from the Indian wars of 1646–47, which resulted in the ceding of a large tract of land (our present North End) by the Setaucus Indians, whose hand-carved flint arrowheads and quartz tools, some of them dating back to the fifteenth century, are on display in a Plexiglas case in a nearby room.

These exhibits are of the first importance, here at the Historical Society. The suggestion that we might use them to promote questionable ends is malicious and absurd. It's precisely by means of our exhibits that we attract the vast majority of our visitors—the groups of elementary school children brought here by their teachers, the residents mildly curious about their town's history, the outsiders with an idle hour or two who have exhausted the modest pleasures of Main Street, the young couples holding hands and stopping in for a look on their way to a beach party or a backyard barbecue. This is in no way to diminish the importance of our valuable research library, with its more than 4,000 volumes on the history of our town in every period, its 500 linear feet of archival material (deeds and legal documents), its manuscript holdings, and its wide-ranging collection of photographs, microfilms, maps, genealogical papers, cemetery records, immigration lists, and military pension registers. Nor do I in any sense mean to slight the numerous activities that are a vital part of our relation to the town: the walking tours, the children's workshops, the preschool crafts program, the adult lecture series. But it remains true that it is principally through our exhibits that we connect most immediately with our visitors, who look to us for some sense, however confused and uncertain, of a common past. Even residents of Portuguese, Italian, and Slovakian descent, whose roots in our town rarely go back before the mid-nineteenth century, are often to be found peering at the illustrations on our eighteenth-century china dinner plates or looking curiously at our display of Puritan costumes. Our holdings include a number of popular permanent exhibits—the Setaucus arrowheads and stone tools, the Revolutionary War artifacts (including a cast-iron eight-pounder fieldpiece and three cannonballs), the seventeenth-century parlor—but we also present a broad array of well-attended temporary exhibits with shifting themes: Costume Fashions in the Victorian and Edwardian Doll, the Setaucus Village, Eighteenth-Century Farm Implements, the Puritan Schoolhouse, Main Street in 1895, the Coming of the Railroad.

Despite the variety and abundance of our exhibits, the artifacts on display represent only a fraction of those stored in our basement rooms, where we have a carefully cataloged and highly heterogeneous collection not open to the public. There, among some twenty thousand objects, you may find telegraph keys, riding crops, glass stereopticon slides, tin windup toys, cedar butter churns, Victorian dollhouses, tulip-globed brass cigar lighters, blunderbusses, Philco radios, Civil War uniforms, oaken well buckets, Edison phonographs with wax cylinders, spinning wheels, hoopskirts, and mahogany folding cameras with nickel trim. This large and always growing collection of artifacts, from which our displays are selected, is itself an incalculably minuscule fraction of objects haphazardly rescued from our past. At best they may be said to possess a representative value. The same is true of our other collections—the letters, diaries, photographs, and official documents of every variety that we accumulate in order to reveal a glimmer of all that's gone. The knowledge that our evidence about the past is fragmentary and incomplete and, like all incomplete things, dangerously inaccurate spurs us to acquire still more evidence, while at the same time we realize with terrible clarity that we can never begin to approach the fullness and precision of the past—and this double knowledge, combined with a gradual change in our conception of history, has led to striking new developments, here at the Historical Society.

The immediate sign of a change is our series of new exhibits, mounted over the past two years. All have come under sharp attack. Perhaps our critics, who are so fertile with objections, might find it refreshing to pause for a few moments and consider whether their views may suffer from a narrow, facile, and insufficient grasp of the historical process. The new displays, mixed in with more conventional ones, include a large glass case filled with four shelves of carefully labeled pieces of litter (cellophane from a lollipop, a scrap of candy wrapper, bits of paper from

Popsicles and toasted almond bars, pieces of potato chip bags and cigarette packs, torn straw wrappers); an eight-hour film showing nothing but the view from above of a backyard lawn containing grass, dandelions, chickweed, and clover, with the shadow of a garage moving gradually in from the left; and an audio booth in which one can listen to snatches of random conversation recorded in the aisles of our largest supermarket. Our critics accuse the displays of being uninstructive, uninteresting, and above all unhistorical. We believe the animus is directed against a change in the understanding of history itself.

History is the study of the past—but what is the past? It is everything that has happened up to the present. Precedence tends to be given to the distant past, which is separated from us less by time than by the absence of immediate sensual knowledge, so that the smallest fragment of a bowl from a seventeenth-century merchant's family seems to contain within itself the revelation of a vanished world. But that same fragment, historically speaking, is of no more importance than yesterday's teacup. The pastness of the past infects all artifacts equally. Cathedrals, stone ax-heads, cereal boxes, the Hanging Gardens of Babylon—all are leveled in the long democracy of the done. For just as, in a single moment of the distant past, an Egyptian comb is of no less historical interest than a pyramid, so in the vast stretch of all pastness a pyramid is of no more historical interest than a Coca-Cola bottle. Our task, as members of the Historical Society, is not to hierarchize the past, but to collect and preserve it.

This view of the past, which began to gain ground among us during the last years of the old millennium, has led to a new conception of the present. It's our view, here at the Historical Society, that the present is *the past made visible.* Close your eyes and open them: in that instant of darkness, the entire world has fallen into the past. It is replaced by another world that itself is only a newer and more visible past. The science of optics informs us that the act of vision is a direct seeing of the past, since we see only after streams of photons, striking the photoreceptors in the retina, are transmuted into electrical impulses that travel along the optic nerve and make their way to the visual cortex. The present is our most recent past. It is also our most complete past. Indeed, we no longer use the word "present," here at the Historical Society, but speak instead of the New Past.

Even the future, viewed historically, is only a past that hasn't yet revealed itself, a past that is taking shape secretly, in dark rooms, behind closed doors that any day now will suddenly fly open from the sheer pressure of accumulation.

Our goal is clear. For the first time, we here at the Historical Society have the chance to capture the past completely, in all its overwhelming variety and luminous, precise detail. Our well-trained staff of researchers and assistant researchers go out each day to observe and classify a world that is already a part of the historical record. Our account includes measurements, descriptions, digital photographs, and, wherever possible, samples of every stop sign, fire hydrant, and telephone pole in our town, every roof slope and chimney, every Monopoly piece and badminton racket, every cobweb in every corner of every attic. We include every soup spoon and sugar maple, every design on the back of every deck of playing cards. As we pursue our work, our desire for completeness increases, and our categories grow more exacting. There are assistants who count the needles of every fir tree and the specks of mica in every roof shingle, others who study the patterns of grass blades flying up behind a power mower and settling onto the cut grass. We record the sounds of dishes and silverware in the kitchens of our town, the exact fall of the shadows of fence posts and street signs. We investigate the bend in a blue rubber band wrapped around a morning newspaper lying on a sun-striped front porch.

In an undertaking of this scope, criticism cannot be eluded or ignored. There are those who say in the accents of self-righteousness that we should stick to the "real" past—to our Indian ax-heads, our Puritan utensils, our Revolutionary War cannonballs. Why else would anyone wish to visit the Historical Society? To such critics we reply that the past you look for is a delusion, a dream composed of a fistful of images snatched at random from the fate that awaits all things. But look around you, in the streets of our town. What do you see? You see, alive in all its vividness, the one past you can fully grasp. History is a scrupulous record of missing evidence—of lost cities, smashed statues, ruined libraries. Now is the only past we'll ever know.

And our past is expanding. The official history, published in 1998, on the occasion of the 350th anniversary of our town's founding, comprises two volumes of 464 and 432 pages, respectively. In the year 2000 we started the Supplementary Series, which grew to 24 volumes in the next few years, and in 2005 we launched the Supplementary Series II, an online project that, if printed, would fill more than 500 volumes. Here one can find the most detailed record of a historical period ever attempted. Nothing is considered too negligible for the attention of our researchers—indeed, the Negligible itself has proved an unusually rich field for investigation. Here, every drawer pull and jar lid and pot-cover knob is accounted for, every hair wave and shirt weave. Here, we record the shapes of lines on the soles of sneakers, we follow the flight of dandelion puffs as they separate from the stalk and drift through the air. This is the exact and multifarious evidence of the New Past, which future generations will study closely while glancing with impatience at their boxful of broken pieces from the Old Past.

Meanwhile, the artifacts pour in. What finds, what treasures of the quotidian!—refrigerator magnets, roof shingles, cracker boxes, Clue boards, mouse pads, hockey sticks, muffin pans, space heaters, fence pickets, night-lights, zip disks, lawn sprinklers, porcelain kittens, maple leaves, wooden ice-cream spoons. Already we've constructed an outbuilding in back, with rows of narrow drawers from floor to ceiling and a deep cellar, and plans are under way for a series of underground display rooms and computerized research facilities.

One newspaper columnist has suggested, with heavy wit, that what we desire is to draw within our walls, piece by piece, our entire town, with its stores and street corners, its attics and backyards, its power lines and paper clips. What he fails to understand is that our town is disappearing daily, hurtling into a past as remote as Sumer. We wish only to make it more visible, before it vanishes entirely.

Recently we've come under attack from those who say that our love of the past represents a flight from life, a retreat into a world of artifacts. Such critics, who tend to be young, save their harshest attacks for our view of the New Past, which, they claim, turns the living, teeming world into a museum. In our defense we argue that most people walk through the world registering a handful of general impressions—tree, dog, nice house—whereas our meticulous and passionate researches multiply the details of the world and increase its being. One group of youths, who call themselves Brothers of the Rising Sun, have interfered with our researchers in the field and have twice broken into our building, smashing contemporary exhibit cases and damaging, perhaps by mistake, a clay pipe belonging to a Setaucus chieftain. What they cannot understand is that they too, with their orange T-shirts, their black jackets adorned with yellow insignia, their nose tattoos and neck rings, their violent gestures and quaint ideas, are part of the historical record.

And so we carry on, here at the Historical Society. Although we scrupulously arrange exhibits of Setaucus canoes and nineteenth-century ropewalks, although we continue to purchase for our library early town documents, histories of the Indian wars, and records of farm and factory production, our hearts are most deeply stirred by the New Past: by the drips of red paint on a can in an open, sun-flooded garage, by the arc of a rubber ball thrown against the side of a white-shingled house on which you can see the ball's bluish shadow, by the dim rainbow trembling in the hose spray aimed at the wet-gleaming side of a car. We can only make guesses about that other past, which stretches back through a few blurry centuries to the black beginnings of the world. But the New Past gives us hope. It stands before us in a nearly unfaded richness. It tempts us with the promise of total precision. Yet even as we record it, even as we reach out to touch it, we see it dissolving before our eyes, revealing a piece of the next past that has already replaced it. For we walk through a world no longer there, toward tomorrows that are only yesterdays. Look! That corner mailbox is an ancient ziggurat. Turn the next corner and you come to Alexandria. For once you accept the New Past, nothing is unworthy of your closest and most reverent attention. Those who accuse us of straying from our duty might ask themselves whether they see one-hundredth of what we see, on any afternoon, on any sidewalk. For us, the sun glinting on a piece of cellophane lying in a patch of roadside weeds speaks more eloquently than the history of Rome. For that's the way we look at things, here at the Historical Society.

A CHANGE IN FASHION

AFTER THE AGE of Revelation came the Age of Concealment. Sleeves flowed along forearms and closed tight at the wrist, hems fell to the ankle, necklines rose above the collarbone. Young women at first resisted the new fashion, which reminded them of old photographs in boring albums on dreary Sunday afternoons, before succumbing to it with fervor. It became stylish to wear dresses that brushed the floor of high school hallways and allowed coy glimpses of polished boot toes; bands of girls strolling through malls wore kerchiefs over their hair and displayed lengthening gloves of lambskin and Italian leather that crept above the elbow toward the middle of the upper arm. Necks slowly disappeared behind rising collars as hat brims grew broader, casting the face in shadow. It was as if, after half a century of reckless exposure, a weariness had overcome women, a yearning for withdrawal, a disenchantment with the obligation to invite a bold male gaze. In every skirt fold and blouse button, one could sense the new longing for hiddenness.

As the fashion for more and more fabric spread from the pages of popular magazines, where the new models posed with turned-aside faces and downcast eyes, to the middle-class housewife and her daughters, a group of emerging designers on both coasts began to attract attention. They were young, imperious, and contemptuous of the recent past. Among the creators the most daring and secretive was one who signed his clothes with a small gold *H* in a blood-red circle. He refused to be photographed; in a spirit of irony or bravado, he called himself Hyperion.

At this time the long style still clung to the shape of the female body. It was Hyperion who took the decisive leap away from the body toward regions of high invention. In a celebrated autumn catwalk show, he shocked viewers by bringing back a version of the Victorian crinoline, with its hoops of flexible steel, and raising it to the level of the shoulders. Now a woman could walk hidden in a hemispheric ripple of wire-supported silk or velvet that fell from her shoulders to the floor. Although the hemi-dress was ridiculed by a number of fashion commentators for its awkwardness, its ugliness, its retro-kitsch jokiness, its air of mockery, others saw in it an expression of liberation from the tyranny of the body. Before the show, the history of women's fashion was a record of shifts of attention from one part of the body to another. With a single design, Hyperion had freed fashion from its long dependence on the female shape.

A brief and unsatisfactory geometric period—the pyramid dress, the octagon dress—was followed by the creation of the free style, which rejected symmetry altogether. Now women adorned themselves in free-floating designs that seemed intent on allowing fabric to explore its inner nature, to fulfill secret necessities. There were dresses with troubling structures that burst from the shoulders and waist and swooped up in arabesques of velvet and satin; aggressively long dresses with silk-lined trains that, raised and fastened about the neck, formed a kind of shimmering and ecstatic plumage; horizontal dresses; dresses like delirium dreams, dresses like feverish blossoms blazing in the heart of impenetrable jungles; dresses composed of synthetic fabrics specially developed to assume the appearance of thunderclouds, of swirling snow, of tongues of fire. It was as if dresses had become stricken with boredom, with impossible desires. Whereas fashion extravagances of the past—the Elizabethan farthingale, the horsehair bustle of the 1870s—had always emphasized and exaggerated some part of the female anatomy, the new shapes ignored the body entirely, while at the same time they seemed to express inner moods, forgotten dreams, buried realms of feeling. Teenage girls in particular embraced the Hyperion free style, with its double pleasure of secrecy and exposure—for they could plunge down, far down, into layers of costume that sheltered them from sight, while rivers of twisting cloth allowed them to bring forth forbidden longings.

Meanwhile the female face, which had hovered somewhat uncertainly above the early Hyperion dresses, began to be absorbed by the new designs. A petal collar, composed of lanceolate shafts of cloth, rose to the hairline; colorful wraps known as neckbands reached above the chin; elaborate head coverings swept down to the bodice. Even more remarkable was the development on the surface of dresses: new shapes sprang from folds of cloth, secondary growths that seemed to lead separate lives, like gargoyles sprouting in the corners of cathedrals.

Although the Hyperion free style was above all notable for its refusal to reveal the female body, commentators were quick to point out that the fashion for concealment was not without an erotics of its own. The direct and simple provocations of the old style—a bare stomach, a nipple pressing through a tight sweater—were replaced by indirection, disguise, and a vague suggestiveness. In the new style, the imagination was said to be stimulated to an unusual degree: beneath those lavish swirls of fabric, playful and at times forbidding, lay a hidden body, inviting discovery. One fashion writer compared the free-style dress to the series of obstacles facing a medieval knight adventuring through a dark forest toward his mistress held captive in the tower of a distant castle guarded by an ogre. That sense of difficulty, of seductive impediment, was increased by elaborations of lingerie permitted by the new volume—beneath the vast skirts bloomed a garden of lace-trimmed petticoats in raspberry chiffon and black organdy, crimson silk half-slips with side slits, stretch-satin and dotted-mesh chemises with ruffle trim. Teenage girls, who a year earlier had reveled in their thongs and V-strings, led the way in adopting an excess of underclothes, holding contests in high school bathrooms to see who was wearing the greatest number of layers, in vivid and hidden colors: sunburst yellow, vermilion, ice blue. But quite apart from this development, which drew attention to new depths of concealment and thus to the veiled body itself, several commentators pointed out that it was not strictly accurate to speak of the complete covering of the female form. Beyond the neckbands and high collars, parts of the face continued to be visible, thereby reminding the observer of unseen portions of the body, which were helplessly summoned to the imagination. In addition, women concealed in Hyperion free-style dresses moved from place to place, so that the creations shook and swayed; now and then, a hidden arm or leg might press visibly against a portion of fabric. Stimulated by the unseen, lashed by the unknown, sexual fantasies became at once more violent and more devious. The new clothing was essentially paradoxical. Women, it was argued, were never more naked than when concealed from view.

Indeed one feature of the new style was its appeal to women who longed to inspire fiery passions but who judged their visible bodies to be inadequate or repellent. Beneath the Hyperion dress a woman could rest secure in the knowledge that her body, safely shut away, could become whatever she wished it to be, down there in the dark below distractions of fabric that seemed to tremble on the edge of dream.

Fashion is an expression of boredom, of restlessness. The successful designer understands the ferocity of that boredom and provides it with new places in which to calm its rage for a while. Even as Hyperion free-style dresses were displayed in photo spreads in international magazines and promoted in vigorous poster campaigns, the designer was preparing his next step. In his eagerly awaited spring/summer collection, he proclaimed the final liberation of costume from the female body. The new dress completed the urge to concealment by developing the bodice upward into a complete covering for the face and head. Now the Hyperion dress entirely enclosed the wearer, who was provided with artful spaces for the mouth, nostrils, and eyes. The new top quickly developed a life of its own. It seemed determined to deny the existence of the head, to use the area between collarbone and scalp as a transitional element, by expanding the idea of a dress upward to include the space above the height of the wearer. Meanwhile the openings for eyes and nostrils, which had drawn attention to the concealed face and threatened to turn the dress into a species of mask, were replaced by an opaque fabric that permitted one-way vision. Women, who had gradually been disappearing into the hidden spaces of the new style, had at last become invisible.

Commentators welcomed the enclosure dress but were divided over its merits. Some argued that it represented the ultimate defense of the female body against visual invasion, while others saw in it the final liberation of costume from its demeaning dependence on the body. One fashion writer praised what she called the vanished woman and compared the enclosure dress to the development of the boudoir, or private sitting room, in the eighteenth-century house—a secret domain in which a woman could be herself, safe from male control. A rival journalist, ignoring women and their desires, spoke only of the new aesthetic of costume, which at last was free to develop in the manner of landscape painting after it had become bold enough to exile the human figure.

And indeed there now began a period of excess, of overabundant fulfillment, as if the banishment of the face had removed some nuance of restraint still present in the earlier collections. Inspired by Hyperion, dresses became fevered with obscure cravings, with sudden illuminations and desolations, and threw themselves into hopeless adventures. Restless and dissatisfied, they grew in every direction; in some instances they exceeded the size of rooms and had to be worn in large outdoor spaces, like backyards or public parks. The vast lower depths of such dresses encouraged coarse speculation. It was said that beneath those coverings, naked women coupled madly with young lovers in the grass. One dress contained in its side a little red door, which was said to lead to a room with a bed, a mirror, and a shaded lamp. Another dress, designed for the wife of a software CEO, rose three stories high and was attached to the back of the house by a covered walkway. A celebrated fashion journalist with a fondness for historical parallels compared these developments to the fanatical elaborations of coiffure in the late eighteenth century, when three-foot castles of hair rose on wire supports. The new dresses were not so much worn as entered—it was as if they wished to carry the structural qualities of fashion to the point at which clothing began to merge with architecture.

Such excesses were not without a touch of desperation, as if the escape of costume from the female body had created in clothes an uncertainty, a sharp malaise. One summer afternoon during a party at an estate in northwestern Connecticut, an unusual immobility in the lavish dresses became apparent. Had the women taken a solemn vow not to move? The stationary costumes, arranged on a lawn that sloped down to a lake, resembled a form of sculpture. Four men, bored or excited by the motionless women, stood before one of them, talking and drinking hard. Suddenly two of the men bent over, grasped the heavy dress by the hem, and lifted it violently into the air. Voices shouted, cheered. Underneath they discovered only the lawn itself, stretching away.

The four men rushed over to the other dresses, yanking them up, knocking them over, tearing at them with their fingers, but the women had disappeared. Later that day they were discovered in the kitchen of a neighbor's house, dressed in old bathrobes and talking among themselves.

For a time the new fashion caught on. Women donned immense dresses and then quietly withdrew, wandering away to do whatever they liked. Dresses, freed at last from bodies, became what they had always aspired to be: works of art, destined for museums and private collections. Often they stood on display in large living rooms, beside pianos or couches.

But the complete separation of clothing from women's bodies created a new confusion. Women no longer knew how to dress, what to wear. Many dressed in a deliberately slatternly way, as if to express their sense of the unbearable distance between the perfection of high costume and the humiliating imperfection of the body it was meant to obliterate. It was as if a superior race of beings had been inserted into the world: the race of costume. A tension was building; there were rumors of an uprising of women, who would overthrow the dresses that had rendered them superfluous. Such talk, however absurd, revealed a longing for something new, for a redemptive leap. People spoke hungrily of new, impossible dresses—dresses worn on the inside of the body, dresses the size of entire towns. Others proposed an Edenic nakedness. As the new season approached, it was clear that something had to happen.

It was at this moment that Hyperion gave his only interview. In it he abjured the fashions that had made him famous; apologized to women for leading them astray; revealed that his name was Ben Hirschfeld, of Brooklyn; and announced his retirement after the coming show. The interview was analyzed relentlessly, attacked as a promotional stunt, dismissed as a hoax. On the nightly news a short, balding man stood under an umbrella as he blinked nervously behind small round lenses and said that yes, his name was Benjamin Hirschfeld, yes, he lived in Brooklyn, but no, he knew nothing about fashion, nothing about clothes, nothing. The public, skeptical and patient, waited.

And the moment came; it was not what anyone had expected. Along the catwalk strolled a tall model in a classic fitted dress, with a trim waist and a full, pleated skirt. Her face, entirely exposed, bore an indolent and haughty look that hadn't been seen for years. The new, impoverished dress represented a repudiation of everything Hyperion had stood for. At the same time, within the culture of the liberated dress, it struck a radical note. Women hesitated; here and there, in a spirit of daring, someone appeared at a party dressed in the new style. One day, as if by secret agreement, the fashion was everywhere. The monstrous old dresses drifted into attics, where young girls, climbing the stairs in search of an abandoned dollhouse or a pair of skates, came upon something looming against the rafters and stopped uneasily before continuing on their way. At dinner parties and family gatherings, people recalled the old style with amusement and affectionate embarrassment, as one might remember an episode of drunkenness. In memory the dresses became more vivid, more remote, until they seemed like brilliant birds rising in dark forests or like distant sunlit towns. Meanwhile the new dresses grew a little shorter, a little longer; slacks and blouses grew tighter, looser. One afternoon in late summer, on a sidewalk printed with the shade of maple leaves and flickers of sun, a woman walking with her young daughter had the sense that she was about to remember something, something about a dress, but no, it was gone, vanished among the overhead leaves already turning, the bits of blue sky, the smell of cut grass, the chimney shadows sharp and black on the sunlit roofs.

A PRECURSOR OF THE CINEMA

EVERY GREAT INVENTION is preceded by a rich history of error. Those false paths, wrong turns, and dead ends, those branchings and veerings, those wild swerves and delirious wanderings—how can they fail to entice the attention of the historian, who sees in error itself a promise of revelation? We need a taxonomy of the precursor, an aesthetics of the not-quite-yet. Before the cinema, that inevitable invention of the mid-1890s, the nineteenth century gave birth to a host of brilliant toys, spectacles, and entertainments, all of which produced vivid and startling illusions of motion. It's a seductive prehistory, which divides into two lines of descent. The true line is said to be the series of rapidly presented sequential drawings that create an illusion of motion based on the optical phenomenon known as persistence of vision (Plateau's Phenakistoscope, Horner's Zoetrope, Reynaud's Praxinoscope); the false line produces effects of motion based on visual illusions of another kind (Daguerre's Diorama, with its semitransparent painted screens and shifting lights; sophisticated magic-lantern shows with double projectors and overlapping views). But here and there we find experiments in motion that are less readily explained, ambiguous experiments that invite the historian to follow obscure, questionable, and at times heretical paths. It is in this twilit realm that the work of Harlan Crane (1844–88?) leads its enigmatic life, before sinking into a neglect from which it has never recovered.

Harlan Crane has been called a minor illustrator, an inventor, a genius, a charlatan. He is perhaps all and none of these things. So little is known of his first twenty-nine years that he seems almost to have been born at the age of thirty, a tall, reserved man in a porkpie hat, sucking on a pipe with a meerschaum bowl. We know that he was born in Brooklyn, in the commercial district near the Fulton Ferry; many years later he told W. C. Curtis that as a child he had a distant view from his bedroom window of the church steeples and waterfront buildings of Manhattan, which seemed to him a picture that he might step into one day. His father was a haberdasher who liked to spend Sundays in the country with oil paints and an easel. When Harlan was thirteen or fourteen, the Cranes moved across the river to Manhattan. Nothing more is known of his adolescence.

We do know, from records discovered in 1954, that Crane studied drawing in his early twenties at Cooper Union and the National Academy of Design (1866–68). His first illustrations for *Harper's Weekly*—"Selling Hot Corn," "The Street Sweeper," "Fire Engine at the Bowery Theater," "Unloading Flour at Coenties Slip"—date from 1869; the engravings are entirely conventional, without any hint of what was to come. It is of course possible that the original drawings (since lost) contained subtleties of line and tone not captured by the crude wood engravings of the day, but unfortunately nothing remains except the hastily executed and poorly printed woodcuts themselves. There is evidence, in the correspondence of friends, to suggest that Crane became interested in photography at this time. In the summer of 1870 or 1871 he set up against one wall of his walk-up studio a long table that became a kind of laboratory, where he is known to have conducted experiments on the properties of paint. During this period he also worked on a number of small inventions: a doll with a mechanical beating heart; an adaptation of the kaleidoscope that he called the Phantasmatrope, in which the turning cylinder contained a strip of colored sequential drawings that gave the illusion of a ceaselessly repeated motion (a boy tossing up and catching a blue ball, a girl in a red dress skipping rope); and a machine that he called the Vivograph, intended to help amateurs draw perfect still lifes every time by the simple manipulation of fourteen knobs and levers. As it turned out, the Vivograph produced drawings that resembled the scrawls of an angry child, the Phantasmatrope, though patented, was never put on the market because of a defect in the shutter mechanism that was essential for masking each phase of motion, and the beating hearts of his dolls kept suddenly dying. At about this time he began to paint in oils and to take up with several artists who later became part of the Verisimilist movement. In 1873 he is known to have worked on a group of paintings clearly influenced by his photographic studies: the Photographic Print Series, which consisted of several blank canvases that were said to fill gradually with painted scenes. By the age of thirty, Harlan Crane seems to have settled into the career of a diligent and negligible magazine illustrator, while in his spare time he painted in oils, printed photographs on albumen paper, and performed chemical experiments on his laboratory table, but the overwhelming impression he gives is one of restlessness, of not knowing what it is, exactly, that he wants to do with his life.

Crane first drew attention in 1874, when he showed four paintings at the Verisimilist Exhibition held in an abandoned warehouse on the East River. The Verisimilists (Linton Burgis, Thomas E. Avery, Walter Henry Hart, W. C. Curtis, Octavius Ward, and Arthur Romney Ropes) were a group of young painters who celebrated the precision of photography and rejected all effects of a dreamy, suggestive, or symbolic kind. In this there was nothing new; what set them apart from other realist schools was their fanatically meticulous concern for minuscule detail. In a Verisimilist canvas it was possible to distinguish every chain stitch on an embroidered satin fan, every curling grain in an open package of Caporal tobacco, every colored kernel and strand of silk on an ear of Indian corn hanging from a slanted nail on the cracked and weatherworn door of a barn. But their special delight was in details so marvelously minute that they could be seen only with the aid of a magnifying glass. Through the lens the viewer would discover hidden minutiae—the legs of a tiny white spider half hidden in the velvet folds of a curtain, a few bread crumbs lying in the shadow cast by a china plate's rim. Arthur Romney Ropes claimed that his work could not be appreciated without such a glass, which he distributed free of charge to visitors at his studio. Although the Verisimilists tended to favor the still life (a briarwood pipe lying on its side next to three burnt matches, one of which was broken, and a folded newspaper with readable print; a slightly uneven stack of lovingly rendered silver coins rising up beside a wad of folded five-dollar bills and a pair of reading glasses lying on three loose playing cards), they ventured occasionally into the realm of the portrait and the landscape, where they painstakingly painted every individual hair in a gentleman's beard or a lady's muff, every lobe and branching vein on every leaf of every sycamore and oak. The newspaper reviews of the exhibition commended the paintings for illusionistic effects of a remarkable kind, while agreeing that as works of art they had been harmed by the baleful influence of photography, but the four works (no longer extant) of Harlan Crane seemed to interest or irritate them in a new way.

From half a dozen newspaper reports, from a letter by Linton Burgis to his sister, and from a handful of scattered entries in journals and diaries, we can reconstruct the paintings sufficiently to understand the perplexing impressions they caused, though many details remain unrecoverable.

Still Life with Fly appears to have been a conventional painting of a dish of fruit on a table: three apples, a yellow pear, and a bunch of red grapes in a bronze dish with repoussé rim, beside which lay a woman's slender tan-colored kid glove with one slightly curling fingertip and a scattering of envelopes with sharply rendered stamps and postmarks. On the side of one of the red-and-green apples rested a beautifully precise fly. Again and again we hear of the shimmering greenish wings, the six legs with distinct femurs, tibias, and tarsi, each with its prickly hairs, the brick-red compound eyes. Viewers agreed that the lifelike fly, with its licorice-colored abdomen showing through the silken transparence of the wings, was the triumph of the composition; what bewildered several observers was the moment when the fly darted suddenly through the paint and landed on an apple two inches away. The entire flight was said to last no more than half a second. Two newspapers deny any movement whatever, and it remains uncertain whether the fly returned to its original apple during visiting hours, but the movement of the painted fly from apple to apple was witnessed by more than one viewer over the course of the next three weeks and is described tantalizingly in a letter of Linton Burgis to his sister Emily as "a very pretty simulacrum of flight."

Waves appears to have been a conventional seascape, probably sketched during a brief trip to the southern shore of Long Island in the autumn of 1873. It showed a long line of waves breaking unevenly on a sandy shore beneath a melancholy sky. What drew the attention of viewers was an unusual effect: the waves could be clearly seen to fall, move up along the shore, and withdraw—an eerily silent, living image of relentlessly falling waves, under a cheerless evening sky.

The third painting, *Pygmalion,* showed the sculptor in Greek costume standing back with an expression of wonderment as he clutched his chisel and stared at the beautiful marble statue. Observers reported that, as they looked at the painting, the statue turned her head slowly to one side, moved her wrists, and breathed in a way that caused her naked breasts to rise and fall, before she returned to the immobility of paint.

The Séance showed eight people and a medium seated in a circle of wooden chairs, in a darkened room illuminated only by candles. The medium was a stern woman with heavy-lidded eyes, a fringed shawl covering her upper arms, and tendrils of dark hair on her forehead. Rings glittered on her plump fingers. As the viewer observed the painting, the eight faces gradually turned upward, and a dim form could be seen hovering in the darkness of the room, above or behind the head of the medium.

What are we to make of these striking effects, which seem to anticipate, in a limited way, the illusions of motion perfected by Edison and the Lumière brothers in the mid-1890s? Such motions were observed in no other of the more than three hundred Verisimilist paintings, and they inspired a number of curious explanations. The "trick" paintings, as they came to be called, were said to depend on carefully planned lighting arrangements, as in the old Diorama invented by Daguerre and in more recent magic-lantern shows, where a wagon might seem to move across a landscape (though its wheels did not turn). What this explanation failed to explain was where the lights were concealed, why no one mentioned any change in light, and how, precisely, the complex motions were produced. Another theory claimed that behind the paintings lay concealed systems of springs and gears, which caused parts of the picture to move.

Such reasoning might explain how a mechanical fly, attached to the surface of a painting, could be made to move from one location to another, but we have the testimony of several viewers that the fly in Crane's still life was smooth to the touch, and in any case the clockwork theory cannot explain phenomena such as the falling and retreating waves or the suddenly appearing ghostly form. It is true that Daguerre, in a late version of his Diorama, created an illusion of moving water by the turning of a piece of silver lace on a wheel, but Daguerre's effects were created in a darkened theater, with a long distance between seated viewers and a painted semitransparent screen measuring some seventy by fifty feet, and cannot be compared with a small canvas hanging six inches from a viewer's eyes in a well-lit room.

A more compelling theory for the historian of the cinema is that Harlan Crane might have been making use of a concealed magic lantern (or a projector of his own invention) adapted to display a swift series of sequential drawings, each one illuminated for an instant and then abolished before being replaced by the next. Unfortunately there is no evidence whatever of beams of light, no one saw a telltale flicker, and we have no way of knowing whether the motions repeated themselves in exactly the same way each time.

The entire issue is further obscured by Crane's own bizarre claim to a reporter, at the time of the exhibition, that he had invented what he called animate paint—a paint chemically treated in such a way that individual particles were capable of small motions. This claim—the first sign of the future showman—led to a number of experiments performed by chemists hired by the Society for the Advancement of the Arts, where at the end of the year an exhibition of third-rate paintings took place. As visitors passed from picture to picture, the oils suddenly began to drip down onto the frames, leaving behind melting avenues, wobbly violinists, and dissolving plums. The grotesque story does not end here. In 1875 a manufacturer of children's toys placed on the market a product called Animate Paint, which consisted of a flat wooden box containing a set of brightly colored metal tubes, half a dozen slender brushes, a manual of instruction, and twenty-five sheets of specially prepared paper. On the advice of a friend, Crane filed suit; the case was decided against him, but the product was withdrawn after the parents of children with Animate Paint sets discovered that a simple stroke of chrome-yellow or crimson lake suddenly took on a life of its own, streaking across the page and dripping brightly onto eiderdown comforters, English-weave rugs, and polished mahogany tables.

An immediate result of the controversy surrounding Crane's four paintings was his expulsion from the Verisimilist group, who claimed that his optical experiments detracted from the aim of the movement: to reveal the world with ultra-photographic precision. We may be forgiven for wondering whether the expulsion served a more practical purpose, namely, to remove from the group a member who was receiving far too much attention. In any case, it may be argued that Crane's four paintings, far from betraying the aim of the Verisimilists, carried that aim to its logical conclusion. For if the intention of verisimilism was to go beyond the photograph in its attempt to "reveal" the world, isn't the leap into motion a further step in the same direction? The conventional Verisimilist wave distorts the real wave by its lack of motion; Crane's breaking wave is the true Verisimilist wave, released from the falsifying rigidity of paint.

Little is known of Crane's life during the three years following the Exhibition of 1874. We know from W. C. Curtis, the one Verisimilist who remained a friend, that Crane shut himself up all day in his studio, with its glimpse of the distant roof of the Fulton Fish Market and a thicket of masts on the East River, and refused to show his work to anyone. Once, stopping by in the evening, Curtis noticed an empty easel and several large canvases turned against the wall. "It struck me forcibly," Curtis recorded in his diary, "that I was not permitted to witness his struggles." Exactly what those struggles were, we have no way of knowing. We do know that a diminishing number of his undistinguished woodcut engravings continued to appear in *Harper's Weekly*, as well as in *Appleton's Journal* and several other publications, and that for a time he earned a small income by tinting portrait photographs. "On a long table at one side of the studio," Curtis noted on one occasion, "I observed a wet cell, a number of beakers, several tubes of paint, and two vessels filled with powders." It remains unclear what kinds of experiment Crane was conducting, although the theme of chemical experimentation raises the old question of paint with unusual properties.

In 1875 or 1876 he began to frequent the studio of Robert Allen Lowe, a leading member of a loose-knit group of painters who called themselves Transgressives and welcomed Crane as an offender of Verisimilist pieties. Crane began taking his evening meals at the Black Rose, an alehouse patronized by members of the group. According to Lowe, in a letter to Samuel Hope (a painter of still lifes who later joined the Transgressives), Crane ate quickly, without seeming to notice what was on his plate, spoke very little, and smoked a big-bowled meerschaum pipe with a richly stained rim, a cherrywood stem, and a black rubber bit as he tilted back precariously in his chair and hooked one foot around a table leg. He wore a soft porkpie hat far back on his head and followed the conversation intently behind thick clouds of smoke.

The Transgressive movement began with a handful of disaffected Verisimilists who felt that the realist program of verisimilism did not go far enough. Led by Lowe, who was known for his spectacularly detailed paintings of dead pheasants, bunches of asparagus, and gleaming magnifying glasses lying on top of newspapers with suddenly magnified print, the Transgressives argued that Verisimilist painting was hampered by its craven obedience to the picture frame, which did nothing but draw attention to the artifice of the painted world it enclosed. Instead of calling for the abolishment of the frame, in the manner of trompe l'oeil art, Lowe insisted that the frame be treated as a transition or "threshold" between the painting proper and the world outside the painting. Thus in a work of 1875, *Three Pears,* a meticulous still life showing three green pears on a wooden table sharply lit by sunlight streaming through a window, the long shadows of the pears stretch across the tabletop and onto the vine-carved picture frame itself. This modest painting led to an outburst of violations and disruptions by Lowe and other members of the group, and their work made its way into the Brewery Show of 1877.

The Transgressive Exhibition—better known as the Brewery Show, since the paintings were housed in an abandoned brewery on Twelfth Avenue near the meatpacking district—received a good deal of unfavorable critical attention, although it proved quite popular with the general public, who were attracted by the novelty and playfulness of the paintings. One well-known work, *The Window,* showed a life-size casement window in a country house. Real ivy grew on the picture frame. *The Writing Desk*, by Robert Allen Lowe, showed part of a rolltop desk in close-up detail: two rows of pigeonholes and a small, partly open door with a wooden knob. In the pigeonholes one saw carefully painted envelopes, a large brass key, folded letters, a pince-nez, and a coil of string, part of which hung carelessly down over the frame. Viewers discovered that one of the pigeonholes was a real space containing a real envelope addressed to Robert Allen Lowe, while the small door, composed of actual wood, protruded from the picture surface and opened to reveal a stoneware ink bottle from which a quill pen emerged at a slant.

Several people reached for the string, which proved to be a painted image. *Grapes,* a large canvas by Samuel Hope, showed an exquisitely painted bunch of purple grapes from which real grapes emerged to rest in a silver bowl on a table beneath the painting. After the first day, a number of paintings had to be roped off, to prevent the public from pawing them to pieces.

In this atmosphere of playfulness, extravagance, and illusionist wit, the paintings of Harlan Crane attracted no unusual attention, although we sometimes hear of a "disturbing" or "uncanny" effect. He displayed three paintings. *Still Life with Fly #2* showed an orange from which the rind had been partially peeled away in a long spiral, half a sliced peach with the gleaming pit rising above the flat plane of its sliced flesh, the hollow, jaggedly broken shell of an almond beside half an almond and some crumbs, and an ivory-handled fruit knife. To the side of the peach clung a vertical fly, its wings depicted against the peach skin, its head and front legs rising above the exposed flesh of the peach. An iridescent drop of water, which seemed about to fall, clung to the peach skin beside the fly. A number of viewers claimed that the fly suddenly left the canvas, circled above their heads, and landed on the upper-right-hand corner of the frame before returning to the peach beside the glistening, motionless drop. Several viewers apparently swatted at the fly as it flew beside them, but felt nothing.

A second painting, *Young Woman,* is the only known instance of a portrait in the oeuvre of Harlan Crane. The painting showed a girl of eighteen or nineteen, wearing a white dress and a straw bonnet with a cream-colored ostrich plume, standing in a bower of white and red roses with sun and leaf-shadow stippling her face. In one hand she held a partly open letter; a torn envelope lay at her feet. She stood facing the viewer, with an expression of troubled yearning. Her free hand reached forward as if to grasp at something or someone. Despite its Verisimilist attention to detail—the intricate straw weave of the bonnet, the individual thorns on the trellis of roses—the painting looked back to the dreary conventions of narrative art deplored by Verisimilists and Transgressives alike; but what struck more than one viewer was the experience of stepping up close to the painting, in order to study the lifelike details, and feeling the unmistakable sensation of a hand touching a cheek.

The third painting, *The Escape,* hung alone in a small dusky niche or alcove. It depicted a gaunt man slumped in the shadows of a stone cell. From an unseen window a ray of dusty light fell slantwise through the gloom. Viewers reported that, as they examined the dark painting, in the twilit niche, the prisoner stirred and looked about. After a while he began to crawl forward, moving slowly over the hard floor, staring with haunted eyes. Several viewers spoke of a sudden tension in the air; they saw or felt something before or beside them, like a ghost or a wind. In the painting, the man had vanished. One journalist, who returned to observe the painting three days in succession, reported that the "escape" took place three or four times a day, at different hours, and that, if you watched the empty painting closely, you could see the figure gradually reappearing in the paint, in the manner of a photographic image appearing on albumen paper coated with silver nitrate and exposed to sunlight beneath a glass negative.

Although a number of newspapers do not even mention the Crane paintings, others offer familiar and bogus explanations for the motions, while still others take issue with descriptions published in rival papers. Whatever one may think of the matter, it is clear that we are no longer dealing with paintings as works of art, but rather with paintings as *performances.* In this sense the Brewery Show represents the first clear step in Harlan Crane's career as an inventor-showman, situated in a questionable realm between the old world of painting and the new world of moving images.

It is also worth noting that, with the exception of Lowe's *Writing Desk,* Transgressive paintings are not trompe l'oeil. The trompe l'oeil painting means to deceive, and only then to undeceive; but the real ivy and the real grapes immediately present themselves as actual objects disruptively continuing the painted representation. Harlan Crane's animate paintings are more unsettling still, for they move back and forth deliberately between representation and deception and have the general effect of radically destabilizing the painting—for if a painted fly may at any moment suddenly enter the room, might not the painted knife slip from the painted table and cut the viewer's hand?

After their brief moment of notoriety in 1877, the Transgressives went their separate ways. Samuel Hope, Winthrop White, and C. W. E. Palmer returned to the painting of conventional still lifes, Robert Allen Lowe ventured with great success into the world of children's book illustration, and John Frederick Hill devoted his remaining years to large, profitable paintings of very white nudes on very red sofas, destined to be hung above rows of darkly glistening bottles in smoky saloons.

Crane now entered a long period of reclusion, which only in retrospect appears the inevitable preparation for his transformation into the showman of 1883. It is more reasonable to imagine these years as ones of restlessness, of dissatisfaction, of doubt and questioning and a sense of impediment. Such a view is supported by the few glimpses we have of him, in the correspondence of acquaintances and in the diary of W. C. Curtis. We know that in the summer of 1878 he took a series of photographs of picnickers on the Hudson River, from which he made half a dozen charcoal sketches that he later destroyed. Not long afterward he attempted and abandoned several small inventions, including a self-cleaning brush: through its hollow core ran a thin rubber tube filled with a turpentine-based solvent released by pressing a button. For a brief time he took up with Eliphalet Hale and the Sons of Truth, a band of painters who were opposed to the sentimental and falsely noble in art and insisted on portraying subjects of a deliberately vile or repellent kind, such as steaming horse droppings, dead rats torn open by crows, blood-soaked sheets, scrupulously detailed pools of vomit, rotting vegetables, and suppurating sores. Crane was indifferent to the paintings, but he liked Hale, a soft-spoken God-fearing man who believed fervently in the beauty of all created things.

Meanwhile Crane continued to take photographs, switching in the early 1880s from wet-collodion plates to the new dry-gelatin process in order to achieve sharper definition of detail. He also began trying his hand at serial photography. At one period he took scores of photographs of an unknown woman in a chemise with a fallen shoulder strap as she turned her face and body very slightly each time. He tested many kinds of printing paper, which he coated with varying proportions of egg white, potassium iodide, and potassium bromide, before sensitizing the prepared paper in a solution of silver nitrate. He told W. C. Curtis that he hated the "horrible fixity" of the photographic image and wished to disrupt it from within. In 1881 or 1882 we find him experimenting with a crude form of projector: to an old magic lantern he attached a large, revolving glass disk of his own invention on which transparent positives were arranged in phase. One evening, to the astonishment of Curtis, he displayed for several seconds on a wall of his studio the Third Avenue El with a train moving jerkily across.

But Crane did not pursue this method of bringing photographs to life, which others would carry to completion. Despite his interest in photography, he considered it inferior to painting.

After attending a photographic exhibition with W. C. Curtis, he declared: "Painting is dead," but a week later at an oyster bar he remarked that photography was a "disappointment" and couldn't compare with paint when it came to capturing the textures of things. What is striking in the career of Harlan Crane is that more than once he seemed to be in the direct line of invention and experimentation that led to the cinema of Edison and the Lumières, and that each time he turned deliberately away. It was as if he were following a parallel line of discovery, searching for an illusion of motion based not on serial photographs and perforated strips of celluloid, but on different principles altogether.

The Phantoptic Theater opened on October 4, 1883. People purchased tickets at the door, passed through a foyer illuminated by brass gas lamps on the walls, and made their way toward an arched opening half concealed by a thick crimson curtain hung on gold rings. The curtain, the arch, and the rings turned out to be images painted on the wall; the actual entrance was through a second, less convincing curtain that opened into a small theater with a high ceiling, worn red-plush seats for some three hundred people, a cut-glass chandelier, and a raised stage with a black velvet curtain. Between the audience and the stage stood a piano. Newspaper reports differ in certain details, but the performance appears to have begun by the emergence from a side door of a man in evening dress and gleaming black shoes who strode to the piano bench, flung out his tails, sat grandly down, threw back his head, and began to play a waltz described variously as "lively" and "melancholy." The hissing gas jets in the chandelier grew quiet and faint as the footlights were turned up. Slowly the black curtain rose. It revealed an immense oil painting that took up the entire rear wall of the stage and was framed on three sides by a polished dark wood carved with vine leaves and bunches of grapes.

The painting showed a ballroom filled with dancers: women with roses and ropes of pearls in their high-piled hair, heavily flounced ball gowns that swept along the floor, and tight-corseted bosoms pressing against low-cut necklines trimmed with lace; men with beards and monocles, tight-waisted tail-coats, and very straight backs. A hearth with a fire was visible in one wall, high windows hung with dark blue velvet curtains in another. As the audience watched and the pianist played his lively, melancholy waltz, the figures in the painting began to dance. Here the newspaper accounts differ. Some say the figures began to waltz suddenly; others report that first one pair of dancers began to move and then another—but it is clear that the figures were moving in a lifelike manner, made all the more convincing by the waltz music welling up from the piano. Other movements are also mentioned: the flames in the fire-place leaped and fell, a man leaning his elbow on the mantel-piece removed his monocle and replaced it in his eye, and a woman with yellow and pink roses in her hair fanned herself with a black silk fan.

The audience, exhilarated by the spectacle of the waltzing figures, soon began to notice a second phenomenon. Some of the dancers appeared to emerge from the ballroom onto the stage, where they continued waltzing. The stage, separated from the first row of seats by the piano and a narrow passageway, gradually seemed to become an extension of the ballroom. But the optical effect was unsettling because the dancers on the stage were seen against a ballroom that was itself perceived as a flat perspective painting—a painted surface with laws of its own. After no more than a minute or two the dancers returned to the painting, where for several minutes they continued to turn in the picture until the last notes of the waltz died away. Gradually—or suddenly, according to one journalist—the figures became immobile. In the auditorium, the gaslights in the chandelier were turned up.

From a door at stage left emerged Harlan Crane, dressed in black evening clothes and a silk top hat that glistened as if wet in the glare of the gas jets. He stepped to the front of the stage and bowed once to enthusiastic applause, sweeping his hat across his body. He rose to wait out the shouts and cheers. Holding up a hand, he invited the audience onto the stage to examine his painting, asking only that they refrain from touching it. He then turned on his heel and strode out of sight.

An assistant came onto the stage, carrying a long red-velvet rope. He suspended the rope between two wooden posts at both ends of the painting, some three feet from its surface.

Members of the audience climbed both sets of side steps onto the stage, where they gathered behind the velvet rope and examined the vast canvas. Sometimes they bent forward over the rope to study the painting more closely through a lorgnette or monocle. In this second phase of the show, the theater may be said to have withdrawn certain of its features and transformed itself into an art museum—one that contained a single painting. The evidence we have suggests that it was in fact an oil painting, with visible brushstrokes, rather than a screen or other surface onto which an image had been cast.

There were three showings daily: at two o'clock, four o'clock, and eight o'clock. Crane, who was present at every performance, never varied his routine, so that one wit said it wasn't Harlan Crane at all, but a mechanical figure, like Kempelen's Chess Player, fitted out with one of Edison's talking machines.

Contemporary accounts speculate lavishly about the secret of the motions, some seeing the Phantoptic Theater as a development of the old Diorama, others arguing that it was done with a specially adapted magic lantern that projected serial images of dancers onto a motionless background. But the motions of the Diorama were nothing like those of the Phantoptic Theater, for Daguerre's effects, produced by artful manipulation of light, were limited to extremely simple illusions, such as lava or masses of snow rushing down the side of a mountain; and the theory of serial projection, while anticipating later advances in the development of the cinema, cannot explain the emergence of the dancers onto the stage. For their part, the dancers onstage are variously explained as real actors appearing from behind a curtain, as images projected onto "invisible" screens, and as optical illusions produced by "hidden lenses" that the writer does not bother to describe. In truth, the riddle of Crane's *Ballroom* illusions has never been solved. What strikes the student of cinema is the peculiar position assumed by Crane and his theater with respect to the history of the illusion of motion. For if in one respect the Phantoptic Theater shares the late-nineteenth-century fascination with the science of moving images, in another it looks back, far back, to a dim, primitive world in which painted images are magical visions infused with the breath of life. Crane's refusal to abandon painting and embrace the new technology of serial photographs, his insistence on creating illusions of motion that cannot be accounted for in the new way, make him a minor, quirky, exasperating, and finally puzzling figure in the prehistory of the cinema, who seizes our attention precisely because he created a riddling world of motion entirely his own.

For a while the daily shows of the Phantoptic Theater continued to draw enthusiastic audiences, even as the press turned its gaze in other directions. By the end of the year, attendance had begun to decline; and by the middle of January the theater rarely held more than a few dozen people, crowded expectantly into the front rows.

We have several glimpses of Crane during this period. In the diary of W. C. Curtis we hear that Crane is hard at work on a new painting for his theater, though he refuses to reveal anything about it; sometimes he complains of "difficulties." One evening in December, Curtis notes with surprise the presence of a youngish woman at the studio, with auburn hair and a "plain, intelligent" face, whom he recognizes as the woman in the chemise. Crane introduced her first as Annie, then as Miss Merrow; she lowered her eyes and quickly disappeared behind a folding screen that stood in one corner of the studio. After this, Curtis saw her now and then on evening visits, when she invariably retreated behind the screen. Crane never spoke of her. Curtis remarks on his friend's "secretive" nature, speculates that she is his mistress, and drops the subject.

One evening at an alehouse, Crane suddenly began to speak of his admiration for Thomas Edison. Unfolding a newspaper, he pointed to an interview in which the inventor insisted on the importance of "chance" in his discoveries. Crane read several passages aloud, then folded the paper and looked up at Curtis. "A methodical man who believes in chance. Now what does that sound like to you, Curtis?" Curtis thought for a moment before replying: "A gambler." Crane, looking startled and then pleased, gave a laugh and a shake of the head. "I hadn't thought of that. Yes, a gambler." "And you were thinking—" "Oh, nothing, nothing—do you have any matches, Curtis, I never seem to—but a methodical man, who believes in chance—tell me, Curtis, have you ever heard a better definition of an artist?"

Not until March of 1884 was a new piece announced. The opening took place at eight o'clock in the evening. The black velvet curtain rose to reveal *Picnic on the Hudson,* a monumental painting that showed groups of picnickers sitting in sun-checked green shade between high trees. Sunlight glowed in sudden bursts: on the corner of a white cloth spread on the grass, on a bunch of red grapes in a silver dish, on the lace sleeve of a lavender dress, on the blue-green river in the background, where sunlit portions of a two-stacked steamer were visible through the trees. As the pianist played a medley of American melodies ("Aura Lee," "Sweet Genevieve," "Carry Me Back to Old Virginny," "I'll Take You Home Again, Kathleen"), *Picnic on the Hudson* began to show signs of life: the second of the steamer's smokestacks emerged fully from behind the trunk of an oak, a squirrel moved along a branch, the hand of a picnicker held out a glistening crystal glass, into which, from the mouth of a wine bottle, poured a ruby-colored liquid. A small boy in boots and breeches and a feathered hat strolled into view, holding in one hand a red rubber ball. A young woman, wearing a straw poke bonnet trimmed with purple and gold pansies, slowly smiled. The several groups of men and women seated on the grass seemed to feel a great sense of peacefulness, in the warm shade, under the trees, on a summer afternoon beside the Hudson. A number of viewers later said that the painting created in them a feeling of deep repose.

As the picnickers relaxed on the riverbank, one of them, a mustached young man in a bowler hat who had been gazing toward the river, turned his head lazily in the direction of the audience and abruptly stopped. The woman in the straw bonnet, following his gaze, turned and stared. And now all the faces of the people in the painting turned to look toward the viewers, many of whom later spoke of feeling, at that moment, a sensation of desire or yearning. Someone in the audience rose and slowly climbed the steps to the stage; others soon followed. Once on the stage, they walked up and down along the painting, admiring its Verisimilist accuracy of detail—the brown silk stitching on the back of a woman's white kid glove, the webbed feet and overlapping feather tips of a tiny seagull sitting on the railing of the steamer, the minuscule fibers visible in the torn corner of a folded newspaper on the grass. Contemporary reports are unclear about what happened next, but it appears that a man, reaching out to feel the canvas, experienced in his fingertips a sensation of melting or dissolving, before he stepped into the painting. Those who entered the painting later reported a "dreamlike feeling" or "a sense of great happiness," but were less clear about the physical act of entry. Most spoke of some kind of barrier that immediately gave way; several felt hard canvas and paint. One woman, a Mrs. Amelia Hartman, said that it reminded her of immersing herself in the ocean, but an ocean whose water was dry. Inside the painting, the figures watched them but did not speak. The mingling seems to have lasted from about ten minutes to half an hour, before the visitors experienced what one described as a "darkening" and another as "stepping into deep shade." The deep shade soon revealed itself to be a corridor lit by dimmed gas jets, which led to a door that opened into the side of the auditorium.

When all the members of the audience had returned to their seats, the pianist drove his music to a crescendo, threw back his head with a great agitation of hair, struck three ringing chords, and stopped. The figures in the painting resumed their original poses. Slowly the curtain came down. Harlan Crane walked briskly out onto the apron, bowed once, and strode off. The showing was over.

Newspaper reviews outdid themselves in their attempts to explain the new range of effects produced by Crane in *Picnic on the Hudson.* The *New York News* proposed a hollow space behind the painting, with actors and a stage set; the picture, an ingenious deception, was nothing but a diaphanous screen that separated the actors from the stage. The proposed solution fails to mention the hardness of the canvas, as reported by many members of the audience, and in any case it cannot explain why no one ever detected anything resembling a "diaphanous screen," or how the mysterious screen vanished to permit entry.

Other explanations are equally unsatisfactory: one columnist described the barrier as an artificially produced "mist" or "vapor" onto which magic-lantern slides were projected, and another suggested that the audience, once it reached the stage, had inhaled an opiate sprayed into the atmosphere and had experienced a shared hallucination.

These explanations, far from revealing the secret of Crane's art, obscured it behind translucent, fluttering veils of language, which themselves were seductive and served only to sharpen the public's curiosity and desire.

Picnic on the Hudson was shown to a packed house every evening at eight o'clock, while *The Ballroom* continued to be displayed daily to diminishing audiences. By early summer, when evening attendance at the Phantoptic Theater showed signs of falling off, a rumor began to circulate that Crane had already started a new work, which would usher in an age of wonder; and it was said that if you listened closely, in the theater, you could hear the artist-showman moving about in the basement, pushing things out of the way, hammering, preparing.

A single anecdote survives from this period. In a dockside restaurant with a view of the Brooklyn ferry across the river, Crane told W. C. Curtis that as a child he had thought he would grow up to be a ferryboat captain. "I like rivers," he said. "I thought I'd travel a lot." Curtis, a well-traveled man who had spent three years in Europe in his twenties, urged Crane to go abroad with him, to Paris and Munich and Venice. Crane appeared to consider it. "Not far enough," he then said. Curtis had also spent six months in China; he immediately began to sing the praises of the Orient. Crane gave "an odd little laugh" and, with a shrug of one shoulder, remarked, "Still not far enough." Then he lit up his pipe and ordered another dish of Blue Point oysters.

We know very little about *Terra Incognita*, which was shown only a single time (February 6, 1885). From the foyer of the Phantoptic Theater, visitors were led down a flight of steps into a dark room illuminated by a few low-burning gas jets in glass lanterns suspended from the ceiling. Gradually the viewers became aware of a painting rising up on all sides—a continuous twelve-foot-high canvas that stretched flat along all four walls and curved at the wall junctures.

The vast, enclosing composition seemed at first to be painted entirely black, but slowly other colors became visible, deep browns and blackish reds, while vague shapes began to emerge. Here the evidence becomes confused. Some claimed that the painting represented a dark cavern with rocks and ledges. Others spoke of a dark sea. All witnesses agreed that they gradually became aware of shadowy figures, who seemed to float up from the depths of the painting and to move closer to the surface. A woman screamed—it isn't clear when—and was harshly hushed. At some point several figures appeared to pass from the surface into the dark and crowded room. Precisely what took place from then on remains uncertain. One woman later spoke of a sensation of cold on the back of her neck; another described a soft pressure on her upper arm. Others, men and women, reported "a sensation of being rubbed up against, as by a cat," or of being touched on the face or bosom or leg. Not all impressions were gentle. Here and there, hats were knocked off, shawls pulled away, hands and elbows seized. One witness said: "I felt as though a great wind had blown through me, and I was possessed by a feeling of sweetness and despair." Someone screamed again. After a third scream, things happened very quickly: a woman burst into tears, people began pushing their way to the stairs, there were cries and shouts and violent shoving. A bearded man fell against the canvas. A young woman in a blue felt hat trimmed with dark red roses sank slowly to the floor.

The commotion was heard by a janitor sweeping the aisles of

the upper theater. He came down to check and immediately ran outside for a policeman, who hurried over and appeared at the top of the stairs with a lantern and a nightstick to witness a scene of dangerous panic. People were sobbing and pushing forward, tearing at one another's bodies, trampling the fallen woman. The policeman was unable to fight his way down. Shrill blows of his whistle brought three more policemen with lanterns, who helped the terrified crowd up the narrow stairway. When it was all over, seven people were hospitalized; the young woman on the floor later died of injuries to the face and head. The painting had been damaged in many places; one portion of canvas showed a ragged hole the size of a fist. On the floor lay broken fans and crushed top hats, torn ostrich plumes, a scattering of dark red rose petals, a mauve glove, an uncoiled chignon with one unraveled ribbon, a cracked monocle at the end of a black silk cord.

Regrettably, newspaper accounts concentrated more on the panic than on the painting. There were the usual attempts at tracing the motions of the figures to hidden magic lanterns, even though not a single visitor reported a beam of light in the darkened, gas-lit room. The penetration of the figures into the room was explained either as a theatrical stunt performed by concealed actors or a delusion stimulated by the heightened anxiety of a crowd in the dark. In truth, we simply cannot explain the reported effects by means of the scant evidence that has come down to us. It is worth noting that no one has ever duplicated the motions produced in the Phantoptic Theater. On strictly objective grounds, we cannot rule out the possibility that Crane's figures in *Terra Incognita* really did what they appeared to do, that is, emerge from the paint and enter the room, perhaps as a result of some chemical discovery no longer recoverable.

By order of the mayor, Crane's theater was closed. Three weeks later, when he attempted to open a second theater, city authorities intervened. Meanwhile the parents of the trampled woman sued Crane for inciting a riot. Although he was exonerated, the judge issued a stern warning. Crane never returned to public life.

In his cramped studio and in neighborhood chophouses we catch glimpses of him over the next few years: a thin-lipped, quiet man, with a clean-shaven face and brooding eyes. He is never without his big-bowled meerschaum with its cherrywood stem and its chewed rubber bit. W. C. Curtis speaks of his melancholy, his long silences. Was he bitter over the closing of his theater, over his brief notoriety that failed to develop into lasting fame? Only once does he complain to Curtis: he regrets, he says, that his "invention" has never been recognized. When he is mentioned in the papers now and then, it is not as an artist or an inventor but as the former proprietor of the Phantoptic Theater.

He is often tired. Curtis notes that Crane is always alone in the evenings when he visits; we hear no further mention of Annie Merrow, who vanishes from the record. For a time Crane returns to his old invention, the Phantasmatrope, attempting to solve the problem of the shutter but abruptly losing interest. He no longer takes photographs. He spends less and less time in his studio and instead passes long hours in coffee shops and cheap restaurants, reading newspapers slowly and smoking his pipe. He refuses to attend art exhibitions. He likes to stroll past the East River piers and ferry slips, to linger before the windows of the sailmakers' shops on South Street. Now and then, in order to pay the rent, he takes a job that he quits after a few weeks: a toy salesman in a department store, a sandwich-board man advertising a new lunchroom. One day he sells his camera for a dollar. He takes long walks into distant neighborhoods, sits on benches at the water's edge, a lean man beside wavering lines of smoke. He appears to subsist on apples and roasted chestnuts bought in the street, on cheap meals in alehouses and oyster bars. He likes to watch the traffic on the East River: three-masted barks, old paddle-wheel towboats and the new screw-propelled tugs, steamboats with funnels and masts.

Suddenly—the word belongs to W. C. Curtis—Crane returns to his studio and shuts himself up day after day. He refuses to speak of his work. At alehouses and night cafés he picks at his food, looks restlessly about, knocks out his pipe on the table, and packs in fresh tobacco with slow taps of his fingertip. Curtis can scarcely see him behind clouds of smoke. "It's like the old days," Curtis notes in his diary, adding ruefully, "without the joy."

One evening, while Crane is raising to his mouth a glass of dark ale, he pauses in midair, as if a thought has crossed his mind, and mentions to Curtis that a few hours ago he rented a room in an old office building on Chambers Street, a few blocks from City Hall Park. Curtis starts to ask a question but thinks better of it. The next day a flurry of hand-lettered signs on yellow paper appears on hoardings and lampposts, announcing a new exhibition on November 1, 1888.

In the small room with its two dust-streaked windows and its rolltop desk, a single painting was on display. Only W. C. Curtis and four of Curtis's friends attended. Crane stood leaning against the opposite wall, between the two windows, smoking away at his pipe. Curtis describes the painting as roughly four feet by five feet, in a plain, varnished frame. A small piece of white paper, affixed to the wall beside it, bore the words SWAN SONG.

The painting depicted Crane's studio, captured with Verisimilist fidelity. Crane himself stood before an easel, with his long legs and a buttoned-up threadbare jacket, gripping his palette and a clutch of brushes in one hand and reaching out with a long fine-tipped brush in the other as he held his head back and stared at the canvas "with a look of ferocity." The walls of the studio were thickly covered with framed and unframed paintings and pencil-and-chalk sketches by Crane, many of which Curtis recognized from Crane's Verisimilist and Transgressive periods. There were also a number of paintings Curtis had never seen before, which he either passes over in silence or describes with disappointing briskness ("another pipe-and-mug still life," "a rural scene"). On the floor stood piles of unframed canvases, stacked six deep against the walls. One such painting, near a corner, showed an arm protruding from the surface and grasping the leg of a chair. The painting on the easel, half finished, appeared to be a preliminary study for *Picnic on the Hudson;* a number of seated figures had been roughly sketched but not painted in, and in another place a woman's right arm, which had been finished at a different angle, showed through the paint as a ghostly arm without a hand. The studio also included a zinc washstand, the corner of a cast-iron heating stove, and part of a thick table, on which stood one of Crane's magic lanterns and a scattering of yellowed and curling photographs showing a young woman in a chemise, with one strap slipping from a shoulder and her head turned at many different angles.

From everything we know of it, *Swan Song* would have been at home in the old Verisimilist Exhibition of 1874. Curtis notes the barely visible tail of a mouse between two stacked canvases, as well as a scattering of pipe ashes on a windowsill. As he and his friends stood before the painting, wondering what was new and different about it, they heard behind them the word "Gentlemen." In truth they had almost forgotten Crane. Now they turned to see him standing against the wall between the two windows, with his pipe in his hand. Smoke floated about him. Curtis was struck by his friend's bony, melancholy face. Weak light came through the dusty windows on both sides of Crane, who seemed to be standing in the dimmest part of the room. "Thank you," he said quietly, "for—" And here he raised his arm in a graceful gesture that seemed to include the painting, the visitors, and the occasion itself. Without completing his sentence, he thrust his pipe back in his mouth and narrowed his eyes behind drifts of bluish smoke.

It is unclear exactly what happened next. Someone appears to have exclaimed. Curtis, turning back to the painting, became aware of a motion or "agitation" in the canvas. As he watched, standing about a foot from the picture, the paintings in the studio began to fade away. Those that hung on the wall and those that stood in stacks on the floor grew paler and paler, the painting on the easel and the photographs on the table began to fade, and Crane himself, with his palette and brush, seemed to be turning into a ghost.

Soon nothing was left in the painting but a cluttered studio hung with white canvases, framed and unframed. Blank canvases were stacked six deep against the walls. The mouse's tail, Curtis says, showed distinctly against the whiteness of the empty canvas.

"What the devil!" someone cried. Curtis turned around. In the real room, Crane himself was no longer there.

The door, Curtis noticed, was partly open. He and two of his friends immediately left the rented office and took a four-wheeler to Crane's studio. There they found the door unlocked. Inside, everything was exactly as in the painting: the easel with its blank canvas, the empty rectangles on the walls, the table with its scattering of blank printing paper, the stacks of white canvases standing about, even the ashes on the windowsill. When Curtis looked more closely, he had the uneasy sensation that a mouse's tail had just darted out of sight behind a canvas. Curtis felt he had stepped into a painting. It struck him that Crane had anticipated this moment, and he had an odd impulse to tip his hat to his old friend. It may have been the pale November light, or the "premonition of dread" that came over him then, but he was suddenly seized by a sense of insubstantiality, as if at any moment he might begin to fade away. With a backward glance, like a man pursued, he fled the empty studio.

Crane was never seen again. Not a single painting or sketch has survived. At best we can clumsily resurrect them through careless newspaper accounts and the descriptions, at times detailed, in the diary of W. C. Curtis. Of his other work, nothing remains except some eighty engravings in the pages of contemporary magazines—mediocre woodblock reproductions in no way different from the hurried hackwork of the time. Based on this work alone—his visible oeuvre—Harlan Crane deserves no more than a footnote in the history of late-nineteenth-century American magazine illustration. It is his vanished work that lays claim to our attention.

He teases us, this man who is neither one thing nor another, who swerves away from the history of painting in the direction of the cinema, while creating a lost medium that has no name. If I call him a precursor, it is because he is part of the broad impulse in the last quarter of the nineteenth century to make pictures move—to enact for mass audiences, through modern technology, an ancient mystery. In this sense it is tempting to think of him as a figure who looks both ways: toward the future, when the inventions of Edison and the Lumières will soon be born, and toward the remote past, when paintings were ambiguously alive, in a half-forgotten world of magic and dream. But finally it would be a mistake to abandon him here, in a shadow-place between a vanished world and a world not yet come into being. Rather, his work represents a turn, a dislocation, a bold error, a venture into a possible future that somehow failed to take place. One might say that history, in the person of Harlan Crane, had a wayward and forbidden thought. And if, after all, that unborn future should one day burst forth? Then Harlan Crane might prove to be a precursor in a more exact sense. For even now there are signs of boredom with the old illusions of cinema, a longing for new astonishments. In research laboratories in universities across the country, in film studios in New York and California, we hear of radical advances in multidimensional imaging, of mobile vivigrams, of a modern cinema that banishes the old-fashioned screen in order to permit audiences to mingle freely with brilliantly realistic illusions. The time may be near when the image will be released from its ancient bondage to cave wall and frame and screen, and a new race of beings will walk the earth. On that day the history of the cinema will have to be rewritten, and Harlan Crane will take his place as a prophet. For us, in the meantime, he must remain what he was to his contemporaries: a twilight man, a riddle. If we have summoned him here from the perfection of his self-erasure, it is because his lost work draws us toward unfamiliar and alluring realms, where history seems to hesitate for a moment, in order to contemplate an alternative, before striding on.

The diary of W. C. Curtis, published in 1898, makes one last reference to Harlan Crane. In the summer of 1896 Curtis, traveling in Vienna, visited the Kunsthistorisches Museum, where a still life (by A. Muntz) reminded him of his old friend. "The pipe was so like his," Curtis writes, "that it cast me back to the days of our old friendship." But rather than devoting a single sentence to the days of his old friendship, Curtis describes the painting instead: the stained meerschaum bowl, the cherrywood stem, the black rubber bit, even the tarnished brass ring at the upper end of the bowl, which we hear about for the first time. The pipe rests on its side, next to a pewter-lidded beer stein decorated with the figure of a hunting dog in relief. Bits of ash, fallen from the bowl, lie scattered on the plain wooden tabletop. In the bowl glows a small ember. A thin curl of smoke rises over the rim.

THE WIZARD OF WEST ORANGE

OCTOBER 14, 1889. BUT THE WIZARD'S on fire! The Wizard is wild! He sleeps for two hours and works for twelve, sleeps for three hours and works for nineteen. The cot in the library, the cot in Room 12. Hair falling on forehead, vest open, tie askew. He bounds up the stairs, strides from room to room, greeting the experimenters, asking questions, cracking a joke. His boyish smile, his sharp eye. Why that way? Why not this? Notebook open, a furious sketch. Another. On to the next room! Hurls himself into a score of projects, concentrating with fanatical attention on each one before dismissing it to fling himself into next. The automatic adjustment for the recording stylus of the perfected phonograph. The speaking doll. Instantly grasps the essential problem, makes a decisive suggestion. Improved machinery for drawing brass wire. The aurophone, for enhancement of hearing. His trip to Paris has charged him with energy. Out into the courtyard!—the electrical lab, the chemical lab. Dangers of high-voltage alternating current: tests for safety. Improved insulation for electrical conductors. On to the metallurgical lab, to examine the graders and crushers, the belt conveyors, the ore samples. His magnetic ore-separator. "Work like hell, boys!" In Photographic Building, an air of secrecy. Excitement over the new Eastman film, the long strip in which lies the secret of visual motion. The Wizard says kinetoscope will do for the eye what phonograph does for the ear. But not yet, not yet! The men talk. What else? What next? A method of producing electricity directly from coal? A machine for compacting snow to clear city streets? Artificial silk? He hasn't slept at home for a week. They say the Wizard goes down to the Box, the experimental room in basement. Always kept locked. Rumors swirl. Another big invention to rival the phonograph? Surpass the incandescent lamp? The Wizard reads in library in the early mornings. From my desk in alcove I see him turn pages impatiently. Sometimes he thrusts at me a list of books to order. Warburton's *Physiology of Animals.* Greene and Wilson, *Cutaneous Sensation.* Makes a note, slams book shut, strides out. Earnshaw says Wizard spent three hours shut up in the Box last night.

OCTOBER 16. Today a book arrived: Kerner, *Archaeology of the Skin.* Immediately left library and walked upstairs to experimental rooms. Room 12 open, cot empty, the Wizard gone. On table an open notebook, a glass battery, and parts of a dissected phonograph scattered around a boxed motor: three wax cylinders, a recording stylus attached to its diaphragm, a voice horn, a cutting blade for shaving used cylinders. Notebook showed a rough drawing. Identified it at once: design for an automatic adjustment in recording mechanism, whereby stylus would engage cylinder automatically at correct depth. Wizard absolutely determined to crush Bell's graphophone. From window, a view of courtyard and part of chemical lab.

Returned to corridor. Ran into Corbett, an experimental assistant. The Wizard had just left. Someone called out he thought Wizard heading to stockroom. I returned down the stairs. Passed through library, pushed open double door, and crossed corridor to stockroom.

Always exhilarating to enter Earnshaw's domain. Those high walls, lined from floor to ceiling with long drawers—hides, bones, roots, textiles, teeth. Pigeonholes, hundreds of them, crammed with resins, waxes, twines. Is it that, like library itself, stockroom is an orderly and teeming universe—a world of worlds—a finitude with aspirations to allness? Earnshaw hadn't seen him, thought he might be in basement. His hesitation when I held up Kerner and announced my mission. Told him the Wizard had insisted it be brought to him immediately. Earnshaw still hesitant as he took out ring of keys. Is loyal to Wizard, but more loyal to me. Opened door leading to basement storeroom and preceded me down into the maze.

Crates of feathers, sheet metal, pitch, plumbago, cork. Earnshaw hesitated again at locked door of Box. Do not disturb: Wizard's strict orders. But Wizard had left strict orders with me: deliver book immediately. Two unambiguous commands, each contradicting the other. Earnshaw torn. A good man, earnest, but not strong. Unable to resist a sense of moral obligation to me, owing to a number of trifling services rendered to him in the ordinary course of work. In addition, ten years younger. In my presence instinctively assumes an attitude of deference. Rapped lightly on door. No answer. "Open it," I said, not unkindly. He stood outside as I entered.

Analysis of motives. Desire to deliver book (good). Desire to see room (bad). Yielded to base desire. But ask yourself: was it only base? I revere the Wizard and desire his success. He is searching for something, for some piece of crucial knowledge. If I see experiment, may be able to find information he needs. Analyze later.

The small room well-lit by incandescent bulbs. Bare of furnishings except for central table, two armchairs against wall. On table a closed notebook, a copper-oxide battery, and two striking objects. One a long stiff blackish glove, about the length of a forearm, which rests horizontally on two Y-shaped supports about eight inches high. Glove made of some solid dark material, perhaps vulcanized rubber, and covered with a skein of wires emerging from small brass caps. The other: a wooden framework supporting a horizontal cylinder, whose upper surface is in contact with a row of short metal strips suspended from a crossbar. Next to cylinder a small electric motor. Two bundles of wire lead from glove to battery, which in turn is connected to cylinder mechanism by way of motor. On closer inspection I see that interior of glove is lined with black silky material, studded with tiny silver disks like heads of pins. "Sir!" whispers Earnshaw.

I switch off lights and step outside. Footsteps above our heads. I follow Earnshaw back upstairs into stockroom, where an experimental assistant awaits him with request for copper wire. Return to library. Am about to sit down at desk when Wizard enters from other door. Gray gabardine laboratory gown flowing around his legs, tie crooked, hair mussed. "Has that book—?" he says loudly. Deaf in his left ear. "I was just bringing it to you," I shout. Holding out Kerner. Seizes it and throws himself down in an armchair, frowning as if angrily at the flung-open pages.

OCTOBER 17. A quiet day in library. Rain, scudding clouds. Arranged books on third-floor gallery, dusted mineral specimens in their glass-doored cabinets. Restless.

OCTOBER 18. That wired glove. Can it be a self-warming device, to replace a lady's muff? Have heard that in Paris, on cold winter nights, vendors stand before the Opera House, selling hot potatoes for ladies to place in their muffs. But the pinheads? The cylinder? And why then such secrecy? Wizard in locked room again, for two hours, with Kistenmacher.

OCTOBER 20. This morning overheard a few words in courtyard. Immediately set off for stockroom in search of Earnshaw. E.'s passion—his weakness, one might say—is for idea of motion photography. Eager to get hold of any information about the closely guarded experiments in Photographic Building and Room 5. Words overheard were between two machinists, who'd heard an experimental assistant speaking to so-and-so from chemical lab about an experiment in Photographic Building conducted with the new Eastman film. Talk was of perforations along both edges of strip, as in the old telegraph tape. The film to be driven forward on sprockets that engage and release it. This of course the most roundabout hearsay. Nevertheless not first time there has been talk of modifying strip film by means of perforations, which some say the Wizard saw in Paris: studio of Monsieur Marey. Earnshaw thrives on such rumors.

Not in stockroom but down in storeroom, as I knew at once by partially open door. In basement reported my news. Excited him visibly. At that instant—suddenly—I became aware of darker motive underlying my impulse to inform Earnshaw of conversation in courtyard. Paused. Looked about. Asked him to admit me for a moment—only a moment—to the Box.

An expression of alarm invading his features. But Earnshaw particularly well qualified to understand a deep curiosity about experiments conducted in secret. Furthermore: could not refuse to satisfy an indebtedness he felt he'd incurred by listening eagerly to my report. Stationed himself outside door. Guardian of inner sanctum. I quickly entered.

The glove, the battery, the cylinder. I detected a single difference: notebook now open. Showed a hastily executed drawing of glove, surrounded by several smaller sketches of what appeared to be electromagnets, with coils of wire about a core. Under glove a single word: HAPTOGRAPH.

Did not hesitate to insert hand and arm in glove. Operation

somewhat impeded by silken lining, evidently intended to prevent skin from directly touching any part of inner structure. When forearm was buried up to elbow, threw switch attached to wires at base of cylinder mechanism.

The excitement returns, even as I write these words. How to explain it? The activated current caused motor to turn cylinder on its shaft beneath the metal rods suspended from crossbar, which in turn caused silver points in lining of glove to move against my hand. Was aware at first of many small gentle pointed pressures. But—behold!—the merely mechanical sensation soon gave way to another, and I felt—distinctly—a sensation as of a hand grasping my own in a firm handshake. External glove had remained stiff and immobile. Switched off current, breathed deep. Repeated experiment. Again the motor turning the cylinder. Sensation unmistakable: I felt my hand gripped in a handshake, my fingers lightly squeezed. At that moment experienced a strange elation, as if standing on a dock listening to water lap against piles as I prepared to embark on a longed-for voyage. Switched off current, withdrew hand. Stood still for a moment before turning suddenly to leave room.

OCTOBER 21. Books borrowed by Kistenmacher, as recorded in library notebook, Oct. 7–Oct. 14: *The Nervous System and the Mind*, *The Tactile Sphere*, *Leçons sur la Physiologie du Système Nerveux*, *Lezioni di Fisiologia Sperimentale*, *Sensation and Pain*. The glove, the cylinder, the phantom handshake. Clear—is it clear?—that Wizard has turned his attention to sense of touch. To what end, exactly? Yet even as I ask, I seem to grasp principle of haptograph. "The kinetoscope will do for the eye what the phonograph does for the ear." Is he not isolating each of the five senses? Creating for each a machine that records and plays back one sense alone? Voices disembodied, moving images without physical substance, immaterial touches. The phonograph, the kinetoscope, the haptograph. Voices preserved in cylinders of wax, moving bodies in strips of nitrocellulose, touches in pinheads and wires. A gallery of ghosts. Cylinder as it turns must transmit electrical impulses that activate the silver points. Ghosts? Consider: the skin is touched. A firm handshake. Hello, my name is. And yours? Strange thoughts on an October night.

OCTOBER 24. This morning, after Wizard was done looking through mail and had ascended stairs to experimental rooms, Kistenmacher entered library. Headed directly toward me. Have always harbored a certain dislike for Kistenmacher, though he treats me respectfully enough. Dislike the aggressive directness of his walk, arms swinging so far forward that he seems to be pulling himself along by gripping onto chunks of air. Dislike his big hands with neat black hairs growing sideways across fingers, intense stare of eyes that take you in without seeing you, his black stiff hair combed as if violently sideways across head, necktie straight as a plumb line. Kistenmacher one of the most respected of electrical experimenters. Came directly up to my rolltop desk, stopping too close to it, as if the wood were barring his way.

"I wish to report a missing book," he said.

Deeper meaning of Kistenmacher's remark. It happens—infrequently—that a library book is temporarily misplaced. The cause not difficult to wrest from the hidden springs of existence. Any experimenter—or assistant—or indeed any member of staff—is permitted to browse among all three tiers of books, or to remove a volume and read anywhere on premises. Instead of leaving book for me to replace, as everyone is instructed to do, occasionally someone takes it upon self to reshelve. An act well meant but better left undone, since mistakes easy to make. Earnshaw, in particular, guilty of this sort of misplaced kindness. Nevertheless I patrol shelves carefully, several times a day, not only when I replace books returned by staff, or add new books and scientific journals ordered for library, but also on tours of inspection intended to ensure correct arrangement of books on shelves. As a result quite rare for a misplaced volume to escape detection. Kistenmacher's statement therefore not the simple statement of fact it appeared to be, but an implied reproach: You have been negligent in your duties.

"I'm quite certain we can find it without difficulty," I said. Rising immediately. "Sometimes the new assistants—"

"Giesinger," he said. *"Musculo-Cutaneous Feeling."*

A slight heat in my neck. Wondered whether a flush was visible.

"You see," I said with a smile. "The mystery solved." Lifted from my desk *Musculo-Cutaneous Feeling* by Otto Giesinger and handed it to Kistenmacher. He glanced at spine, to make certain I hadn't made a mistake, then looked at me with interest.

"This is a highly specialized study," said he.

"Yes, a little too specialized for me," I replied.

"But the subject interests you?"

Hesitation. "I try to keep abreast of—developments."

"Excellent," he said, and suddenly smiled—a disconcerting smile, of startling charm. "I will be sure to consult with you." Held up book, tightly clasped in one big hand, gave a little wave with it, and took his leave.

The whole incident rich with possibility. My responsibility in library is to keep up with scientific and technical literature, so that I may order books I deem essential. Most of my professional reading confined to scientific journals, technical periodicals, and institutional proceedings, but peruse many books as well, in a broad range of subjects, from psychology of hysteria to structure of the constant-pressure dynamo; my interests are wide. Still, it cannot have failed to strike Kistenmacher that I had removed from shelves a study directly related to his investigations in Box.

Kistenmacher perfectly well aware that everyone knows of his secretive experiments, about which many rumors. Is said to enjoy such rumors and even to contribute to them by enigmatic hints of his own. Once told Earnshaw, who reported it to me, that there would soon be no human sensation that could not be replicated mechanically. At time I imagined a machine for production of odors, a machine of tastes. Knows of course that I keep a record of books borrowed by staff, each with name of borrower. Now knows I have been reading Giesinger on musculo-cutaneous feeling.

What else does he know? Can Earnshaw have said something?

OCTOBER 26. A slow day. Reading. From my desk in alcove I can see Wizard's rolltop desk with its scattering of books and papers, the railed galleries of second and third levels, high up a flash of sun on a glass-fronted cabinet holding mineral specimens. The pine-paneled ceiling. Beyond Wizard's desk, the white marble statue brought back from Paris Exposition. Winged youth seated on ruins of a gas street-lamp, holding high in one hand an incandescent lamp. The Genius of Light. In my feet a rumble of dynamos from machine shop beyond stockroom.

OCTOBER 28. In courtyard, gossip about secret experiments in Photographic Building, Room 8, the Box. A machine for extracting nutrients from seaweed? A speaking photograph? Rumors of hidden workrooms, secret assistants. In courtyard one night, an experimental assistant seen with cylinders under each arm, heading in direction of basement.

OCTOBER 29. For the Wizard, there is always a practical consideration. The incandescent lamp, the electric pen, the magnetic ore-separator. The quadruplex telegraph. Origin of moving photographs in study of animal motion: Muybridge's horses, Marey's birds. Even the phonograph: concedes its secondary use as instrument of entertainment, but insists on primary value as business machine for use in dictation. And the haptograph? A possible use in hospitals? A young mother dies. Bereft child comforted by simulated caresses. Old people, lingering out their lives alone, untouched. Shake of a friendly hand. It might work.

NOVEMBER 3. A momentous day. Even now it seems unlikely. And yet, looked at calmly, a day like any other: experimenters in their rooms, visitors walking in courtyard, a group of schoolchildren with their teacher, assistants passing up and down corridors and stairways, men working on grounds. After a long morning decided to take walk in courtyard, as I sometimes do. Warmish day, touch of autumn chill in the shade. Walked length of courtyard, between electrical lab and chemical lab, nodding to several men who stood talking in groups. At end of yard, took a long look at buildings of Phonograph Works. Started back. Nearly halfway to main building when aware of sharp footsteps not far behind me. Drawing closer. Turned and saw Kistenmacher.

"A fine day for a walk," he said. Falling into step beside me.

Hidden significance of Kistenmacher's apparently guileless salutation. His voice addressed to the air—to the universe—but with a ripple of the confidential meant for me. Instantly alert. Common enough of course to meet an experimenter or machinist in courtyard. Courtyard after all serves as informal meeting place, where members of staff freely mingle. Have encountered Kistenmacher himself innumerable times, striding along with great arms swinging. No, what struck me, on this occasion, was one indisputable fact: instead of passing me with habitual brisk nod, Kistenmacher attached himself to me with tremendous decisiveness. So apparent he had something to say to me that I suspected he'd been watching for me from a window.

"My sentiment exactly," I replied.

"I wonder whether you might accompany me to Room 8," he then said.

An invitation meant to startle me. I confess it did. Kistenmacher knows I am curious about experimental rooms on second floor, just up stairs from library. These rooms always kept open—except Room 5, where photographic experiments continue to be conducted secretly, in addition to those in new Photographic Building—but there is general understanding that rooms are domain of experimenters and assistants, and of course of the Wizard himself, who visits each room daily in order to observe progress of every experiment. Kistenmacher's invitation therefore highly unusual. At same time, had about it a deliberate air of mystery, which Kistenmacher clearly enjoying as he took immense energetic strides and pulled himself forward with great swings of his absurd arms.

Room 8: Kistenmacher's room on second floor. On a table: parts of a storage battery and samples of what I supposed to be nickel hydrate. No sign of haptograph. This in itself not remarkable, for experimenters are engaged in many projects. Watched him close door and turn to me.

"Our interests coincide," he said, speaking in manner characteristic of him, at once direct and sly.

I said nothing.

"I invite you to take part in an experiment," he next remarked. An air of suppressed energy. Had sense that he was studying my face for signs of excitement.

His invitation, part entreaty and part command, shocked and thrilled me. Also exasperated me by terrible ease with which he was able to create inner turmoil.

"What kind of experiment?" I asked: sharply, almost rudely.

He laughed—I had not expected Kistenmacher to laugh. A boyish and disarming laugh. Surprised to see a dimple in his left cheek. Kistenmacher's teeth straight and white, though upper left incisor is missing.

"That," he said, "remains to be seen. Nine o'clock tomorrow night? I will come to the library."

Noticed that, while his body remained politely immobile, his muscles had grown tense in preparation for leaving. Already absolutely sure of my acceptance.

When I returned to library, found Wizard seated at his desk, in stained laboratory gown, gesturing vigorously with both hands as he spoke with a reporter from the *New York World.*

NOVEMBER 5. I will do my utmost to describe objectively the extraordinary event in which I participated on the evening of November 4.

Kistenmacher appeared in library with a punctuality that even in my state of excitement I found faintly ludicrous: over fireplace the big clock-hands showed nine o'clock so precisely that I had momentary grotesque sense they were the false hands of a painted clock. Led me into stockroom, where Earnshaw had been relieved for night shift by young Benson, who was up on a ladder examining contents of a drawer. Looked down at us intently over his shoulder, bending neck and gripping ladder-rails, as if we were very small and very far away. Kistenmacher removed from pocket a circle of keys. Held them up to inform Benson of our purpose. Opened door that led down to basement. I followed him through dim-lit cellar rooms piled high with wooden crates until we reached door of Box. Kistenmacher inserted key, stepped inside to activate electrical switch. Then turned to usher me in with a sweep of his hand and a barely perceptible little bow, all the while watching me closely.

The room had changed. No glove: next to table an object that made me think of a dressmaker's dummy, or top half of a suit of armor, complete with helmet. Supported on stand clamped to table edge. The dark half-figure studded with small brass caps connected by a skein of wires that covered entire surface. Beside it the cylinder machine and the copper-oxide battery. Half a dozen additional cylinders standing upright on table, beside machine. In one corner, an object draped in a sheet.

"Welcome to the haptograph," Kistenmacher said. "Permit me to demonstrate."

He stepped over to figure, disconnected a cable, and unfastened clasps that held head to torso. Lifted off head with both hands. Placed head carefully on table. Next unhooked or unhinged torso so that back opened in two wings. Hollow center lined with the same dark silky material and glittery silver points I had seen in glove.

Thereupon asked me to remove jacket, vest, necktie, shirt. My hesitation. Looked at me harshly. "Modesty is for schoolgirls." Turning around. "I will turn my back. You may leave, if you prefer."

Removed my upper clothing piece by piece and placed each article on back of a chair. Kistenmacher turned to face me. "So! You are still here?" Immediately gestured toward interior of winged torso, into which I inserted my arms. Against my skin felt silken lining. He closed wings and hooked in place. Set helmet over my head, refastened clasps and cable. An opening at mouth enabled me to breathe. At level of my eyes a strip of wire mesh. The arms, though stiff, movable at wrists and shoulders. I stood beside table, awaiting instructions.

"Tell me what you feel," Kistenmacher said. "It helps in the beginning if you close your eyes."

He threw switch at base of machine. The cylinder began to turn.

At first felt a series of very faint pin-pricks in region of scalp. Gradually impression of separate prickings faded away and I became aware of a more familiar sensation.

"It feels," I said, "exactly as if—yes—it's uncanny—but as though I were putting a hat on my head."

"Very good," Kistenmacher said. "And this?" Opened my eyes long enough to watch him slip cylinder from its shaft and replace with new one.

This time felt a series of pin-pricks in region of right shoulder. Quickly resolved into a distinct sensation: a hand resting on shoulder, then giving a little squeeze.

"And this?" Removed cylinder and added another. "Hold out your left hand. Palm up."

Was able to turn my armored hand at wrist. In palm became aware of a sudden sensation: a roundish smooth object—ball? egg?—seemed to be resting there.

In this manner—cylinder by cylinder—Kistenmacher tested three additional sensations. A fly or other small insect walking on right forearm. A ring or rope tightening over left biceps. Sudden burst of uncontrollable laughter: the haptograph had re-created sensation of fingers tickling my ribs.

"And now one more. Please pay close attention. Report exactly what you feel." Slipped a new cylinder onto shaft and switched on current.

After initial pin-pricks, felt a series of pressures that began at waist and rose along chest and face. A clear tactile sensation, rather pleasant, yet one I could not recall having experienced before. Kistenmacher listened intently as I attempted to describe. A kind of upward-flowing ripple, which moved rapidly from waist to top of scalp, encompassing entire portion of body enclosed in haptograph. Like being repeatedly stroked by a soft encircling feather. Or better: repeatedly submerged in some new and soothing substance, like unwet water. As cylinder turned, same sensation—same series of pressures—recurred again and again. Kistenmacher's detailed questions before switching off current and announcing experiment had ended.

At once he removed headpiece and set it on table. Unfastened back of torso and turned away as I extracted myself and quickly began to put on shirt.

"We are still in the very early stages," he said, back still turned to me as I threw my necktie around collar. "We know far less about the tactile properties of the skin than we do about the visual properties of the eye. And yet it might be said that, of all the senses"—here a raised hand, an extended forefinger—"touch is the most important. The good Bishop Berkeley, in his *Theory of Vision,* maintains that the visual sense serves to anticipate the tangible. The same may be said of the other senses as well. Look here."

Turned around, ignoring me as I buttoned my vest. From his pocket removed an object and held it up for my inspection. Surprised to see a common fountain pen.

"If I touch this pen to your hand—hand, please!—what do you feel?"

Extended hand, palm up. He pressed end of pen lightly into skin of my palm.

"I feel a pressure—the pressure of the pen. The pressure of an object."

"Very good. And you would say, would you not, that the skin is adapted to feel things in that way—to identify objects by the sense of touch. But this pen of ours is a rather large, coarse object. Consider a finer object—this, for example."

From another pocket: a single dark bristle. Might have come from a paintbrush.

"Your hand, please. Concentrate your attention. I press here—yes?—and here—yes?—and here—no? No? Precisely. And this is a somewhat coarse bristle. If we took a very fine bristle, you would discover even more clearly that only certain spots on the skin give the sensation of touch. We have mapped out these centers of touch and are now able to replicate several combinations with some success."

He reached over to cylinders and picked one up, looking at it as he continued. "It is a long and difficult process. We are at the very beginning." Turning cylinder slowly in his hand. "The key lies here, in this hollow beechwood tube—the haptogram. You see? The surface is covered with hard wax. Look. You can see the ridges and grooves. They control the flow of current. As the haptogram rotates, the wax pushes against this row of nickel rods: up here. Yes? This is clear? Each rod in turn operates a small rheostat—here—which controls the current. You understand? The current drives the corresponding coil in the glove, thereby moving the pin against the skin. Come here."

He set down cylinder and stepped over to torso. Unfastened back. Carefully pulled away a strip of lining.

"These little devices beneath the brass caps—you see them? Each one is a miniature electromagnet. Look closely. You see the wire coil? There. Inside the coil is a tiny iron cylinder—the core—which is insulated with a sleeve of celluloid. The core moves as the current passes through the coil. To the end of each core is attached a thin rod, which in turn is attached to the lining by a fastener that you can see—here, and here, and all along the lining. Ah, those rods!"

He shook his head: "A headache. They have to be very light, but also stiff. We have tried boar's bristle—a mistake!—zinc, too soft; steel, too heavy. We have tried whalebone and ivory. These are bamboo."

Sighing. "It is all very ingenious—and very unsatisfactory. The haptograms can activate sequences of no more than six seconds. The pattern then repeats. And it is all so very—clumsy. What we need is a different approach to the wax cylinder, a more elegant solution to the problem of the overall design."

Pause—glance at sheet-draped object. Seemed to fall into thought. "There is much work to do." Slowly reached into pocket, removed ring of keys. Stared at keys thoughtfully. "We know nothing. Absolutely nothing." Slowly running his thumb along a key. Imagined he was going to press tip of key into my palm—my skin tingling with an expected touch—but as he stepped toward door I understood that our session was over.

NOVEMBER 7. Last night the Wizard shut himself up in Room 12: seven o'clock to three in the morning. Rumor has it he is still refining the automatic adjustment for phonograph cylinder. Hell-bent on defeating the graphophone. Rival machine produces a less clear sound but has great practical advantage of not requiring the wax cylinder to be shaved down and adjusted after each playing. The Wizard throws himself onto cot for two hours, no more. In the day, strides from room to room on second floor, quick, jovial, shrewd-eyed, a little snappish, a sudden edge of mockery. A university man and you don't know how to mix cement? What do they teach you? The quick sketch: fixed gaze, slight tilt of head. Try this. How about that? Acid stains on his fingers. The Phonograph Works, the electrical lab, the Photographic Building. Alone in a back room in chemical lab, quick visit to Box, up to Room 5, over to 12. The improved phonograph, moving photograph, haptograph. Miniature phonograph for speaking doll. Ink for the blind, artificial ivory. A machine for extracting butter directly from milk. In metallurgical lab, Building 5, examines the rock crushers, proposes refinements in electromagnetic separators. A joke in the courtyard: the Wizard is devising a machine to do his sleeping for him.

I think of nothing but the haptograph.

NOVEMBER 12. Not a word. Nothing.

NOVEMBER 14. Haptograph will do for skin what phonograph does for ear, kinetoscope for eye. Understood. But is comparison accurate? Like phonograph, haptograph can imitate sensations in real world: a machine of mimicry. Unlike phonograph, haptograph can create new sensations, never experienced before. The upward-flowing ripple. Any combinations of touch-spots possible. Why does this thought flood my mind with excitement?

NOVEMBER 17. Still nothing. Have they forgotten me?

NOVEMBER 20. Today at a little past two, Earnshaw entered library. Saw him hesitate for a moment and look about quickly—the Wizard long gone, only Grady from chemical lab in room, up on second gallery—before heading over to my desk. Handed me a book he had borrowed some weeks before: a study of the dry gelatin process in making photographic plates. Earnshaw's appetite for the technical minutiae of photography insatiable. And yet: has never owned a camera and unlike most of the men appears to have no desire to take photographs. Have often teased him about this passion of his, evidently entirely mental. He once said in reply that he carries two cameras with him at all times: his eyes.

Touché.

"A lot of excitement out there," I said. Sweeping my hand vaguely in direction of Photographic Building. "I hear they're getting smooth motions at sixteen frames a second."

He laughed—a little uncomfortably, I thought. "Sixteen? Impossible. They've never done it under forty. Besides, I heard just the opposite. Jerky motions. Same old trouble: sprocket a little off. This is for you."

He reached inside jacket and swept his arm toward me. Abrupt, a little awkward. In his hand: a sealed white envelope.

I took envelope while studying his face. "From you?"

"From"—here he lowered his voice—"Kistenmacher." Shrugged. "He asked me to deliver it."

"Do you know what it is?"

"I don't read other people's mail!"

"Of course not. But you might know anyway."

"How should—I know you've been down there."

"You saw me?"

"He told me."

"Told you?"

"That you'd been there too."

"Too!"

Looked at me. "You think you're the only one?"

"I think our friend likes secrets." I reached for brass letter-opener. Slipped it under flap.

"I'll be going," Earnshaw said, nodding sharply and turning away. Halfway to door when I slit open envelope with a sound of tearing cloth.

"Oh there you are, Earnshaw." A voice at the door.

Message read: "Eight o'clock tomorrow night. Kmacher."

It was only young Peters, an experimental assistant, in need of some zinc.

NOVEMBER 20, LATER. Much to think about. Kistenmacher asks Earnshaw to deliver note. Why? Might easily have contrived to deliver it himself, or speak to me in person. By this action therefore wishes to let Earnshaw know that I am assisting in experiment. Very good. But: Kistenmacher has already told Earnshaw about my presence in room. Which means? His intention must be directed not at Earnshaw but at me: must wish me to know that he has spoken to Earnshaw about me. But why? To bind us together in a brotherhood of secrecy? Perhaps a deeper intention: wants me to know that Earnshaw has been in room, that he too assists in experiment.

NOVEMBER 21, 3:00. Waiting. A walk in the courtyard. Sunny but cold: breath-puffs. A figure approaches. Bareheaded, no coat, a pair of fur-lined gloves: one of the experimenters, protecting his fingers.

NOVEMBER 21, 5:00. It is possible that every touch remains present in skin. These buried hapto-memories capable of being reawakened through mechanical stimulation. Forgotten caresses: mother, lover. Feel of a shell on a beach, forty years ago. Memory-cylinders: a history of touches. Why not?

NOVEMBER 21, 10:06 P.M. At two minutes before eight, Earnshaw enters library. I rise without a word and follow him into stockroom. Down stairway, into basement. Unlocks door of experimental room and leaves without once looking at me. His dislike of Box is clear. But what is it exactly that he dislikes?

"Welcome!" Kistenmacher watchful, expectant.

Standing against table: the dark figure of a human being, covered with wires and small brass caps. On table: a wooden frame holding what appears to be a horizontal roll of perforated paper, perhaps a yard wide, partially unwound onto a second reel. Both geared to a chain-drive motor.

A folding screen near one wall.

"In ten years," Kistenmacher remarks, "in twenty years, it may be possible to create tactile sensations by stimulating the corresponding centers of the brain. Until then, we must conquer the skin directly."

A nod toward screen. "Your modesty will be respected.

Please remove your clothes behind the screen and put on the cloth."

Behind screen: a high stool on which lies a folded piece of cloth. Quickly remove my clothes and unfold cloth, which proves to be a kind of loincloth with drawstring. Put it on without hesitation. As I emerge from behind screen, have distinct feeling that I am a patient in a hospital, in presence of a powerful physician.

Kistenmacher opens a series of hinged panels in back of figure: head, torso, legs. Hollow form with silken lining, dimpled by miniature electromagnets fastened to silver points. Notice figure is clamped to table. Can now admit a man.

Soon shut up in haptograph. Through wire mesh covering eyeholes, watch Kistenmacher walk over to machine. Briskly turns to face me. With one hand resting on wooden frame, clears throat, stands very still, points suddenly to paper roll.

"You see? An improvement in design. The key lies in the series of perforations punched in the roll. As the motor drives the reel—here—it passes over a nickel-steel roller: here. The roller is set against a row of small metallic brushes, like our earlier rods. The brushes make contact with the nickel-steel roller only through the perforations. This is clear? The current is carried to the coils in the haptograph. Each pin corresponds to a single track—or circular section—of the perforated roll. Tell me exactly what you feel." Throws switch.

Unmistakable sensation of a sock being drawn on over my left foot and halfway up calf. As paper continues to unwind, experience a similar but less exact sensation, mixed with prickles, on right foot and calf. Kistenmacher switches off current and gives source reel a few turns by hand, rewinding perforated paper roll. Switches on current. Repeats sensation of drawn-on socks, making small adjustment that very slightly improves accuracy in right foot and calf.

Next proceeds to test three additional tactile sensations. A rope or belt fastened around my waist. A hand: pressing its spread fingers against my back. Some soft object, perhaps a brush or cloth, moving along upper arm.

Switches off current, seems to grow thoughtful. Asks me to close eyes and pay extremely close attention to next series of haptographic tests, each of which will go beyond simple mimicry of a familiar sensation.

Close my eyes and feel an initial scattering of prickles on both elbows. Then under arms—at hips—at chin. Transformed gradually into multiple sensation of steady upward pushes, as if I've been gripped by a force trying to lift me from ground. Briefly feel that I am hovering in air, some three feet above floor. Open my eyes, see that I haven't moved. Upward-tugging sensation remains, but illusion of suspension has been so weakened that I cannot recapture it while eyes remain open.

Kistenmacher asks me to close eyes again, concentrate my attention. At once the distinct sensation of something pressing down on shoulders and scalp, as well as sideways against rib cage. A feeling as if I were being shut up in a container. Gradually becomes uncomfortable, oppressive. Am about to cry out when suddenly a sensation of release, accompanied by feeling of something pouring down along my body—as though pieces of crockery were breaking up and falling upon me.

"Very good," says Kistenmacher. "And now one more?"

Again a series of prickles, this time applied simultaneously all over body. Prickles gradually resolve themselves into the sensation—pleasurable enough—of being lightly pressed by something large and soft. Like being squeezed by an enormous hand—as if a fraternal handshake were being applied to entire surface of my skin. Enveloped in that gentle pressure, that soft caress, I feel soothed, I feel more than soothed, I feel exhilarated, I feel an odd and unaccountable joy—a jolt of well-being—a stream of bliss—which fills me to such bursting that tears of pleasure burn in my eyes.

When sensation stops, ask for it to be repeated, but Kistenmacher has learned whatever it was he wanted to know.

Decisively moves toward me. Disappears behind machine. Unlatches panels and pulls them apart.

I emerge backward, in loincloth. Carefully withdraw arms from torso. Across room see Kistenmacher standing with back to me. Yellowish large hands clasped against black suit-jacket.

Behind screen begin changing. Kistenmacher clears his throat.

"The sense of sight is concentrated in a single place—two places, if you like. We know a great deal about the structure of the eye. By contrast, the sense of touch is dispersed over the entire body. The skin is by far the largest organ of sense. And yet we know almost nothing about it."

I step out from behind screen. Surprised to see Kistenmacher still standing with back to me, large hands clasped behind.

"Good night," he says: motionless. Suddenly raises one hand to height of his shoulder. Moves it back and forth at wrist.

"Night," I reply. Walk to door: turn. And raising my own hand, give first to Kistenmacher, and then to haptograph, an absurd wave.

NOVEMBER 22. Mimicry and invention. Splendor of the haptograph. Not just the replication of familiar tactile sensations, but capacity to explore new combinations—pressures, touches, never experienced before. Adventures of feeling. Who can say what new sensations will be awakened, what unknown desires? Unexplored realms of the tangible. The frontiers of touch.

NOVEMBER 23. Conversation with Earnshaw, who fails to share my excitement. His unmistakable dislike of haptograph. Irritable shrug: "Leave well enough alone." A motto that negates with masterful exactitude everything the Wizard represents. And yet: his passion for the slightest advance in motion photography. Instinctive shrinking of an eye-man from the tangible? Safe distance of sight. Noli me tangere. The intimacy, the intrusiveness, of touch.

NOVEMBER 24. Another session in Box. Began with several familiar sensations, very accurate: ball in palm, sock, handshake, the belt. One new one, less satisfactory: sensation of being stroked by a feather on right forearm. Felt at first like bits of sand being sprinkled on my arm; then somewhat like a brush; finally like a piece of smooth wood. Evidently much easier for pins to evoke precise sensations by stimulating touch-spots in limited area than by stimulating them in sequence along a length. Kistenmacher took notes, fiddled with metallic brushes, adjusted a screw. Soon passed on to sensations of uncommon or unknown kind. A miscellaneous assortment of ripples, flutters, obscure thrusts, and pushes. Kistenmacher questioned me closely. My struggle to describe. Bizarre sensation of a pressure that seemed to come from inside my skin and press outward, as if I were going to burst apart. At times a sense of disconnection from skin, which seemed to be slipping from my body like clothes removed at night. Once: a variation of constriction and release, accompanied by impression that I was leaving my old body, that I was being reborn. Immediately followed by sensation, lasting no more than a few seconds, that I was flying through the air.

NOVEMBER 26. Walking in courtyard. Clear and cold. Suddenly aware of my overcoat on my shoulders, the grip of shoe leather, clasp of hat about my head. Throughout day, increased awareness of tactile sensations: the edges of pages against my fingers, door handle in palm. Alone in library, a peculiar sharp impression of individual hairs in my scalp, of fingernails set in their places at ends of my fingers. These sensations vivid, though lasting but a short time.

NOVEMBER 27. The Wizard's attention increasingly consumed by his ore-separating machinery and miniature mechanisms of speaking doll. The toy phonograph—concealed within tin torso—repeatedly malfunctions: the little wax cylinders break, stylus becomes detached from diaphragm or slips from its groove. Meanwhile, flying visits to the Box, where he adjusts metallic brushes, studies take-up reel, unhinges back panels, sketches furiously. Leaves abruptly, with necktie bunched up over top of vest. Kistenmacher says Wizard is dissatisfied with design of haptograph and has proposed a different model: a pine cabinet in which subject is enclosed, except for head, which is provided with a separate covering. The Wizard predicts haptograph parlor: a room of cabinet haptographs, operated by nickel-in-slot mechanism. Cabinet haptograph to be controlled by subject himself, by means of a panel of buttons.

NOVEMBER 28. Another encounter with Earnshaw. Distant. Won't talk about machine. So: talked about weather. Cold today. Mm hmm. But not too cold. Uh-huh. Can't tell what makes him more uncomfortable: that I know he takes part in experiment, or that he knows I do. Talked about frames per second. No heart in it. Relieved to see me go.

NOVEMBER 29. Fourth session in Box. Kistenmacher meticulous, intense. Ran through familiar simulations. Stopped machine, removed roll, inserted new one. Presented theory of oscillations: the new roll perforated in such a way as to cause rapid oscillation of pins. Oscillations should affect kinesthetic sense. At first an unpleasant feeling of many insects attacking skin. Then: sensation of left arm floating away from body. Head floating. Body falling. Once: sensation of flying through air, as in previous session, but much sharper and longer lasting. My whole body tingling. Returned to first roll. Skin as if rubbed new. Heightened receptivity. Seemed to be picking up minuscule touches hidden from old skin. Glorious.

NOVEMBER 29, LATER. Can't sleep for excitement. Confused thoughts, sudden lucidities. Can sense a new world just out of reach. Obscured by old body. What if a stone is not a stone, a tree not a tree? Fire not fire? Face not face? What then? New shapes, new touches: a world concealed. The haptograph pointing the way. Oh, what are you talking about? Shut up. Go to bed.

NOVEMBER 30. Kistenmacher says Earnshaw has asked to be released from experiment—the Wizard refuses. Always the demand for unconditional loyalty. In it together. The boys. "Every man jack of you!"

Saw Earnshaw in courtyard. Avoiding me.

DECEMBER 1. This morning the Wizard filed a caveat with Patents Office, setting forth design of haptograph and enumerating essential features. A familiar stratagem. The caveat protects his invention, while acknowledging its incompleteness. In the afternoon, interviews in library with the *Herald*, the *Sun*, and the *Newark News*. "The haptograph," the Wizard says, "is not yet ready to be placed before the public. I hope to have it in operation within six months." As always, prepares the ground, whets the public appetite. Speaks of future replications: riding a roller coaster, sledding down a hill. Sensations of warmth and cold. The "amusement haptograph": thrilling adventures in complete safety of the machine. The cabinet haptograph, the haptograph parlor. Shifts to speaking doll, the small wax cylinders with their nursery rhymes. In future, a doll that responds to a child's touch. The Wizard's hands cut through the air, his eyes are blue fire.

The reporters write furiously.

Kistenmacher says that if three more men are put on job, and ten times current funds diverted to research, haptograph might be ready for public in three years.

DECEMBER 2. Lively talk in courtyard about haptograph, the machine that records touch. Confusion about exactly what it is, what it does. One man under impression it operates like phonograph: you record a series of touches by pressing a recording mechanism and then play back touches by grasping machine. Someone makes a coarse joke: with a machine like that, who needs a woman? Laughter, some of it anxious. The Wizard can make anything. Why not a woman?

DECEMBER 3. Arrived early this morning. Heard voices coming from library. Entered to find Wizard standing at desk, facing Earnshaw. Wizard leaning forward, knuckles on desk. Nostrils flared. Cheek-ridges brick-red. Earnshaw pale, erect—turns at sound of door.

I, hat in hand: "Morning, gentlemen!"

DECEMBER 5. Fifth session in Box. Kistenmacher at work day and night to improve chain-drive mechanism and smooth turning of reels. New arrangement responsible for miracles of simulation: ball in palm, handshake, the sock, the hat. Haptograph can now mimic perfectly the complex sensation of having a heavy robe placed on shoulders, slipped over each arm in turn, tied at waist. Possible the Wizard's predictions may one day be fulfilled.

But Kistenmacher once again eager to investigate the unknown. Change of paper rolls: the new oscillations. "Please. Pay very close attention." Again I enter exotic realms of the tactile, where words become clumsy, obtuse. A feeling—wondrous—of stretching out to tremendous length. A sensation of passing through walls that crumble before me, of hurtling through space, of shouting with my skin. Once: the impression—how to say it?—of being stroked by the wing of an angel. Awkward approximations, dull stammerings which cannot convey my sense of exhilaration as I seemed to burst impediments, to exceed bounds of the possible, to experience, in the ruins of the human, the birth of something utterly new.

DECEMBER 6. Is it an illusion, a trick played by haptograph? Or is it the revelation of a world that is actually there, a world from which we have been excluded because of the limitations of our bodies?

DECEMBER 6, LATER. Unaccustomed thoughts. For example. Might we be surrounded by immaterial presences that move against us but do not impress themselves upon the touch-spots of our skin? Our vision sharpened by microscopes. Haptograph as the microscope of touch.

DECEMBER 7. Ever since interview, the Wizard not once in Box. His attention taken up by other matters: plans for mining low-grade magnetite, manufacture of speaking dolls in Phonograph Works, testing of a safe alternating current. The rivalry with Westinghouse. Secret experiments in Photographic Building.

DECEMBER 8. My life consumed by waiting. Strong need to talk about haptograph. In this mood, paid visit to stockroom. Earnshaw constrained, uneasy. Hasn't spoken to me in ten days. I pass on some photographic gossip. Won't look me in the eye. Decide to take bull by horns. So! How's the experiment going? Turns to me fiercely. "I hate it in there!" His eyes stern, unforgiving. In the center of each pupil: a bright point of fear.

DECEMBER 9. There are documented cases in which a blind person experiences return of sight. Stunned with vision: sunlight on leaves, the blue air. Now imagine a man who has been wrapped in cotton for forty-five years. One day cotton is removed. Suddenly man feels sensations of which he can have had no inkling. The world pours into his skin. The fingers of objects seize him, shake him. Touch of a stone, push of a leaf. The knife-thrust of things. What is the world? Where is it? Where? We are covered in cotton, we walk through a world hidden away. Blind skin. Let me see!

DECEMBER 10. This afternoon, in courtyard, looked up and saw a hawk in flight. High overhead: wings out, body slowly dipping. The power of its calm. A sign. But of what? Tried to imagine hawkness. Failed.

DECEMBER 11. Long morning, longer afternoon. Picked up six books, read two pages in each. Looked out window four hundred times. Earnshaw's face the other day. Imprint of his ancestors: pale clerics, clean-cheeked, sharp-chinned, a flush of fervor in the white skin. Condemning sinners to everlasting hellfire.

DECEMBER 12. A night of terrors and wonders. Where will it end?

Kistenmacher tense, abrupt, feverish-tired. Proceeded in his meticulous way through familiar mimicries. Repeated each one several times, entered results in notebook. Something perfunctory in his manner. Or was it only me? But no: his excitement evident as he changed rolls. "Please. Tell me exactly." How to describe it? My skin, delicately thrummed by haptograph, gave birth to buried powers. Felt again that blissful expansion of being—that sense of having thrown off old body and assumed a new. I was beyond myself, more than myself, un-me. In old body, could hold out my hand and grasp a pencil, a paperweight. In new body, could hold out my hand and grasp an entire room with all its furniture, an entire town with its chimneys and salt-shakers and streets and oak trees. But more than that—more than that. In new skin I was able to touch directly—at every point on my body—any object that presented itself to my mind: a stuffed bear from childhood, wing of a hawk in flight, grass in a remembered field. As though my skin were chock-full of touches, like memories in the brain, waiting for a chance to leap forth.

Opened my eyes and saw Kistenmacher standing at the table. Staring ferociously at unwinding roll of paper. Hum and click of chain-drive motor, faint rustle of metallic brushes. Closed my eyes . . .

. . . and passed at once into wilder regions. Here, the skin becomes so thin and clean that you can feel the touch of air—of light—of dream. Here, the skin shrinks till it's no bigger than the head of a pin, expands till it stretches taut over the frame of the universe. All that is, flowing against you. Drumming against your skin. I shuddered, I rang out like a bell. I was all new, a new creature, glistening, emerging from scaly old. My dull, clumsy skin seemed to break apart into separate points of quivering aliveness, and in this sweet cracking open, this radiant dissolution, I felt my body melting, my nerves bursting, tears streamed along my cheeks, and I cried out in terror and ecstasy.

A knock at the door—two sharp raps. The machine stopped. Kistenmacher over to door.

"I heard a shout," Earnshaw said. "I thought—"

"Fine," Kistenmacher said. "Everything is fine."

DECEMBER 13. A quiet day, cold. Talk of snow. The sky pale, less a color than an absence of color: unblue, ungray: tap water. Through the high arched windows, light traffic on Main. Creak of wagons, knock of hooves. In library fireplace, hiss and crackle of hickory logs. Someone walking in an upper gallery, stopping, removing a book from a shelf. A dray horse snorts in the street.

DECEMBER 14. A sense within me of high anticipation, mixed with anxiousness. Understand the anticipation, but why the other? My skin alert, watchful, as before a storm.

DECEMBER 15. A new life beckons. A shadow-feeling, an on-the-vergeness. Our sensations fixed, rigid, predictable. Must smash through. Into what? The new place. The there. We live off to one side, like paupers beside a railroad track. The center cannot be here, among these constricting sensations. Haptograph as a way out. Over there. Where?

Paradise.

DECEMBER 17. Disaster.

On evening of sixteenth, Kistenmacher came to fetch me at eight o'clock. Said he hadn't been in Box for two days—a last-minute snag in automatic adjustment of phonograph required full attention—and was eager to resume our experiments. Followed him down steps to basement. At locked door of Box he removed his ring of keys. Inserted wrong one. Examined it with expression of irritable puzzlement. Inserted correct one. Opened door, fumbled about. Switched on lights. At this point Kistenmacher emitted an odd sound—a kind of terrible sigh.

Haptograph lay on floor. Wires ripped loose from fastenings. Stuck out like wild hair. Back panels torn off, pins scattered about. On the floor: smashed reels, a chain from the motor, a broken frame. Wires like entrails. Gashed paper, crumpled lumps. In one corner I saw the dark head.

Kistenmacher, who had not moved, strode suddenly forward. Stopped. Looked around fiercely. Lifted his right hand shoulder-high in a fist. Suddenly crouched down over haptograph body and began touching wires with great gentleness.

Awful night. Arrived at library early morning. Earnshaw already dismissed. Story: On night of December 16, about seven o'clock, a machinist from precision room, coming to stockroom to pick up some brass tubing, saw Earnshaw emerging from basement. Seemed distracted, fidgety, quite unlike himself. After discovery of break-in, machinist reports to Wizard. Wizard confronts Earnshaw. E. draws himself up, stiff, defiant, and in sudden passionate outburst resigns, saying he doesn't like goings-on "down there." Wizard shouts, "Get out of here!" Storms away. End of story.

Kistenmacher says it will take three to five weeks to repair haptograph, perforate a new roll. But the Wizard has ordered him to devote himself exclusively to speaking doll. The Wizard sharp-tempered, edgy, not to be questioned. Dolls sell well but are returned in droves. Always same complaint: the doll has stopped speaking, the toy phonograph concealed in its chest has ceased to operate.

DECEMBER 18. No word from Kistenmacher, who shuts himself up in Room 8 with speaking doll.

DECEMBER 19. The Wizard swirling from room to room, his boyish smile, a joke, laughter. Go at it, boys! Glimpse of Kistenmacher: drooping head, a big, punished schoolboy. Can Wizard banish disappointment so easily?

DECEMBER 20. Earnshaw's destructive rage. How to understand it? Haptograph as devil's work. The secret room, naked skin: sin of touch. Those upright ancestors. Burn, witch!

DECEMBER 20, LATER. Saw Kistenmacher walking in courtyard. Forlorn. Didn't see me.

DECEMBER 20, LATER. Or did he?

DECEMBER 20, STILL LATER. Worried about fate of haptograph. Felt we were on the verge. Of what? A tremendous change. A revolution in sensation, ushering in—what, exactly? What? Say it. All right. A new universe. Yes! The hidden world revealed. The haptograph as adventure, as voyage of discovery. In comparison, the phonograph nothing but a clever toy: tunes, voices.

Haptograph: instrument of revelation.

Still no word.

DECEMBER 21. The Wizard at his desk, humming. Sudden thought: is that a disappointed man? The haptograph destroyed, Kistenmacher broken-hearted, the Wizard humming. A happy man, humming a tune. How could I have thought? Of course only a physical and temporary destruction. The machine easily reconstructed. But no work ordered. Takes Kistenmacher off job. Reign of silence. Why this nothing? Why?

Perhaps this. Understands that haptograph is far from complete. Protected by caveat. Sees Kistenmacher's growing obsession. Needs to wrest his best electrical experimenter from a profitless task and redirect his energies more usefully. So:

destruction of machine an excuse to put aside experiment. Good. Fine. But surely something more? Relief? Shedding of a tremendous burden? The machine eluding him, betraying him—its drift from the practical, its invitation to heretical pleasures. Haptograph as seductress. Luring him away. A secret desire to be rid of it. No more! Consider: his sudden cheerfulness, his hum. Ergo.

And Earnshaw? His hostility to experiment serves larger design. By striking in rage at Wizard's handiwork, unwittingly fulfills Wizard's secret will. Smash it up, bash it up. Earnshaw as eruption of master's darkness, emissary of his deepest desire. Burn! Die! The Wizard's longing to be rid of haptograph flowing into Earnshaw's hatred of haptograph as wicked machine. Two wills in apparent opposition, working as one. Die! Inescapable conclusion: arm raised in rage against Wizard's work is the Wizard's arm.

Could it be?

It could be.

Kistenmacher entombed with speaking doll. The Wizard flies from room to room, busies himself with a hundred projects, ignores haptograph.

No one enters the Box.

DECEMBER 30. Nothing.

FEBRUARY 16, 1890. Today in courtyard overheard one of the new men speak of haptograph. Seemed embarrassed when I questioned him. Had heard it was shaped like a life-size woman. Was it true she could speak?

Already passing into legend. Must harden myself. The experiment has been abandoned.

Snow in the streets. Through the high windows, the clear sharp jingle of harness bells.

Perhaps I dreamed it all?

Have become friendly with Watkins, the new stockroom clerk. A vigorous, compact man, former telegraph operator, brisk, efficient, humorous; dark blond side-whiskers. His passion for things electrical. Proposes that, for a fee, the owner of a telephone be permitted to listen to live musical performances: a simple matter of wiring. The electric boot, the electric hat. Electric letter opener. A fortune to be made. One day accompanied him down to storeroom, where he searched for supply of cobalt and magnesium requested by an assistant in electrical lab who was experimenting on new storage battery. Saw with a kind of sad excitement that we were approaching a familiar door. "What's in there?"—couldn't stop myself. "Oh that," said Watkins. Takes out a ring of keys. Inside: piles of wooden crates, up to ceiling. "Horns and antlers," he said. "Look: antelope, roebuck, gazelle. Red deer. Walrus tusks, rhino horns." Laughter. "Not much call for these items. But heck, you never can tell."

A dream, a dream!

No: no dream. Or say, a dream, certainly a dream, nothing but a dream, but only as all inventions are dreams: vivid and impalpable presences that haunt the mind's chambers, escaping now and then into the place where they take on weight and cast shadows. The Wizard's laboratory a dream-garden, presided over by a mage. Why did he abandon haptograph? Because he knew in his bones that it was commercially unfeasible? Because it fell too far short of the perfected phonograph, the elegant promise of kinetoscope? Was it because haptograph had become a terrible temptress, a forbidden delight, luring him away from more practical projects? Or was it—is it possible—did he sense that world was not yet ready for his haptograph, that dangerous machine which refused to limit itself to the familiar feel of things but promised an expansion of the human into new and terrifying realms of being?

Yesterday the Wizard spent ten hours in metallurgical lab. Adjustments in ore-separator. "It's a daisy!" Expects it to revolutionize the industry. Bring in a handsome profit.

The haptograph awaits its time. In a year—ten years—a century—it will return. Then everyone will know what I have come to know: that the world is hidden from us—that our bodies, which seem to bring us the riches of the earth, prevent the world from reaching us. For the eyes of our skin are closed. Brightness streams in on us, and we cannot see. Things flow against us, and we cannot feel. But the light will come. The haptograph will return. Perhaps it will appear as a harmless toy in an amusement parlor, a playful rival of the gustograph and the odoroscope. For a nickel you will be able to feel a ball in the palm of your hand, a hat sitting on your head. Gradually the sensations will grow more complex—more elusive—more daring. You will feel the old body slipping off, a new one emerging. Then your being will open wide and you will receive—like a blow—like a rush of wind—the in-streaming world. The hidden universe will reveal itself like fire. You will leave yourself behind forever. You will become as a god.

I will not return to these notes.

Snow on the streets. Bright blue sky, a cloud white as house paint. Rumble of dynamos from the machine shop. Crackle of hickory logs, a shout from the courtyard. An unremarkable day.